The Mother Next Door

BOOKS BY LEAH MERCER

A Secret in the Family
A Mother's Lie
Why She Left

Who We Were Before
The Man I Thought You Were
The Puzzle of You
Ten Little Words

The Mother Next Door

LEAH MERCER

bookouture

Published by Bookouture in 2023

An imprint of Storyfire Ltd.
Carmelite House
50 Victoria Embankment
London EC4Y 0DZ

www.bookouture.com

ISBN: 978-1-83790-318-4
eBook ISBN: 978-1-83790-317-7

PROLOGUE

The river pulled at the shape floating in its waters, playfully passing it from one wave to the next, completely oblivious to the panic and fear of the women watching from the bank. Sharp tendrils of cold currents buffeted the limp body around one bend and then another, long hair trailing like a tail. Shouts and sirens faded, and there was only silence as the waters carried the motionless bounty forward, far from the sharp screams rending the clear-skied afternoon.

Away from the small broken shoe, spinning in the shallows like a talisman from the past.

Away from the horror of what had happened; the terror of the day.

Away from life.

ONE
FIONA
5.30 P.M.

'Come on, come on,' Fiona Bryson muttered, tapping her fingers on the steering wheel as she waited for the traffic light to turn green. It was almost 5.30, and she should have picked up her ten-year-old twins from Lou's thirty minutes ago. She would have, too, if it hadn't been for the terrible traffic on the way home. Thank God, Lou was one of those women who rolled with whatever was thrown at them, making even the dullest detour seem fun. How she had the energy between her own kids and a full-time job, Fiona had no idea.

Where *was* Lou anyway? Fiona glanced at her next-door neighbour's house as she pulled into the drive, surprised that it was still dark. She and the kids should have been home from school long ago, but her Range Rover was nowhere to be seen. Painted a glossy lime green with shiny chrome, it was almost impossible to miss. Only an uber-stylish, uber-confident woman like Lou could get away with that.

Fiona smiled, remembering the first time she'd seen it parked in the drive next door, five years ago now. She'd expected an older couple to purchase the tidy 1970s-style bungalow, but instead Lou had burst outside clutching her two kids' hands, full of energy and light, perfectly matching the van outside. She was recently divorced, she'd explained, and she couldn't have seemed happier. She couldn't have looked more beautiful either, her glossy dark hair and dewy olive skin a marked contrast to Fiona's faded ginger locks and pale, tired face. An interior designer, Lou had gutted the inside of the bungalow, making it like a showroom – her calling card, she'd laughed, to get more business around the village.

She'd gone from strength to strength, slotting easily into the small Surrey commuter town and making friends with everyone she came across. Her place was usually heaving with kids who stayed after school until their parents could get them, but it was still immaculate when Fiona was finally able to pick up her own two. Lou always managed to look so well put together, without an inch to spare, despite saying she wouldn't set foot in a gym if you paid her. Fiona would have hated her if she hadn't become such a great friend and confidante. She'd made life in this town bearable.

She pulled up Lou's contact and hit 'call', wondering if she had taken the kids on an afternoon walk. It was only February, but the evenings were starting to lengthen. The sky was bright blue, the sun warm on her back despite predictions of a coming storm. The news had been full of warnings of gale-force winds and record rainfall, but right now the day couldn't be more picture perfect. It would be just like Lou to decide on the spur of the moment to enjoy some nature – Fiona's worst nightmare with all the kids in tow, but Lou was like Mary Poppins when it came to those kinds of things. She'd probably got so caught up in the fun that she'd forgotten to call.

Fiona's brow furrowed as the mobile rang out. That was odd; Lou always said that any missed call was a missed opportunity. Why wasn't she answering? She let herself into the house and put down her handbag, unable to resist straightening the cushions on the sofa. Her mum's mantra had always been 'agreeable home, agreeable family', obsessively cleaning each day as if she was afraid her new husband would leave her over one speck of dirt. Fiona had to admit there was something therapeutic about putting your house in order, like slotting every little item in place kept all threatening emotions tucked neatly away too. Sighing, she picked up her mobile again to call the school. They would have rung if the kids were still there, but she wanted to make sure they were with Lou. If they were, she had nothing to worry about.

'Hi, this is Fiona Bryson,' she said, when the secretary answered in a harried voice, probably hating the fact that she was still in the building. 'Tabitha and Timothy's mum,' she added, knowing the woman would have no idea who she was unless she identified herself by her offspring. 'They were meant to go home with Lou Drayton – Charina and Saish's mum – today. Do you know if she picked them up?'

'Yes, I believe so,' the secretary responded. 'I'm sure I saw her loading them into her car, along with a few other kids. She was right on time, as always. More than I can say for a lot of other parents around here,' she added darkly.

'Thank you.' Fiona clicked off, then sank onto the sofa. Until Lou had taken over the school run, she herself had been one of those parents who was rarely on time, despite her best efforts. She probably should find a job closer to home, but she'd been at the accountancy firm for years now, and there were never enough minutes in the day to begin searching. Thank goodness Lou had moved in. Fiona had no idea what she'd do without her.

She stared out the window, taking in the large trees that blocked any ray of light brave enough to attempt entry. God, she hated this place. Nick had fallen in love with the sprawling double-fronted house the first time they'd seen it, but Fiona had felt instant revulsion. The way it overlooked the houses around it reminded her of the place she and her mum had moved into when her mother had remarried. Fiona hadn't wanted to leave their cosy flat, but her mother had said they had no choice: with three new stepchildren to contend with, she knew they needed somewhere much bigger. She'd squeezed Fiona's hand, begged her not to make a fuss and asked her to pitch in and help pack up. Fiona had bit her lip and done just that. She'd have done anything for her mum to be happy again, and soon, biting her lip and pitching in became second nature. She wouldn't be the one to make her mother sad the way her father had done. She didn't want to make anyone she loved angry or upset.

So even though the thought of moving back to her home-town had made her want to run, she'd done the same thing when Nick had declared himself tired of London life, deeming the picture-postcard village where Fiona had grown up the perfect combination of country life and easy access to London. He loved the sparkling river that ran through the town, evoking images of the kids paddling on its banks and playfully splashing in its shallows.

Fiona had swallowed down the rising darkness, forcing away the nightmarish images that tumbled through her mind. She couldn't think of the river. She *wouldn't* think of the river. At least this house was some distance from its meandering path, although the memories – and the people who'd played a part in them – were never far away. But the place was big enough that there was always something to keep her busy, and between the house and the kids, family life thankfully enveloped her.

Eleven years later, Nick still loved Holmwood, even though his busy job in London meant he was rarely around to experi-ence the joys of village life. Fiona sighed, thinking of her husband. These days, they were more like flatmates than husband and wife, only passing in the hallway with hurried logistics about the kids. That was normal, though, right? But maybe if they'd spent more time together, she wouldn't have... She pushed the memory from her head, shoving aside the accompanying guilt.

Nothing happened, she told herself for the millionth time. At least she didn't think so. Anyway, there was no point dredging it all up now. Better to tuck it neatly away at the back of the closet, like she had with the dress Lou had given her to wear that night. Only Lou knew about the party, and she wouldn't say anything. Fiona hadn't even needed to ask.

She sighed, telling herself to relax. If Lou was with Tabitha and Tim, they were fine. Lou was the most careful driver she'd ever seen, so an accident was out the question. Perhaps her beloved Range Rover had broken down – she kept saying how she had to take it to be serviced soon. Or maybe... Fiona shook her head. Who knew?

Wherever they were, all that mattered was that the children were safe with her best friend. Soon they'd be home, filling the space with their voices and demands. And until then, she'd do her best to savour this rare moment of peace.

After she'd wiped down the countertops and put away the dishes, of course.

TWO
ALISON
5.30 P.M.

Alison Evans got to her feet and stretched, admiring in the shiny mirrors of her gym how her muscles popped. She'd worked hard over the years to achieve this physique, and despite advancing age – forty was knocking on the door – she was in the best shape of her life.

Pity the gym wasn't, she thought, slumping in a chair to fill out yet another loan application. Given her past rejections and the dire state of the gym's finances, she knew it was probably in vain, but she had to try. She had to do everything she could to keep the place afloat, especially given what she'd already put on the line.

The gym was worth it, though. It was her first baby, something she'd nurtured ever since she'd opened it sixteen years ago. It was the one thing that belonged to her and her alone, her escape when she felt like she didn't fit in the home Greg had inherited from his father – the home she'd remortgaged to try to pump more money into her business. The home her husband didn't *know* she'd remortgaged. A shot of fear and guilt went through her. She'd never done anything behind his back before.

Lou started coming every day at lunch, and they'd fallen into the routine of having a quick coffee at the café once she finished her workout. Thrilled to have finally met someone who seemed to love exercising as much as she did, Alison had plucked up the courage and invited her for a drink one night. But Lou had shaken her head, saying with a grin that her body was a temple and she didn't touch alcohol. Alison's heart had plummeted, sure it was only an excuse. The very next day, though, Lou had invited her out for dinner. They'd talked for hours, and when they found out they had kids at the same school, Lou had offered to pick Gabby up whenever Alison needed. They'd been firm friends ever since, and Alison – who'd steered clear of female friends since secondary school – appreciated Lou in a way she never had anyone else. Besides Greg, of course.

'Speak of the devil,' she muttered, as his name flashed up on her mobile screen. She turned off the treadmill and stepped onto solid ground.

'Hi, babe.' She grabbed a towel and wiped her face. 'What are you and Gabs up to? Did she manage to find her inhaler at school?' Gabby's asthma flared up when she was stressed. Alison had given her some medicine to bring into school, which she'd promptly lost in the depths of her locker.

'Actually...' Greg drew out the word, and Alison shook her head as she sat down to do some leg presses. By the sound of things, the inhaler was long gone, and the last thing she needed was a long queue at the pharmacy on the way home. But Greg's next words jolted her. 'Gabby isn't home yet,' he said. 'Didn't you tell me that woman from the gym was going to drop her off after school?' Greg had never met Lou since he was always too busy at the shop during the day to hit the gym or do the school run.

'What? She's not home?' Alison stopped, her mind

whirring. Maybe she'd got it wrong. Maybe Lou had said she'd bring Gabby to her house to give Alison more time, and then Alison could pick her up from there. Or perhaps she'd said she'd drop her by around supper. If Alison was being honest, she'd been reading through yet another loan application at the time and hadn't really been paying attention.

'Let me call Lou,' she said. 'I'm sure Gabby is over at hers. I'll talk to you later.'

'You should probably start making your way home soon. The police are asking everyone to stay in tonight because of the storm. They're worried the river might burst its banks and cause flooding.'

The river. Alison swallowed at the thought of dark water engulfing the land. 'I won't be long. Love you.' She hung up, guilt flowing through her again. She did love him – so much. There wasn't a day that went by when she didn't thank her lucky stars they'd met all those years ago. He'd been one of the very first clients at the gym where she'd done her personal trainer apprenticeship. He'd been trying to regain strength after breaking his ankle skiing, and for the first time, a man had seen her as competent and successful, rather than the chubby, dull teen who sometimes flashed up when she peered in the mirror. And he hadn't just seen her as a trainer, either, but as a woman – a beautiful one. He was always complimenting her dark eyes and the cheekbones that had appeared after she'd slimmed down. She'd drunk that in, using his vision to buoy her up.

She hit Lou's contact and waited for her friend's cheery voice to come on the line, but all she could hear was the tinny ring. She clicked off and went back inside the office, breathing out slowly to quell the growing unease. Lou was probably giving the kids one of her snack-time specials they all seemed to love, or helping them with their homework. She'd probably been so busy that she hadn't even heard about the storm – or maybe she was in the car dropping Gabby off right now. But... Alison grabbed her keys, Greg's words about flooding ringing in her head. Suddenly, all she wanted was to have her daughter with her, safe and sound. She'd head home first to see if Gabby was back. It was on the way to Lou's anyway.

Then she had to sort out this gym.

THREE
JASMINE
5.30 P.M.

'All done!' Chloe sang out, throwing the needle in the sharps bin as Jasmine sat up. 'You've gone a bit redder than usual in some spots, boss. Want to stay here for a bit while your skin calms down? I don't have another client booked in for the next hour.'

Jasmine looked at her watch: 5.30 p.m. Thankfully, Lou had said she could pick up Juniper from school today and take her back to hers, but she'd be dropping her home any second. There wasn't time to linger, no matter how bad her face appeared. She grabbed the mirror from her employee, grimacing at the swollen injection sites on her face that looked like she'd been stung by a swarm of very angry bees. It would calm down by tomorrow, but right now she looked a state. Botox was worth it, though, and as the owner of the town's premier beauty salon, she owed it to herself and her business to look the best she could.

'I've got to get going,' she said, sliding gracefully off the treatment bed. She smoothed her shirt and straightened her knee-length leather skirt, admiring the way it clung to her slender curves.

'Perfect,' Aidan had growled, as he ran a hand down her bottom this morning as she got ready for work. Brushing back her long blonde hair and sweeping blusher over her smooth skin, she'd had to agree. She was a long way from the girl who'd grown up in a dingy bedsit, spending hours trying to make charity-shop clothes resemble something from the catwalk; trying to hide that she and her mum often got by solely on the generosity of the nearby church's food bank. Even though she was starving, Jasmine would refuse to eat the free school lunch simply to prove she didn't need it, making a point to mock the kids who did, to show how far removed she was from them. In reality, she was poorer than everyone.

She couldn't wait to get home now and slather her face in ice, trying to banish the redness by the time Aidan returned from work. She knew he didn't care – he'd told her loads of times that he preferred her without make-up, without Botox, just as she was – but *she* cared. *Just as she was* evoked memories of huddling under scratchy blankets with greasy hair and unwashed skin, and she couldn't bear the thought.

She said goodbye to Chloe, kept her head down and went out to the car, manoeuvring expertly out of the packed car park. The traffic was terrible, cars clogging the town's high street as everyone tried to get home before 'the storm of the century' hit. Jasmine rolled her eyes as she joined the stream, shielding her eyes from the setting sun. As usual, people were leaping at the chance for a bit of drama to escape their boring lives. There wasn't even a cloud in the sky!

She hummed along to the radio as she drove the short distance to her home on the outskirts of the village, in a gated community that had been built four years earlier. It was all the way across town from where her mother still lived in that same cramped bedsit, not that Jasmine ever visited her. As soon as she had wandered through the house, breathing in the fresh paint and that wonderful new-carpet smell, she knew this was it.

Everything was shiny and fresh, with no marks marring the surface... perfect. It reminded her of when she and the kids from the estate used to cruise around on their beat-up bicycles for hours, exploring construction sites and fantasising about living in such places.

Aidan hadn't been a huge fan, labelling it soulless, but she'd got Lou in to customise the space for them, and her friend couldn't have done a better job. Done up in dark grey and stark white, it looked like a show home. Even better, actually.

Jasmine smiled, thinking of the first time she'd seen Lou, five years ago now. It had been the first day of the school year, and Juniper had been starting Year 1. She'd been so small, so gorgeous, with her baby-blonde hair and bright shiny patent shoes with the tiniest of heels. Jasmine had hugged her close, desperate to protect her before releasing her into the bustling building. School had been a battle for Jasmine – and an opportunity to finally escape. She'd been determined never to let anyone see where she really came from, but that had meant every day was an obstacle course with hidden barriers that could trip her up. Thankfully, Juniper would never have to suffer or strive like she had. She would make sure of it.

She'd just released Juniper when she spotted the most beautiful woman she'd ever seen – apart from herself, of course – with flowing black hair cascading in soft shiny waves down her back, big brown eyes and an olive complexion to die for. Jasmine's expert eye detected she was wearing the latest Burberry mac, and her flats were the same Chanel ones she herself had been coveting for an age. She gave her daughter one last squeeze and sent her off with a cheery goodbye.

'Are you new here?' she'd asked, desperate to be the first to get all the gossip for the mums' WhatsApp group. She'd wanted to claim Lou as her friend too. Two beautiful women like them together – they'd cause quite a stir.

'Yes, we just moved into town. I'm Lou. My daughter is in Year 1 and my son is starting Reception.'

'I have a daughter in Year 1 too! I'm Jasmine. Nice to meet you.' She held out a hand, and Lou took it in a nice, firm grip, confidently maintaining eye contact.

'Oh good!' Lou smiled. 'It's nice to meet someone who can enlighten me on the ins and outs of this place. I need you, Jasmine.' She grinned wider, and Jasmine suddenly felt like she needed Lou too.

They'd become good friends, with Lou turning up to the beauty salon for regular manicures and pedicures, then staying on for a cocktail or three with Jasmine. Jasmine was dying to get her hands on her skin and hair – she'd be a fantastic model for the salon – but Lou just laughed, saying she never cut her hair and her skin was just fine, thank you. When Jasmine found out she was an interior designer, she hadn't given hiring her a second thought.

Jasmine pulled into her large drive, glancing at her watch and blinking with surprise: almost six. Bloody traffic! It'd taken for ever to get home. Thank God she'd given Juniper a key for delays like this. Was she inside now?

'Juni?' she called, as she swung open the door. 'Juniper? Are you here?'

But the house was dark and quiet, her voice bouncing off the stark surfaces. Wherever she was, Juniper clearly wasn't home. Maybe Lou was stuck in traffic too, or perhaps she'd taken Juniper back to her place again – she understood how much Jasmine hated to leave her daughter on her own, and she knew how sensitive Juniper was too. When Jasmine had told her that Juniper had been accused of bullying someone in the class, Lou had been livid, saying that some people liked to play the victim card and that they were probably jealous. Jasmine had nodded, thinking Lou was spot on. Juniper was beautiful, and kids were going to be jealous of her. It was bound to cause problems, like it had for Jasmine. Lou didn't know the half of it.

No one knew, and no one ever would.

No one except two others, and they would keep quiet.

Jasmine grabbed her mobile and dialled Lou's number, leaving a message that if Juniper was still there, she'd swing by as soon as she was ready to come home. Like all the kids, Juniper loved Lou, even going as far as saying she wanted to be her when she grew up. The words had stung Jasmine, but she had understood. If she was being honest, part of her wanted to be Lou too. She was naturally confident and well put together; Jasmine suspected she hadn't faced one tenth the troubles in her childhood that she herself had. Jasmine might be every inch as confident as Lou now, but she'd had to fight to get there.

She threw her bag on the leather sofa and made a beeline for the fridge. Alcohol after Botox was a definite no-no, but one little sip never did any harm. She poured a slug of wine into a glass, then sank down onto the sofa, kicking off her high heels. The wine cooled her throat as it slid down, and she sighed in pleasure. Nothing was better than the first mouthful after a very long day.

Not even Botox.

FOUR
TABITHA
5.30 P.M.

I never knew it was possible to need the toilet this badly. I'm absolutely bursting, *desperate* to do a wee. I've needed to go since Geography, but I didn't want to put up my hand – Mrs Callan always asks if it's 'absolutely necessary' and if you say yes, everyone laughs – so I had to hold it. Then Lou showed up, and before I could say anything, she'd hurried me and Tim into the car, saying she had to leave quickly.

Tim didn't want to go with her for some reason. He was dawdling, like Mum says, spending ages packing his bag. Lou didn't get annoyed like Mum does, though. She just grabbed his shoulders and laughingly pushed him to the car. Juniper and Gabby piled in too, and I groaned. They're in Year 6, the year above me, and I hate listening to Juniper telling Gabby how ugly she is all the time. I wish Gabby would thump her and shut her up, but she sits there and takes it.

The second we were in the car, I knew I wouldn't be able to hold it long. We'll be home soon, I told myself, trying not to wriggle; trying to block out Juniper's horrible whispering in the seat in front of me. Then Juniper turned, snatched my pink leopard-skin headband and put it on her head, laughing and saying it looked better on her. Tears came to my eyes because it *did*. I thought it would look amazing on me – I begged Mum to buy it – but the pink is awful next to my ginger hair. I only wear it every day because Mum paid so much for it.

I could tell Juniper wanted me to beg for it back, but honestly, I was glad she'd taken it. I asked Lou where Charina and Saish were – I love Charina; she's nothing like Gabby or Juniper – but she said they were going to their dad's house and that she'd agreed to pick us all up, as usual.

Everything was fine until we got stuck in traffic. We're *still* stuck – we've been here for what feels like hours, and I honestly think I might wet myself. I'm trying every little thing I can think of not to focus on how much I need the loo, but it's not working. By the way Lou keeps tapping the wheel and looking at her phone, I can tell she wants to get home as fast as I do, so I don't want to bother her.

'Right.' She lets out a puff and pulls a U-turn so suddenly that Tim crashes against me. I breathe in and screw up my face, trying with all my might not to wee.

'What's wrong with you?' he asks, sliding off his head-phones. Finally, we're moving, the car picking up speed as we flash down the motorway. It seems like we're getting further from home, not closer, but I'm sure Lou knows what she's doing. Anyway, I need to wee so badly that I really can't think about anything else.

'I'm desperate for the loo,' I say through gritted teeth. How much longer is this going to take?

'Lou!' Tim leans forward and taps her on the shoulder. 'Tabitha needs a wee. You need to stop before she wets herself.'

Juniper snorts, and even Gabby giggles, and I want to kill my brother. Typical Tim, not even asking me if I want Lou to stop. All our lives he's charged ahead without looking back.

'Can you hold it a bit longer?' Lou asks, meeting my eyes in the rear-view mirror. We're going even faster now, and some-

She turned down the heat on the hob and flopped onto the sofa, allowing her eyes to close for a second. When was the last time she'd been home alone? She couldn't recall, but she remembered now how much she hated it. Being alone left too much space in her mind – too much time for memories – and that was the last thing she wanted. That was the very reason she'd left Holmwood in the first place.

She sighed, thinking of those first few months in London when she'd known no one. It had been such a relief that she'd never have to worry about running into people from her past. She'd met Nick at the coffee shop around the corner from her flat, and they'd soon become friends, sharing a brew each morning before heading off in separate directions for work. When he'd asked her out, she hadn't even hesitated before saying yes. What could be better than dating your best – your only – friend?

She hadn't had much experience with men, but she hadn't been the least bit nervous, and even though she'd never felt the spark everyone seemed to talk about, she loved how safe she felt when he was around. He gave her new life a centre – a direction. He told her over and over how much he loved her kind and gentle nature. She'd drink in his words, telling herself he was right and that whatever had happened was in the past. She *was* the person he believed her to be, and as long as she was with him, she could believe that too.

When he'd asked her to marry him, the future seemed to open up before her, burying the past even deeper. She knew Nick would never let her down; not like her own father had when he'd left. He had told her in no uncertain terms how he felt about people who cheated, and that had made her even more sure he was for her.

Regret rushed through her, and she opened her eyes. How could she have done... whatever it was she'd done at that bloody work do? She hadn't meant to. She loved Nick. She missed him;

missed sitting and talking for hours. These days, she'd be happy with a smile, never mind an actual conversation. He left for the commute to London at 6 a.m., and she couldn't remember the last time he'd been home before 10 p.m. Usually, both she and the twins had passed out by then.

The sound of a car pulling in next door cut into her thoughts. Finally, Lou and the kids were home! She shrugged on an old cardigan hanging in the entryway and shoved her feet into shoes before going outside, eager to talk to Lou and find out what on earth had happened.

The wind whipped her hair across her face, and she pushed it back. Her heart sank when she realised it wasn't Lou's Range Rover in the drive; it was a car she didn't recognise. She squinted, trying to make out the driver. Who was that? And where were the kids?

'Hi there,' a man said, getting out of the car. Fiona blinked as his face came into focus in the dim light. It was Krish, Lou's ex-husband. She had met him a few times when he'd come to pick up the children, and he seemed nice enough. Fiona had tried to ask Lou why they hadn't lasted, but Lou always changed the subject.

'Hi.' She smiled, trying to peer through the car windows to see if Lou and the kids were inside. Perhaps the Range Rover had broken down, after all, and Lou had rung Krish to come get them, although why she still wasn't answering the phone was a mystery. 'Are you the cavalry, then? Did Lou ring you?'

'Cavalry?' Krish looked puzzled. 'Lou did call to say that something had come up, and she couldn't get the kids from school. She asked me to take them back to mine – she sounded a bit stressed.'

Fiona smiled and nodded, but her mind was whirring. Something had come up? Was that why Lou wasn't answering her phone? And asking Krish to collect all the kids was one thing but taking them back to his place was another. For goodness' sake, Fiona barely knew him. She was sure he was fine, but she didn't want her children at a near-stranger's house. She bit her lip, thinking how she might need to have a word with Lou. But then again, maybe not. This was more than likely a one-off.

'Well, thank you so much,' she said, walking over to the car. Why were the kids taking so long to get out? 'I appreciate you bringing them home.' She wrenched open the door, blinking in surprise as she spotted only Charina and Saish. Where were her two? She turned to look at Krish, who appeared as confused as she was.

'Sorry, did you think I had yours?' he asked. 'Lou only asked me to get Charina and Saish. I'm just here because Charina needed her teddy bear.' He smiled. 'Almost twelve and she still can't go to sleep without that thing. She's had it since she was a baby.'

Fiona nodded, but she barely heard his words as she remembered the school saying Lou *had* picked up Tabitha and Tim. But why would she get them and not her own children?

Where the hell *were* they?

'What is it?' Krish asked, clocking her expression.

'Lou picked up my twins today, like she said she would,' Fiona began slowly, trying to make sense of it. 'But I haven't been able to reach her.' She gestured to the house. 'And they're still not home.'

Krish's eyebrows flew up. 'What?'

'The school said she got them right after the bell rang. I can't understand where they might be, especially with the storm coming.' A flash of fear went through her. What was going on? Then she breathed in. Whatever was happening, at least they were safe with Lou. They were almost like her own family.

Krish frowned. 'I don't know,' he said. 'She never mentioned picking up other children, and I certainly didn't see her when I went to get my two.' He shook his head. 'I don't understand why she would get yours and not these guys, but I'm sure she has a good reason. As to where they are...' He paused. 'Traffic is awful, but it shouldn't take this long to get home from school. Maybe they've broken down somewhere. I know the Range Rover was due to be serviced. Lou told me it was making a funny noise.'

Fiona let out a breath. 'Yes, I was thinking that might be it too.'

'Look, you go back inside. I'll ring around the garages in the area and see if they've ended up at one of them. I don't know why she hasn't called you, but maybe her mobile ran out of power. I reckon they're all tucked away somewhere warm and cosy, and she's busy making this into some great game for the kids. You know what she's like.' He said this so affectionately that Fiona wondered if he still had feelings for her.

'Okay. Call as soon as you know anything, okay?'

Krish nodded. 'I will. And let me know if she comes home, all right? But don't worry. I'm sure everything is fine.'

'I'm sure it is. Thanks, Krish.'

Fiona went back into the warmth of her house, breathing in the homely scent of the curry. Krish was right: everything would be fine; no need to get so anxious. She gave the saucepan yet another stir. When Lou and the kids got home, she'd ask Lou to join them for supper. Her best friend and her children gathered around the dining table as the weather closed in would be a perfect ending to the day.

SIX

ALISON

6.30 P.M.

Alison stifled a yawn as she pulled into her driveway. With everyone in a rush to get home before the storm, traffic had clogged the high street. It'd taken ages to move a few metres. Her body was still zinging with restless energy, but her mind was exhausted, numbed by filling out application after application. Far from being a relaxing place, being home didn't make her feel any better. Not only was it a reminder of all she had risked for the gym, but if it hadn't been for Greg insisting they move in after his dad had died, she never would have chosen to live here.

The treetops swayed and twisted in the wind as she got out of the car. She gazed up at the house, taking in the stone exterior and the gaping windows. It was a huge six-bedroom structure, and she should feel lucky to live here – she should feel safe; but somehow it had the opposite effect, as if she had to cower from the walls looming over her. She'd tried to convince Greg a few times over the years to render the outside in a nice creamy colour and to rearrange the heavy, dark furniture inside, but he would just say 'maybe later' and put off the discussion. She knew how close he'd been to his father. This place was a reminder of him... so much so that he never wanted to change a thing.

Light shone from the windows, and even from outside the house, she could hear the tinny bass pounding through the walls. Gabby must be home. She'd recently discovered a love of music – any music, as long as it was at ear-splitting levels. She sighed, thinking that Lou could have called to say that she'd dropped her off.

'Hey,' she said to Greg, as she came into the kitchen. He was making something that smelled delicious but looked like it involved every ingredient in the pantry. She paused, noticing that the music was coming from the speaker in the corner. She turned it down, and silence filled the room.

'Gabs still not here?' she asked, cocking her head for any sound in the cavernous house. Greg shook his head, and she grabbed her mobile and dialled Lou again to say she was on her way now, but once more it went through to voicemail. She left a quick message asking Lou to call, worry clutching at her heart. Why wasn't she picking up? Could she have had an accident? Her breath came faster as images of grinding metal, bloodied faces and agonised screams filled her head.

Stop, she told herself. Everything will be all right. But as much as she tried to convince herself, she knew from experience that sometimes the worst did happen. And ever since she'd had Gabby, she couldn't help thoughts creeping in that the worst could happen to the person she loved most. When her daughter was diagnosed with asthma, Alison had thought that maybe it was payback time for what she'd done when she was young. Gabby was doing fine, though. She *was* fine. And Alison was fine now too – more than fine. She'd left her past behind, the same way she'd left the weak, fearful girl behind. She was a different person now.

'I'll go get her now. Be back in a bit.'

'Be careful out there, and don't stay too long, okay? I'm

cooking up a storm special, and I need you and Gabs to appreciate it while it's hot.' Greg wrapped his arms around her and gave her a sloppy kiss on the cheek, and she couldn't help laughing despite the worry inside. He always made her laugh – in fact, he'd said it was his mission, right from the very start. He'd told her she looked so serious, as if the weight of the world was on her shoulders, and it was his job to make everything a little lighter. And he had. She couldn't have asked for a better partner or father for her child. Guilt surged through her when she thought of the secret she was keeping, and she pushed it away. She'd fix everything with the house. She *would*.

She got back into the car and set off across town to where Lou lived, in a bungalow she'd completely remodelled. With the gym, school and her own house all conveniently located within a one-mile radius, Alison didn't get over to that side of town often – she'd only been to Lou's a few times, since they usually met up at the gym. That was fine with her, actually. She was happy keeping to her little corner of the world. Even if it wasn't the house she'd dreamed of, at least there were no bad memories to contend with.

She had no patience to wait in traffic again, so instead of taking the high street, she manoeuvred onto the motorway that looped around Holmwood. It might be further, but at least it would be smoother – no stops and starts. She pressed the pedal down and the car picked up speed. God, it was dark out here, and unlike town, the road was practically deserted. Huge trees loomed by the roadside, and Alison remembered that this part of the motorway cut through a protected woodland, with the forest stretching for miles. The river that meandered through town bisected a section of the road a few miles ahead. She swallowed, remembering Greg's warning. Thank goodness she'd be exiting before the river, although her relief had nothing to do with fear of flooding and everything to do with bad memories.

Rain splattered onto the windscreen, and she fumbled for

the wipers, almost missing a lime-green vehicle on the hard shoulder. Wait! Was that Lou's? She slowed, then jerked her own car onto the shoulder and put on the emergency lights. It *was* Lou's car. It had to be – there weren't many lime-green Range Rovers out there. But what was it doing parked in the dark on the side of the motorway? That was insanely dangerous! Had she run out of petrol? Had she broken down?

Alison leapt from the car, pulling her jacket more closely around her. God, it was absolutely pouring now, and the Range Rover was a good half-mile behind her. She started to jog, her legs strong and powerful, quelling the uneasy feeling inside. On either side of the road, the woods spread out like a thick woollen blanket that could either soothe or suffocate you. She shivered and forced her legs faster.

Finally, she reached the Range Rover. It was dark inside, and she gingerly tried a door, surprised when it opened easily. Why on earth would Lou leave the car like this, on the side of the road, with the doors unlocked? She sucked in air as she spotted Lou's mobile in the cup holder by the driver's seat. That was why she hadn't answered, then: she'd left it here. But *why*? Alison's heart thumped faster when she noticed the kids' school bags and jackets inside. If the car had broken down or run out of petrol and Lou had had to call a rescue service, why would they leave all their things here?

They wouldn't. Something wasn't right. Lou was never without her phone, even at the gym. And Alison didn't know about Lou's kids, but Gabby never left her school bag anywhere. She couldn't because then she wouldn't have her inhaler with her – if she'd even found it at school today, which was highly unlikely. Her gut clenched as a fresh bout of fear hit. That meant that wherever Gabby was now, she didn't have it.

She took a few quick breaths to calm her racing pulse, then grabbed her mobile and called the police. After telling them where she was and explaining what she'd found, she leaned against the car, the cool of the metal sinking through her thin jacket. The sweat from her run had dampened the jumper underneath, and she could feel the rain starting to penetrate. To warm up and steady herself, she did a few quick lunges, feeling ridiculous as the headlights of passing cars lit her figure. She kept her gaze away from the dark woods at the side of the road, focusing instead on the lights coming towards her on the horizon.

At last, a police car pulled up on the shoulder beside her, and a man got out. Alison hurried towards him.

'Hi, thanks for coming so quickly. This is the car.' She gestured towards the vehicle. 'The driver's name is Lou Drayton, and she had my daughter Gabby with her, as well as her own two kids. She picked them up from school hours ago now.' She gulped, thinking how long ago that had been. Where were they?

'Okay.' The officer nodded. 'Let me take down the registration number, and I'll get our base to run it through the system. Just to make sure you have the right car and all.' He smiled in what he probably thought was a reassuring way but instead was downright patronising.

'All right.' Alison did another few quick lunges, trying to keep her worry under control while she waited. Everything would be fine. This was *Lou* they were talking about. She had never met a more capable woman.

After what felt like for ever, the officer came back.

'So we ran the registration number, and it looks like the car is registered to a Krish Khutale.'

Alison tilted her head. Krish Khutale? Where had she heard that name before? Then it hit her. Krish was Lou's ex-husband. She didn't talk much about him, but she'd mentioned him once or twice when it was his turn to have the kids. 'That makes sense,' she said. 'He's Lou's ex-husband.'

The office nodded. 'Yes, our officers have just spoken to him. He has his kids with him right now.'

'*His* kids?' Every muscle in Alison's body stiffened. 'So where's my daughter?' She gestured towards the car. 'I know Lou collected her from school today. Her things are inside, along with some other bags.' She bit her lip. If those bags didn't belong to Charina and Saish, then whose were they? Had Lou picked up other kids too?

'Maybe she called someone else to come and get them if she had car troubles?' The officer looked the vehicle up and down, as if he could identify the problem by sight.

'But if someone came to get them, why would they leave all their things? Lou's phone is still there. And the children's coats and school bags. It's as if they were planning to come back again – or they left in a hurry.' She shivered as a thought hit. 'Do you think it was one of those carjackings or something? That maybe someone forced them from the car? Range Rovers are always in demand, aren't they?'

The officer gave her a condescending look, and Alison stifled the urge to smack him. 'Since the car's still here, love, I really don't think so.'

She had to admit he had a point.

'Maybe they're planning to come back and get their things,' he said. 'Can you think of who she might have rung?'

She tilted her head. It could be anyone. Lou did have lots of friends; it was amazing how quickly she'd slotted into life here, navigating the school scene more easily than Alison – who had always lived here – ever would.

'Why don't you get on one of those WhatsApp groups you mums always have and ask there? I swear my wife spends half her life on that thing.'

Alison raised an eyebrow. *You mums*? As the female owner of a gym, she'd faced more than her fair share of sexism, from suppliers to clients. Usually, she challenged them to a bench press, smiling when she crushed them.

'Maybe,' she said slowly. As stupid as this officer was, he did have a point: she could post on the WhatsApp group and see if Lou had picked up any other kids from the class. Maybe she had reached out to one of them for help. But why she hadn't called Alison to at least let her know what was happening, she had no idea.

'I'm sure they're fine, and that she's taken them somewhere warm and dry,' the officer said, his eyes kind now. 'You know this woman, right? She's a responsible adult who both you and your daughter trust?'

Alison nodded. Thank goodness. Whatever had happened, at least Gabby was with Lou. 'Yes, she's a family friend. My daughter has been with her many times. I'd trust her with my life.' Gabby *was* her life.

'All right then.' The officer smiled. 'Look, I'll tell our units around town to keep an eye out. It's still early, and I'm certain they'll be back before long. The best thing you can do, especially in this weather, is to head home. We'll call if we spot them. Okay?'

Alison nodded. What choice did she have? Anyway, she wanted to send a message to the other mums in the WhatsApp group and see if anyone responded. Maybe the officer was right, and finding them was as simple as that. She thought of Gabby without her inhaler, and panic washed over her.

Please God, may it be as simple as that.

She gave the officer her details, then started jogging towards her own car, the fresh night air making her feel more centred, more solid again. She turned her face upwards, the cold rain stinging her cheeks. As she glanced back, the lime-green Range Rover was growing smaller and smaller in the distance.

SEVEN

JASMINE

7 P.M.

Jasmine took another swig of wine, surprise sweeping through her when she noticed the bottle was almost three-quarters empty. How had that happened? Sighing, she tore her gaze from the telly, where three women were fighting over a man with a very big nose, and glanced at the shiny chrome clock – one of the very few pieces she'd allowed to grace the walls. Her eyes popped. Seven already? Where the *hell* was Juniper?

She took another gulp, irritation shooting through her as she remembered that tomorrow was school photo day and she had to dye Juniper's hair tonight. What had started off as a beautiful baby blonde had darkened over time, and now her daughter needed her roots done every six weeks to hide the mousy brown. If she wasn't home soon, they'd be up until all hours.

She grabbed her mobile and texted Juniper to see if Lou was dropping her off soon or if she needed someone to get her. Her irritation increased when the phone remained silent. Juniper had begged for the latest iPhone, and even though kids weren't officially allowed to have mobiles in school, Jasmine had smoothed the way by telling Juniper's teacher it helped her anxiety – and offering her a free gift certificate for the salon. But what was the point if Juniper couldn't be arsed to text her own mother? Jasmine sat back, wondering what to do. Should she head out now to get Juniper from Lou's or wait until Aidan got home? As director of sales for a luxury car dealership, he worked even harder than she did, but he always made it home in time for dinner.

Her heart sank as she looked in the mirror. The redness of the injection sites had faded a little, but she still looked a state. There was no way she could show her face like this – and particularly to Lou, who didn't need to do the maintenance Jasmine did to keep up her looks. Jasmine had casually mentioned Botox once, expecting Lou to chime in about how she did the same, but instead she'd screwed up her nose as if she'd encountered a bad smell, saying she hated needles and wasn't about to stick one in her face for beauty's sake. Jasmine had never mentioned it again.

Plus, she'd already had more than half a bottle of wine. Not that it affected her driving, of course. In fact, she was a much better driver after she'd had a few drinks, but there was no way she'd risk it after what had happened last week. Lou had been furious. Jasmine grimaced as the memory filtered in.

The school had rung to say that Juniper was still waiting to be picked up, and Jasmine had glanced at her watch in horror. How had it got so late? She must have drifted off, she'd thought, shrugging on her cashmere cardi, running a brush through her hair and rinsing her empty wine glass in the sink. She rubbed her eyes, blinking to clear her vision. She must have been exhausted! It wasn't like her to sleep so deeply in the late afternoon.

She slid her feet into flats, grabbed the keys and got into the car. As she snapped on the radio and sang along, the wind and sun streamed through the sunroof, and even though it was only February, the air felt so nice on her hot cheeks. She pulled into the school's car park a few minutes later, and over to the main entrance, where Juniper was waiting, along with Lou's two children, Charina and Saish. That was a surprise: usually, Lou was here promptly at pickup, but maybe they'd stayed late for some reason.

'Get in, baby,' she said to Juniper, not caring about her daughter's cringe. Usually, it bothered her, but right now she was on a blissful cloud all of her own. 'Are you two still waiting for your mum?' she asked Lou's kids. 'She's late today!' It felt rather good saying those words.

But Charina shook her head. 'Not really. I had after-school practice for the maths competition, and Saish had to stay late too.'

Jasmine tilted her head. 'Maths competition? What's that?'

Charina darted a glance at Juniper, her cheeks colouring. 'The school chose a few kids in each year to take part. Loads of schools up and down the country are doing it.'

'Oh.' Jasmine raised her eyebrows, her chest tightening. Why hadn't they asked Juniper too? She was clever. Surely, she deserved a shot. 'Actually, now that I remember, the school did ask Juniper to take part. She was too busy, though – what a shame. Right, baby?'

Juniper didn't even respond, just slammed the car door.

'Would you both like a ride home then?' Jasmine asked, her voice high and slightly manic even to her own ears. 'I can give your mum a quick call and tell her we're on our way; there's no need for her to come now.'

Charina and Saish looked at each other, and then Charina nodded. 'Okay. Thank you.'

They climbed into the car and Jasmine started the engine. She cranked up the music and drove home, singing along at the top of her voice and smiling as the kids – even Juniper – joined in to Taylor Swift. When they pulled up in front of Lou's house, the kids all tumbled out with huge smiles on their faces. She followed, nearly tripping as her shoe caught the edge of the floor mat. Christ, she really needed to get that fixed.

She turned to face Lou, who was staring at her with a stony expression. 'Aren't you going to say thank you?' she trilled, wondering why Lou was so dour. Oh, had she forgotten to ring to say she'd bring them home? She hadn't told the school she was taking them either. Maybe that was why. Maybe the school had called to say they were missing. Whoops.

'You've been drinking.' Lou's normally warm voice was like ice, and Jasmine let out an incredulous laugh. Lou was hardly one to talk! Didn't she always drive home after all those cocktails at the salon? But then... She tilted her head, a sudden realisation bursting through the haze. Lou didn't really drink. She'd sip at her glass while Jasmine downed hers, and when she left, it would still be half-full.

'It was only a drop,' she said, taking a step back. 'For God's sake, get over yourself.' She laughed to make the words sound lighter, but they came out strained and tense.

But Lou didn't laugh. Instead, she moved closer, looking Jasmine straight in the eye. Jasmine fought the urge to flinch. There was something in the way Lou was staring at her... with such intensity, as if she could see through her; as if she could see that little girl who'd grown up with nothing. She stepped away, trying to hold back those uncomfortable feelings inside her.

'Just a drop,' Lou repeated. 'I don't believe that. I know you, Jasmine,' she said in that same cold, low voice, and Jasmine shuddered.

She doesn't know me, she told herself, trying to regain her balance. Of course she doesn't. She only knows the beautiful, successful woman I am now.

'I know how you drink. It's never a drop.'

Jasmine blinked, trying to think of something to say. Lou was right, but so what? A few drinks were nothing. She could

handle way more than that. She *did* handle way more than that
– regularly.

'You put your own daughter's life in danger,' Lou continued. 'And now you've put my kids' lives in danger too.' She was
practically shaking now, the fury streaming off her. 'You could
have had an accident. They could have died, but you didn't
even think about that, did you? What kind of a mother are you?'

Jasmine's mouth dropped open, and anger spurted through
her. She could understand Lou being a little upset. Maybe she
shouldn't have driven, even though she knew the alcohol hadn't
affected her. But to imply that she wasn't a loving mother,
well... She knew from personal experience exactly what a bad
mother was, and she was far, far from it. Lou was way out of
line.

She squinted, peering closely at her friend. Something was
different. Was it because she'd never seen Lou angry? For a split
second, she seemed like another person, a stranger. Then
Jasmine blinked, and Lou was back to her usual self.

'Look,' she was saying in a softer tone, as if she realised she'd
gone too far. 'If you need help, maybe you should talk to Aidan.
I can call him now to come and get you if you want.' She took
Jasmine's arm and propelled her to the front terrace, where two
chairs were perfectly positioned outside the door. Jasmine tried
to jerk away, but Lou's grip was firm. 'Why don't I do that,' she
said, sliding out her mobile. 'You shouldn't drive.'

'No!' Jasmine's hand shot out and batted the phone away.
'Don't tell Aidan.' Aidan thought she was perfect; that she was
everything he'd ever wanted. She couldn't bear the notion of
him knowing differently. Anyway, she didn't have a problem.
'I'll call an Uber to get home.'

Lou stared at her with that intense look. 'These things have
a way of coming out,' she said. 'The sooner you tell the truth,
the better for everyone.' Her words swirled around them in the

air, and for a minute, everything else faded away, and it was only the two of them, standing in a timeless landscape.

Then Jasmine forced a little laugh. 'Oh my goodness, Lou, the *drama*! Everything will be fine.' She got out her mobile and ordered an Uber, and a minute or two later, a car pulled into the drive.

'Come on, Juni,' she said gaily to her daughter, who'd been watching with wide eyes. 'Let's go home.'

She waved as they drove away, shaking her head at Lou's solemn face as her words rang in her mind. What was up with her tonight? Lou knew she was a great mother! Something must have happened in her past to make her react like that... maybe a friend who had died from drink-driving or something. That had nothing to do with Jasmine. Jasmine would show she was the bigger person and not take offence.

Lou must have recognised she'd gone too far, because the next time they'd seen each other, she was back to her normal self, and the incident was never mentioned again. Jasmine would have appreciated an apology for such harsh words, but if Lou was happy to move on, then so was she. It was a non-event anyway. Still, there was no need to trigger Lou once more by showing up after drinking, even if she could handle her booze. She'd wait until Aidan got home and ask him to go and get Juniper. In the meantime, she poured herself another drink and turned up the TV.

A few minutes later, as she was drifting off to sleep, a *bing* from her mobile jolted her awake. Finally! Lou must be messaging to say she was bringing Juniper home – or maybe her daughter had deigned to text back. She wiped her eyes and grabbed the phone, annoyance stirring when she noticed it was the class WhatsApp group. She was even more annoyed when she saw the message was from Alison.

God, *Alison*. That was the last person she wanted to hear from: in her opinion, people from the past were best kept there. She'd been far from pleased to see Alison at the school gate the first day of nursery, and when she'd found out Juniper was in the same class as Alison's daughter, well... she'd gone home and had a few shots, even as she told herself it didn't matter.

Alison hadn't changed a bit from secondary school. She might have lost a lot of weight and bulked up – too much, if you asked Jasmine – but she was the same whingy girl she always had been. How could they have ever been friends? Well, not really friends. Jasmine had tolerated her, mainly because of how Alison had looked up to her, with a mixture of envy and awe, and Jasmine had needed that. Lou was right: Alison was jealous, then and now.

She shook her head, thinking of how Alison had blamed poor Juniper for bullying her daughter, Gabby. All Juniper had done was send Gabby a photo she'd taken. It wasn't her fault if other children had drawn horrible things on the photo before it was sent. Of course Alison had blamed her, though. Juniper had vehemently denied it, and Jasmine had believed her wholeheartedly. Juniper didn't need to buoy herself up by taking others down. She had everything already.

She clicked open the WhatsApp message, eyes bulging when she read that Lou had also picked up Gabby from school, that Alison had found her car empty by the side of the road, and that the police had been called. Did anyone know where they might be? Did anyone else have kids that Lou had picked up today, and had they heard anything?

Jasmine put down the phone, her mind spinning as guilt sloshed through her. So Juniper hadn't been at Lou's all this time. Where had she been then? Where was she *now*? And why the hell wasn't she responding to her texts?

Her phone was going crazy as all the class mums piled in, eager to get a piece of the action, but none of them knew anything. She barely even heard Aidan come in through the barrage of messages, glancing up only when he switched off the TV.

'Hey, babe. God, it's good to be home. It's awful out there right now.' He sat down beside her. He was so handsome, and normally she would have taken a moment to appreciate that, but not tonight. 'What's happening?'

She turned to face him, noticing with surprise that he was soaking wet. It must really be pouring out there. Unease grew inside her as she remembered the coming storm. Maybe the media hadn't been exaggerating, after all. 'Juniper isn't back from school yet,' she said, trying to keep the panic from her voice. 'Lou picked her up today so I could get my face done.' Absently she lifted a hand, thinking that Aidan hadn't even commented. But then he'd seen the aftermath of so many rounds of Botox, he was used to it now. She was even making inroads into convincing him to get it done himself. 'I've been trying to get in touch, but I thought they were just busy over at Lou's house.'

'Busy until now? It's gone seven, and the police are telling everyone to keep off the roads. The storm is definitely starting.' Aidan looked at his watch, and Jasmine felt her colour rising. She really should have noticed sooner.

'Then I got a message from another mum on the WhatsApp group, saying that Lou's car has been found by the side of the road and she and the kids are nowhere to be seen. No one can get in touch with them.' She could barely believe she was saying these words, but there had to be an explanation. Everything would be okay.

'Did you call the police?' Aidan looked suddenly frantic. He doted on Juniper; did everything for her. She was his princess, and he would do all he could to protect her. They both would.

'No,' Jasmine said. 'I—'

'You decided to sit there and down a bottle of wine,' he

finished before she could. 'Christ, Jasmine. Your daughter is missing in what's going to be the worst storm for years!' He grabbed the phone from her. She listened as he rang the police and told them all the details, looking at her for confirmation when he wasn't sure. Then he ended the call and picked up his car keys.

'Where are you going? I thought you said the police don't want people driving?' Jasmine couldn't stand the anger in his eyes; the way he was looking at her. His gaze speared deep inside of her, right to her core, and for an instant she heard Lou's words echoing in her mind: *What kind of a mother are you?* She pushed them aside. Lou hadn't meant it, and Juniper would be fine. She wasn't missing. She was with the most responsible, capable person Jasmine had ever met. Aidan didn't know Lou like she did.

'Did you know that Lou's children are safe with her ex-husband?' Aidan said, his voice shaking. 'That he picked them up from school, but Lou took Juniper and some other kids and disappeared? Something's not right.'

Jasmine jerked back at the words. Why would Lou take other children and not her own? What the hell? She swallowed, fear shooting through her as she recalled the expression on Lou's face that day. Jasmine had had the same exact thought: something wasn't right. *Did* she know Lou, after all? She dismissed the thought. There had to be an explanation. 'No, I didn't know,' she said. 'I—'

'Of course you didn't.' Aidan shook his head. 'I'm going to drive around and see if I can find them. The police said that all their units are aware, they're keeping an eye out, and to call if Juniper's still missing in a couple of hours. But I don't care what they say; I don't care if it's a bloody *hurricane* out there. I'm not going to sit around and wait. Nothing can keep me from my daughter.' He didn't say it, but Jasmine knew the rest of his sentence was 'unlike you'.

'I'm coming too,' she said, her face reddening more when she realised she was slurring. She blinked, trying to clear her vision as she got up from the sofa.

Aidan gave her that look again, and she glanced away. He was just upset, she told herself. He didn't think she was a bad mother any more than Lou did. He was always saying how wonderful she was with Juniper. She winced as she recalled those early days when Aidan had gone back to work, and she'd been trapped in the house with a newborn who wouldn't stop crying. She'd gone out into the back garden with a bottle and drunk until she couldn't hear the crying any more, exactly like her own mother used to. Maybe she wasn't so different from mum, she'd thought bleakly, desperately swigging to block out that thought too. She'd cut short the long maternity leave she'd planned and gone back to work, and things had got better. She *was* a good mother. She was nothing like her mum. She would give Juniper everything. She'd never let her down or make her feel worthless.

'You stay here,' Aidan said. 'Someone needs to be home in case she comes back. And you're in no state to come with me.'

Jasmine almost protested that she was fine, but then she remembered the Botox, and realised he was probably talking about how she looked. He was right too. She couldn't be seen outside like this, and it was nice of him to show he cared. 'Okay.' She sat back down on the sofa. 'Keep in touch, all right?'

Aidan nodded and went out the door, and she closed her eyes. God, she needed another drink.

EIGHT
FIONA
7.15 P.M.

Fiona paced back and forth across the lounge. The TV and the radio were blaring, filling the silence she was desperate to banish, but somehow the place felt emptier than ever. Nick still wasn't home, despite her efforts to reach him – not that it surprised her. He'd had so many late-night meetings recently that she was lucky if he was back before midnight. Any other woman might be suspicious, she supposed, but the thought of her hard-working, steadfast husband being with someone else was so ridiculous she couldn't even conjure it. But then... She sighed as regret gripped her. Would he ever have thought that of her? Not that she'd been with someone else, of course. Had she? God, she was never drinking tequila again.

The phone rang and she grabbed it, her heart picking up pace when she saw it was Krish. Had he found the kids? Were they okay?

'Have you found them?' The words tumbled out before she could even say hello.

'I'm so sorry to disappoint you, but no, I haven't,' Krish answered, and her heart dropped. She sank onto the sofa. 'I tried calling local garages and recovery services. I even called the hospital, on the off chance one of the kids was poorly or had had an accident.' She sucked in her breath at the very thought. 'But no luck anywhere,' he continued. 'Then the police got in touch.'

Fiona froze. The police?

'They found Lou's Range Rover by the side of the motor-way,' he said. 'The ring road that goes around the village.'

She let out her breath in relief. 'So the car did break down. But why would Lou be on the ring road? That's not on her way home.'

'I don't know,' Krish said, sounding just as confused. 'And actually, it didn't break down. The police say it works fine, and the petrol tank is almost full. I can't understand why on earth she would stop on the hard shoulder. That's such a dangerous thing to do.'

Fiona swallowed, fear beginning to build inside.

'And she left her mobile in the car, along with her coat. The kids left all their things too. I don't get it.'

Fiona was silent, trying to understand. Why would they leave their things? Where would they go? Had someone forced Lou to stop, maybe? Her mind ran through endless scenarios, none of them seeming like they could be real.

'When I told the police that your children were with Lou and you haven't been able to reach them, they said they'd ring to get more information from you,' he said. 'I gave them your number.'

'Okay,' Fiona said, trying to focus on what Krish was saying – trying not to think of her children alone in the wind and rain by the side of the road... or wherever they were.

They're not alone, she reminded herself, trying to keep breathing through the panic and fear. Whatever had happened, at least they were with Lou, someone they trusted; someone they looked up to. And Lou would protect them from whatever she could, Fiona knew that with every fibre of her being.

She said goodbye to Krish, then went into the kitchen and took the curry off the hob, covering the saucepan. The kids could eat it when they finally got home. Because they would be home tonight. Of course they would. This was Holmwood. Nothing bad could happen here. She swallowed, pushing back her own awful memories. Nothing bad could happen with *Lou* here.

'Hi, guys!' The side door opened, and Nick came in, gazing around in surprise. 'Where is everyone?'

Fiona was so happy to hear his voice and to have him home that she didn't even answer. She threw herself into his arms, hugging him tightly against her despite the fact that he was dripping wet. Hurt zinged through her that he didn't hug her back; simply manoeuvred her aside and looked over her shoulder. 'Kids?' he called. 'Come say hi!'

'Nick.' She put a hand on his arm. 'The kids aren't here.'

He turned towards her. 'What do you mean they aren't here? Where are they? Is there something on at school? The radio said everyone should be sheltering now from the storm.'

'Nothing's on at school.' She breathed in, trying to conjure up the words. As soon as she said them, it would seem way too real. 'Lou picked them up, but...' she swallowed, 'no one knows where they are.'

Nick drew back. 'What?'

'The police found Lou's car on the side of the road, with her phone in it along with the kids' things, but they weren't there. At first, we thought she might have broken down, but the tank is full and all seems fine. And her own kids are with her ex.' Fiona shook her head, trying to stay calm. 'I can't imagine it's anything too terrible, right? I mean, they're with Lou. At least...' Her voice trailed off at the terror on Nick's face. Usually, he was the one reassuring her, but he looked absolutely horrified. Colour had drained from his cheeks, making his dark-blue eyes appear even darker.

'Nick?' She reached out a hand to steady him. He seemed about to keel over. 'It will be fine, I'm sure. They'll be back soon. There's some curry if you're hungry, and—'

'Curry?' Nick repeated the word as if he couldn't take it in. 'Have you talked to the police? What did they say?'

Fiona flinched at his urgent tone. She'd never heard him sound so frantic before. 'No, but Lou's ex, Krish, has been in touch with them and told them everything. He said they'll call.'

'Right.' Nick grabbed his bag and went up the stairs.

'Where are you going?' she called after him.

'I'm not going to wait. I'm ringing the police right now.' His voice filtered down from the bedroom.

Fiona wiped the counter as the door slammed closed to keep out the noise from the telly and radio. Thank God he was home and she didn't have to wait this out alone. His presence made her feel better already, even if he did seem shaky. But that made sense: Nick didn't know Lou as well as she did. He didn't know how much she cared about the kids; how she'd do anything to keep them from coming to harm. Fiona loved how he'd sprung into action the second he'd come in. She bit her lip, thinking that maybe she should have called the police herself, but Krish had said they would ring. Anyway, it wasn't like the twins were in any real danger. The weather might be terrible, but Lou would have found somewhere dry and warm.

She turned off the radio and TV, trying to make out the low rumble of Nick's voice from upstairs. She would have liked to be with him when he called, but the police knew everything from Krish anyway, and there wasn't much she could add. Maybe they had already found Lou and the kids. They couldn't have gone too far.

Eventually, Nick came back downstairs. His face was still

white, his normally neat hair was a mess and his eyes looked wild. Her heart sank. Clearly, the children hadn't been found. Fear shot through her. Had the police told him something even worse?

'Everything okay?' she asked timidly.

'Of course not,' he snapped. 'Our children are missing.'

She coloured, realising how stupid her question had been. 'I mean did the police say anything more? What did they tell you?'

He stood opposite her, and she leaned towards him, longing to feel safe in the comfort of his arms. 'They said they've raised the risk level now that there's no sign of Lou and the kids and it's getting later with worsening weather. They're continuing to search the town, and they may extend the area.'

'Raised the risk level?' Fiona frowned. She was glad to have the police on the case, but it couldn't be that serious, surely. 'And how far are they going to search? If Lou and the children were on foot, they couldn't have gone far, could they? Do you think someone picked them up from the roadside and took them somewhere?'

'I really don't know. I suppose anything's possible.' Nick's face twisted. 'I sent them a recent picture of the twins so they have it on file. They also wanted to know what the kids were wearing today. Their school uniforms, right?'

Fiona nodded, shuddering as she pictured Timothy and Tabitha in their thin uniforms out in the cold and wet. It was good to know the police were gathering details, but surely there was no need to provide such information. She was certain they'd be found soon, safe and sound. 'Tabitha had on that leopard-print headband too,' she said. It wasn't her daughter's usual style, but she'd seen it at a boutique when they'd gone Christmas shopping in London a couple of months ago. If Fiona closed her eyes, she could almost hear the Christmas carols; see the lights and excitement reflected in her daughter's eyes.

They'd been browsing in the children's section, cooing over cool pleather leggings and flashy trainers, when Tabitha had spotted the pink satin headband. It was a ridiculous price from a brand Fiona didn't recognise, but Tabitha had begged for it. Fiona had never been trendy – her mum would never splurge on anything frivolous, and she hadn't been one to beg – but she couldn't resist saying yes. Tabitha had turned to her with glowing eyes and a huge smile, and she'd worn the headband every day since.

'Okay, I'll let them know.' Nick rubbed his eyes, then turned towards her. 'It wasn't only our kids, apparently. The police said there were other children in the car too. They found their bags and coats.'

'Other children?' Krish hadn't told her that, but maybe he hadn't known. 'Did the police say who?' It could be anyone, really – Lou was friends with so many parents, she had a different carload of children almost every day.

'The officer told me their names, but I didn't recognise them. Sorry, I can't remember.' He swallowed. 'I was more concerned with ours.'

Fiona nodded, thinking of other families going through the same thing as them right now. Who were they? Would she know them? At least they all had Lou on their side, and that would give them some comfort. 'Come here,' she said to Nick, sitting down on the sofa and patting the cushion next to her. 'It will be okay. The kids are with Lou. She'll keep them safe.' It was a strange role reversal for her to be comforting him, but he looked as if he needed it.

He just stared at her, then sat down in a chair across from her. He was only a few feet away, but somehow it felt like miles.

'Nick?' She scooted closer to him, reaching out to touch his hand. 'Are you all right?' There was a strange expression on his face – a look that made her think he wanted to tell her something important, but that he wasn't sure how to start. Once more she longed for the days when they could talk easily.

He paused for a minute, then nodded. 'I'm fine,' he said. He smiled, but it was more like a grimace, and his eyes still looked strange. 'You're right. Lou will keep them safe. She will.'

But somehow it sounded more like a plea than a promise.

NINE

ALISON

8 P.M.

Alison forced her legs faster on the cross trainer, her breath tearing at her throat. She should be upstairs with Greg. She *wanted* to be upstairs with Greg. But seeing his panic when she'd told him what she'd found made the horrific thoughts circling her brain spin even faster, so she'd fled to the exercise room in the basement to try to get rid of the fear. Feeling the power of her muscles was the only thing that made her strong inside, and she needed to harness that power for Gabby. She couldn't let it drain away now.

Her WhatsApp dinged yet again, and she slowed and grabbed it from her pocket, heart sinking when it was just another mum saying how worrying it must be but that she was sure the kids would turn up soon. Alison looked at the time. It was past eight now, and she'd heard nothing. That fear she'd felt when she'd spotted Lou's car abandoned at the side of the road was only growing, despite countless reassurances from the multitude of mums, and no matter how much distance she covered on her exercise machines.

She scanned the messages, noting that everyone in the class but Jasmine had responded. She shook her head. No surprise there: Jasmine was probably annoyed that Alison was getting some attention. Jasmine didn't speak to her anyway, not even acknowledging her presence, and that was more than fine with Alison – the less they had to do with each other, the better. There was nothing more to talk about; they'd decided that long ago. If only Jasmine's daughter would leave Gabby alone too.

Alison sighed, thinking of the day Gabby had come home shaking with sobs and streaked to her room. She had only been able to prise out what had happened after several hours of asking over and over. Through her tears, Gabby had revealed that Juniper had taken a very uncomplimentary photo of her and then sent it to everyone, complete with various annotations. The incident had struck fear into Alison's heart because it was a reminder of what had happened decades earlier; of how something like this could start a whole chain of events that could never be reversed. Ever. It was almost as if history was repeating itself, unleashing its pent-up vengeance on those Alison loved most, just like she'd feared.

She pounded the cross trainer furiously, remembering how she'd spent most of secondary school afraid of being picked on. She might have been heavyset as a child, but she was never fat. She was shy, though, and an easy target for bullies. It had been so bad that one day she'd run away with a bottle of her mum's Nurofen. Her parents had found her before she'd had a chance to do anything, and she'd spent the last half of Year 7 at home. She'd only agreed to return to school after she'd moved to a secondary school in a new area, where no one knew her.

She'd been so relieved when one of the prettiest girls in her tutor group, Jasmine, had chosen to bully someone else. As long as that girl was in the firing line, Alison was safe. In a strange turn of events, she even became friends with Jasmine herself, though she'd never been able to believe that Jasmine really wanted to be friends with her. She wasn't even sure she liked Jasmine, but it was better to be on the side of the bully than against her. Alison knew that for a fact. Every day she'd spent with Jasmine, though, she'd been terrified she would be her next victim. And that terror, well... it had propelled her to do things she never would have done otherwise.

She sighed, trying to push away those memories. Her mobile started ringing, and she quickly hit answer. 'Hello?'

'It's Jasmine.'

Alison blinked. It was as if Jasmine had somehow invaded her thoughts and come from the past into her present. Why was she calling?

'I saw your message,' Jasmine continued. 'Lou picked up Juniper too.'

Alison froze. *Juniper?* The girl who was tormenting Gabby? Oh my God. Poor Gabby. She winced, picturing her daughter sitting beside Juniper, listening to her whisper horrible things for hours on end, wherever they were. It was bad enough that her daughter was missing, but... What was Juniper doing in the car anyway? Alison hadn't known Jasmine and Lou were friends, but then Lou was friendly with everyone.

Lou would be able to keep the two girls separated, she thought suddenly, taking a deep breath. She knew the situation.

'So have you heard anything?' Jasmine asked. 'I've tried texting both Juniper and Lou, and neither one is answering.' Her tone was more irritated than worried, and Alison shook her head. It was the same tone Jasmine had always used when one of them was slow or didn't do what she wanted straight away. It might be decades later, but she hadn't changed.

'I haven't heard anything from them yet,' she responded. 'The police rang earlier to request a photo of Gabby, though, as well as asking what she was wearing. At least they're taking this seriously now.'

'Yes, Aidan called them. He made sure they actually did something,' Jasmine said, and Alison bit her lip at the implication that she hadn't been able to get through to them. Well, she hadn't, had she? The officer had told her they'd simply keep an eye out, nothing more.

'Let me know if you hear anything,' Jasmine continued in that commanding tone.

'Same,' Alison managed to say before the phone clicked in her ear. Slowly, she set it down, the silence weighing on her as thoughts swirled in her head. She picked up a heavy weight, feeling her muscles work as she lifted it easily. This wasn't the past. Jasmine might not have changed, but she had. She was strong now. She wasn't the same fearful girl who'd been so afraid that she'd let Jasmine bully her into doing the very worst thing of her life.

But Gabby wasn't strong – not yet – and Alison couldn't let her carry the same scars.

She had to come back home soon, before something terrible happened.

TEN

FIONA

8 P.M.

Fiona jumped at the sound of knocking on the door. The doorbell had needed fixing for ages, but despite her many reminders to Nick to have a look, he'd never had the time. She glanced at her husband. He'd been sitting in the same spot, frozen, as she buzzed around him, straightening the tea towels and putting away dishes. She had to do *something* – the minutes had been unbearable as they waited, every muscle tense. She longed to make it better, but she had no idea what to say. The only thing that would make everything okay was having Tabitha and Timothy back home. And with every second that passed, it was getting harder and harder to keep the worry and fear in check, especially as the wind howled outside and rain lashed the windowpanes.

But Lou was with them, she reminded herself for the millionth time. Whatever had happened and wherever they were, Lou was there too. In the midst of everything, that was something for which she'd be eternally grateful.

She jerked at the sight of the police on the doorstep, her heart racing at their sombre faces. Oh God. What had happened? By the looks of things, it clearly wasn't something good.

'Hello, I'm PC Samar Gandhi,' the man said, 'and this is the family liaison officer, Steph Brisby.' Fiona nodded, barely able to take in their names amidst her racing mind and pounding heart. Family liaison officer? They didn't need that... did they?

'Can we come in?' the woman – Steph – asked, when Fiona didn't move from the door.

'Oh, of course. Yes, do come in.' She ushered them inside, then waited while they sloughed off their sodden jackets. 'I think you spoke to my husband on the phone.'

Officer Gandhi glanced at Nick, nodding. 'We wanted to update you on where we're at,' he said, and Fiona felt something inside her unwind. *Phew.* Just an update. 'We've been searching the area around the motorway, and we found an item we think might belong to Tabitha.'

Fiona sucked in her breath. 'An item? Can I see it?'

He took out a clear plastic evidence bag and handed it to her. She stared at it for a minute, the world turning dark as she realised what was inside the bag. It was a pink leopard-print headband, which she knew instantly belonged to Tabitha.

What had happened? How had it come off her daughter's head? Tabitha wouldn't have taken it off willingly, Fiona knew that much. She loved that thing. And... She froze. Was that *blood*? Her heart pounded and nausea swirled inside as she noticed that half of the headband was no longer pink, but a dark red where blood had dried.

Oh my God. Oh... She ran to the cloakroom and was sick into the toilet. This couldn't be happening. It couldn't be. The room churned around her, and she was sick again. Then she felt a hand on her back, and she lifted her head to see Steph holding out a glass of water. She took it gratefully, rinsing her mouth, then drinking some down.

'I know it's hard,' Steph said. 'But we can't jump to any

conclusions right now.' She took Fiona's arm and led her back to the sofa. 'The fact that we haven't found anything else is a good thing in a way. It means your daughter is all right and able to keep moving. Head wounds bleed a lot, and if your daughter was seriously injured, she wouldn't have made it far.'

Fiona nodded, then glanced over at her husband. He looked like a statue; like he was barely breathing. 'But where did you find it? Keep moving *where?*'

'It was at the bottom of the bank by the motorway, right before the treeline starts,' Officer Gandhi said. 'We believe they may have entered the woods.'

Fiona drew in a breath. The forest by the motorway stretched for miles, large trees and undulating hills punctuated only by a small lake in the middle and a lookout up a steep cliff. The river marked its boundary on one side, with the town's growing suburbs on the other. It was popular with hikers, and every few years someone would get lost in its depths. Sometimes, it would take days to find them – if they *were* even found. And to be out there in this weather...

'But why would they have gone into the woods? Do you think...' She paused, that fear circling through her again. 'Do you think they were running from something? From someone?' Nick was staring at the officer, his face mirroring her fear. She longed to move over beside him, to drink in his warmth and strength, but there was no room.

'It's possible. At this point, we just don't know.' He shook his head. 'We're examining all CCTV footage of the area to see if another vehicle picked them up, but it will take some time. We'll continue to search the banks and the perimeter of the woods as long as we can safely do so. We're also marshalling our specialist search-and-rescue team should we need to enter the woodland. The children may be hiding, waiting for someone to come.' He glanced at Steph, then back to Nick and Fiona.

'Is there anything else you'd like to share with us?' Officer

Gandhi turned to Fiona. 'You said you're good friends with Lou. How did she seem with you recently? Did you notice any unusual behaviour?'

Fiona's brow furrowed. 'How did she seem? What do you mean? She seemed how she always is: a great friend.' She paused. 'Lou would give you the clothes off her back if you needed them. She's that kind of neighbour... that kind of friend. She'd never do anything to hurt me or the children.' Why were they asking this? she wondered. Surely, they couldn't suspect Lou of something. But they didn't know her, she supposed. They had to entertain any possibility.

'Before we go, we'd like to collect DNA samples for the children. Just to have on hand,' Officer Gandhi added quickly, seeing Fiona's expression. 'An old toothbrush, maybe, or a hairbrush will do.'

She nodded and went upstairs to the bathroom, grabbing the kids' toothbrushes, then handing them to the officer back downstairs. Her eyes filled with tears as he put them into plastic bags. They should be here to use them right now. They shouldn't be out in the darkness, alone. The headband flashed into her mind, and she covered her mouth.

'Right, we'll leave you now,' Officer Gandhi said. 'Steph will keep you posted on anything more we find. And please feel free to call her at any time, right, Steph?'

She nodded and squeezed Fiona's arm.

Fiona showed them out, then closed the door behind them and turned to Nick. The house was so quiet without the twins. 'Nick, I'm scared. Tabitha...' The words eked out of her, expanding until they filled the whole space with fear and darkness. No matter what she must have tried, Lou hadn't been able to protect the kids. And now... now they were out there in the storm, her daughter injured and the others in who knew what state, running from something not even the police understood yet. 'If Lou hasn't been able to keep them safe, then they must

really be at risk.' She shook her head, still unable to believe this
was happening. 'God, can you believe they were asking me
about Lou? Do you think they suspect she's involved? That's
crazy.'

She waited for him to nod and agree; to fold her into his
arms – to say they would do something to make it better, to
come up with a solution like he always did – but instead he
stayed frozen in place, that same strange look on his face.

'I need to tell you something,' he said, his voice shaking.
'And I need you to stay quiet until I'm finished.' Fiona opened
her mouth, but he put up a hand. '*Please.* Please let me get this
out.' He looked so tortured that she nodded and followed him
silently to the sofa, sitting down beside him. But even though
they were now only inches apart, it still felt like miles.

He swallowed, and she could see his hands trembling. It
was so unlike him that worry shot through her. What on earth
was he going to say?

'I want you to know that nothing happened,' he began, and
she felt the unease twist deeper. 'But lately, maybe for the past
three or four months, we've been spending a lot of time
together.'

Fiona's head felt light, as if she was going to float up, up and
away from here... as if she was going to watch all of this unfold
from above. 'We?' The word came out as a whisper. Who did he
mean? Who was he spending a lot of time with? And what did
this have to do with Lou and the children going missing?

'Lou,' Nick said, and she felt herself drift loose from her
moorings. *Lou?* Nick had been spending time with Lou? Her
next-door neighbour Lou? Her best *friend*? But when? And how
could she not have noticed?

It couldn't be anything, she told herself frantically, trying to
calm down, to anchor herself again. Lou would never do
anything. And Nick, well... Nick always said he'd never betray
her trust; that he'd never forgive anyone who did such a thing.

Whatever it was, it was just neighbourly friendliness. Lou was like that. With his conscience and all, maybe Nick was feeling a little guilty, but there was nothing to feel guilty about. There couldn't be.

'Sometimes, before I'd come home, I'd go over to hers,' he said. Fiona's mouth dropped open in disbelief, anger stirring within her. All those nights she'd been alone here, crawling into bed by herself, and Nick had been right next door. Right next door with *Lou*. She pictured Lou's perfect clothes, perfect skin, perfect hair, quickly followed by her own sallow skin, lank locks and serviceable clothing that no one in their right mind would call stylish, and her certainty slipped. *Could* something have happened?

'I was coming home late from work one night, and I noticed her front door was swinging open in the wind. I rang the bell to tell her to close it, and she invited me in to try a whisky we'd been talking about.'

Fiona tilted her head. Whisky? Lou didn't drink whisky. In fact, Fiona had never really seen her drink at all. She always said she was saving her liver for when she was older and had nothing better to do than binge-drink and watch telly.

'I went inside, and we got chatting.' He sighed and met her eyes, and she flinched from the sadness in them. 'It was nice to actually talk to someone. Not that I'm saying that's an excuse, but... well, I feel like we barely speak any more.' Fiona swallowed, thinking how he was echoing what she'd thought herself. If they'd both felt that way, then why had neither of them bothered to change it? she wondered. Why had *she* never bothered to change it?

'I found myself popping by each night, and staying longer each time.' He looked away. 'And then last night... well, that's when it all changed.'

Fiona felt herself lock onto him, snapping back into her body with a vengeance. *When it all changed*? What did he mean? *Had* something happened? And why was he telling her about it now?

'Lou tried to kiss me,' he continued, and Fiona stared, unable to say anything; unable to right herself. 'She did kiss me, actually. I want to be honest with you. I was so shocked that it took me a second to pull away. Maybe I was naïve, but I really thought we were just friends. But now...' He dropped his head. 'Now I see that maybe we were more. We'd connected on an emotional level.'

Fiona's gut twisted, and bile rose in her throat. She'd been craving that emotional connection with her husband once more, and instead he'd had it with Lou. He'd *kissed* Lou. And Lou... She swallowed, thinking she might be sick again.

'Nothing really happened,' Nick repeated, but she shook her head. Something *had* happened. She could deal with a quick kiss. Hell, she'd done something similar herself, and she knew it meant nothing to her. But an emotional connection? That was worse. That was so much worse. 'I love you. I love our family. I shouldn't have spent so much time with Lou. It was wrong. I see that. And...' his eyes glistened with tears, and he rubbed them furiously, 'I think this thing with Lou might be the reason the children are missing. I told the police about it earlier. That's when they began really searching... why they started to take it seriously.'

Fiona frowned, trying to understand. 'You think that because you pulled away from Lou, she took our children?' That was crazy. No one tore someone else's life apart – kidnapped their children – because of one spurned advance.

But Nick nodded. 'You didn't see her, Fiona. She was so angry. It was like she became someone else. When I told her I couldn't... that I couldn't do that to you... I've never seen her look like that. Honestly, I couldn't get out of there fast enough.' He breathed in. 'And then today, the very next day, she disappeared with the kids. She disappeared, and... and she might have hurt Tabitha, by the looks of things. Oh God.' The blood-encrusted headband flashed into Fiona's mind again, and she winced. 'I can't bear the thought that our daughter is hurt because of me. Because of what I did.'

Fiona watched as he clutched his head, trying to absorb the fact that Lou hadn't been the friend she'd thought. That she'd tried to kiss her husband, and that... Could she have really taken the kids? And hurt Tabitha too? She loved Tabitha. Didn't she? But then Fiona had thought Lou loved her, too, and that they were friends. And yet the whole time, she'd been having late-night chats with Nick behind Fiona's back. She'd tried to kiss him. How could she do that?

And if she could do that, what else was she capable of?

'But... but there were other kids there too, right? If this is to get back at you, why would she take them?' Fiona asked, still trying to understand.

'I don't know,' Nick said. 'Maybe she got roped into driving them last minute. I'm not sure we can reason things out – anyone who would do something like this isn't thinking sensibly. And the way she reacted last night, well, it was clear to me that something was off.'

Fiona shuddered. She'd thought the kids would be safe because they'd been with Lou. She never could have imagined that Lou was behind all of this... that Lou was the one she should be worried about.

'I need to make this right,' Nick said, his eyes wild. 'I'm going to text Lou to say I'm sorry; that I never meant to hurt her. I'll say that we'll tell the police it's all been a big mistake and that we won't need to take this any further. Just let the kids come home.'

Fiona shook her head. 'There's only one problem,' she said. 'Lou doesn't have her mobile. How are you going to reach her?'

Nick's face drained of colour. 'Shit,' he said, rubbing his eyes. 'But I need to do something. I can't sit here and wait around. I *can't*.' He looked at her, and for the first time in weeks, it felt like he actually saw her. 'I really am so sorry. I don't know what I was thinking. I do love you.' He took her hand. 'If we're together, Lou can't hurt us. She can't break us. She can't tear up our family.'

Fiona nodded, but she couldn't help wondering about the secret that Lou did know, one that very well might tear them apart. But that had just been one night, and Nick had been going behind her back for weeks – no, months. Pain twisted her insides again. He would have to understand a slip-up, no matter what promises they'd made. Wouldn't he?

But she couldn't think about that right now. All that mattered was the kids – getting them back before anything else happened. God, Lou. She still couldn't believe it. Lou and her *husband*. They seemed so different. What on earth had they talked about all those nights?

And why couldn't he have talked to *her*?

'I'm going to call the police again and see if there's anything more we can do,' Nick said, getting to his feet. He stared down at her. 'I promise I'll make this up to you and the kids. Nothing will ever come between us again.'

Fiona swallowed as she watched him disappear up the stairs. She hoped he was right.

ELEVEN
TABITHA
8 P.M.

It's dark and cold. My legs are tired, but I can't stop. The trees bend and swoop in the wind above us, and rain drops onto us through thick boughs. Every time I slow, Tim grabs my arm and drags me deeper into the woods. We don't talk. We just keep moving forward, moving away. I shut my eyes against the image of Juniper's face, bloodied and dazed, the dripping crimson so bright against the dull, wintry land, as if it's been Photoshopped in art class. Who did that to her? Is she okay?

It's not real, I tell myself, my heart pounding. It can't be real.

But I know it is. It's not a horror film. It's real, and it's my fault. If only I hadn't needed to use the loo so badly, we'd never have stopped, and maybe none of this would have happened. I still don't know exactly what did happen, but I know it was something bad, something from a horror film, and everyone knows what happens in horror films: the kids get killed first.

We shouldn't have run. We should have helped, but Lou was there. Lou will make sure Juniper is okay. And by the look on Lou's face and the way she was yelling, I think she was telling us to go into the woods to hide. So I followed my brother

– younger by only two minutes, but always ahead of me. Gabby caught us up before we got too far into the forest, and she's plodding along beside us now as we push between trees, tripping over rocks and roots in the dark. My face stings from the branches that slap into my cheeks, my feet are soaking, and the strap on one of my school shoes has broken. I'm still desperate for a wee, and I really wish I'd listened to Mum and worn my trousers instead of the skirt I insisted on. Gabby's lips are blue, and I can tell by the way she keeps pulling her thin jumper around her that she's as cold as I am.

'Can we stop now?' I ask Tim for the millionth time, as he keeps moving forward. I've told him over and over that the best thing to do when you're lost in the woods is to sit down and let people come and find you. That's what they told us in Brownies anyway. But he won't listen to me. He just shakes his head, says that we don't want to be found, and keeps urging us on, away from the crashing behind us. I want to ask him what happened, but I haven't the breath, and part of me doesn't really want to know. It's easier to focus on what's in front of us.

But even Tim looks tired and a little scared now. We're out here on our own, and we've no idea where we are. He puts a finger to his lips. We all fall silent, and there's nothing but the sound of the wind in the trees. Usually, I like that sound, but now it reminds me how alone we really are.

'Should we make a shelter?' I ask through numb lips. We made a pretty good den together on our last trip to a National Trust place. There are plenty of dead branches around, and it shouldn't be too hard. I grimace as a drop of water splashes through the trees and onto my forehead. I don't know how waterproof anything we build will be, though.

'Look.' Tim points towards something in the distance. Squinting in the darkness, I can make out a little cabin positioned on the edge of a lake. The water glistens in the night, looking almost like a pool of black ink. I swallow against the fear rising up. We'll be okay, I tell myself. Whatever we were running from, we'll be fine.

'Do you think someone is in there?' I ask, as we trudge through the undergrowth towards it. My heart lifts at the thought of a warm fire, a cup of hot chocolate... a phone. Where is Juniper when you need her? She's always going on and on about her phone. I picture all that blood on her face, and fear jolts through me. I hope she's okay.

But my heart drops again when Tim shakes his head. 'Doesn't look like it. It might be a fishing hut or a bird hide, and they probably don't use it this time of year. But maybe we can find some food and water there, and at least we'll have somewhere to keep dry.' I nod and follow him towards it, wishing for the millionth time that I was as calm and capable as him. He always seems to know what to do, unlike me. And even if I did, would people listen? I try to talk, but the only one who ever acknowledges me is Tim. Even Mum's too distracted by stuff to really listen.

We push on through the woods towards the cabin, which I'm starting to think isn't real at all. Finally, we get there, soaked through now and absolutely freezing, and of course the door is locked.

'What now?' I ask, barely able to get the words out.

Tim, Gabby and I all stare at each other. I cup my hands and peer through the window. Inside I can make out a narrow bed, a counter lined with cupboards, and a rough wooden chair in the corner. Never has something so basic looked so welcoming.

Tim takes a big gulp of air and throws himself at the door. Nothing. He tries again, and still nothing. Then Gabby, who's a bit bigger than Tim, has a go, and amazingly, it bursts open. We all spill inside, closing the door behind us. It's freezing in here, but at least we're out of the rain and wind. There is a stack of woolly jumpers, an old mac, and thick blankets on the bed. It's still pitch black, and we knock over countless items trying to wrap ourselves in the warm things, but we'll fix all of that in the morning. I'm sure whoever owns this cabin won't mind. Right now, with these four walls around us, I feel safe for the first time since Tim dragged me into the forest what feels like hours ago.

My mind flashes to Juniper and Lou on the grassy bank. Where are they right now? Is Juniper okay? Are they in the woods too, trying to escape like we did? Or...

I meet Tim's eyes, trying to be brave. I need to know. 'Tim, what happened?' I ask. 'Why did we run?'

He blinks, and I think how I've never seen him look so exhausted. His face is white, and his dark hair looks even darker against the pale skin.

'I hate her,' he says, his mouth twisting around the words, his eyes flashing.

I stare in surprise. 'What do you mean? Juniper?' I can understand that, but...

He shakes his head. 'No, not Juniper. *Lou.*'

'Lou?' What on earth? How can he hate Lou? She's so nice – the sort of mum everyone wants to have, me included. She's Mum's best friend, and I kind of feel like she's my best friend too. I've never told Mum this, but I don't have a lot of friends in school. The other girls can sit and talk about TikTok, hair and make-up for ages every break time. I'm not allowed to watch TikTok, I have no clue what to do with my hair, and the few times I tried to put on make-up, Tim took one look at me and burst out laughing. Sometimes, I feel like they're all speaking another language that I'll never be able to understand, and when I asked Mum to teach me how to use mascara, she patted my arm and told me I look fine as I am.

But Lou seems to get it – to understand that I feel alone... *lonely.* She's started showing me how to straighten my curly hair, and she even lets me have a sneaky peek at TikTok – as long as I don't tell my mum, she laughs. That night we spent at Lou's when Mum had a work party, I stayed up chatting with her for ages after everyone else went to sleep. She was so interested: asking loads of questions about everything, from what our family likes to do to my favourite school dinners. I love spending time with her, and I've even started going over sometimes after supper. Mum's so busy tidying everything up that she doesn't even realise I'm gone.

Tim stares at me now, and once again I feel like he's years older. 'I went to Lou's last night to give back Saish's game. I couldn't sleep, but I knew she was awake because all the lights were on.' He bites his lip. 'And I saw Dad with her.' His jaw clenches, and I raise my eyebrows. Dad? With Lou? I didn't even know they talked. But what's the big deal? 'They were laughing and joking around. Dad looked so happy.' His face twists. 'And then they kissed.'

His voice is so low that at first I'm not sure I've heard what he said. He couldn't have said *kissed*. I shake my head and laugh. 'Kissed? No. No way.'

Tim nods. 'I ran back home after that, and Dad came in soon after. But I know what I saw.' His face is set in that stubborn look, and I know I'll never be able to convince him it's nothing. Maybe they did kiss, but adults do, don't they? Mum's always kissing her friends on the cheek. That's probably what Tim saw. Lou wouldn't do anything like that to Mum... anything like that to me.

'I don't want to be anywhere near her,' Tim's saying now, his voice tight with anger. 'I don't want to see that fake smile, listen to her laugh, breathe the same air.' I keep staring. I've never heard him talk like this. 'So when she stopped the car so you could go to the loo, I had to get away from her. I didn't want to stay there any longer.'

My mouth drops open. 'So that's it?' I ask. 'We're lost in the woods because you didn't want to breathe the same air as *Lou*?' My voice rises as I think of how I trusted him, of how we kept moving deeper and deeper into the forest, of how I should have just told him to *stop*.

'I didn't mean for us to get lost,' he says. 'I thought we'd hang out in the trees for a bit to make her scared or something. I don't know. I didn't mean for everyone else to follow. And when I saw Lou running after us, I didn't want her to catch us, so I kept going.'

I keep staring. I still can't believe what I'm hearing. I'm glad there's no axe murderer chasing us, but still... 'But what about Juniper?' I ask. 'How did she get hurt?'

Tim shakes his head. 'I didn't see what happened.'

We all freeze as we hear footsteps crashing through the trees, the noise getting nearer and nearer. Is help on the way? I'm closest to the window, so I pop my head up. Two figures, one bigger than the other, are making their way through the dark forest towards us. In the dim light I can't see their faces, and Tim squints beside me.

'It's Lou,' he says, his voice tight with tension. 'Lou and Juniper.'

As soon as I hear the words, a whoosh of relief goes through me. Juniper's okay! And Lou's here too. Thank God. Whatever Tim thought he saw, he can't be right. Lou loves us – she loves our family. And now she's here to save us. She'll get us home safe and sound.

Just as I think that, there's a huge noise outside, like a gunshot, then the sound of something crashing to the ground. My heart jumps into my throat, and Tim and I stare at each other before turning to look out the window again. I catch my breath. A massive tree has splintered and fallen, narrowly missing the cabin – and Lou and Juniper, thank goodness.

I run to the door to open it, but Tim grabs my arm. 'What are you doing? Don't let her in.'

I stare at him. 'Are you *serious*?' He's not thinking straight. A tree almost fell on her... and us. We might be sheltered, but

THE MOTHER NEXT DOOR 69

it's still not safe to stay here. We need Lou to get us out of this, and Juniper might need help. I shake my head. I always listen to Tim. I always follow him. I followed him into the woods, and I kept running. I didn't ask him anything, like always. And look where we are now.

Something bursts inside me. I never think on my own. If I had, I wouldn't be in this stupid forest freezing my butt off for nothing. And I'm not going to let Lou and Juniper freeze out there either. This time I'm not going to listen to my brother. I *am* going to think for myself.

I jerk from his grip and push open the door, right when Lou and Juniper reach it. 'Lou!' I cry, throwing myself against her. Beside me, I can almost feel the anger radiating off Tim. But I don't care. He can be angry all he likes.

She comes into the small space, pulling a dazed Juniper behind her, and I feel something inside me relax. I was right to let her in. Lou is here. She's here, and she'll take care of us. She is my best friend, after all.

Finally, I've made the right move.

Fiona leaned against the kitchen counter, staring at her mobile and willing it to ring with the news that her children had been found. The heavy air swirled around her, pressing down, as she tried to breathe... tried to understand why Lou was doing this; *how* she could do this. Was she simply angry and wanted revenge – to scare Nick by taking away the people he held dearest? If Lou had wanted to damage their marriage, she could have told him Fiona's secret.

Why hadn't she?

Maybe Nick was wrong, she thought now. Maybe this had nothing to do with him at all.

Her phone bleeped, and she scooped it up. It was a message from... She squinted at the name. From Juniper, Jasmine's daughter. *Jasmine*. Fiona stared at the screen, her mind spinning. She would never forget how her heart had dropped when she'd spotted the familiar face at the school gates. This was the very reason she hadn't wanted to move back here: so she'd never have to confront her past. And then to see Alison too... Their eyes had met and they'd all turned away, as if repelled by an invisible force. They'd kept their distance from each other ever since.

Why was Juniper texting her? Ah, yes. She'd put Fiona's number into her mobile one day when Tabitha had been assigned her as a partner in the school badminton club and they'd had to arrange practices. Fiona hadn't been able to believe that an eleven-year-old had her own top-end iPhone, but she'd been happy that the girls could organise everything themselves and she wouldn't have to talk to Jasmine. Maybe this was about next week's match.

She clicked open the message, the phone almost dropping from her hand when she read the words on the screen.

> *It's Lou. I have your children. I'll return them when you tell the truth.*

Fiona blinked, so many thoughts swarming through her head that she couldn't grasp on to anything. Why did Lou have Juniper's phone? Was Juniper one of the kids she'd picked up? She must be. Her stomach twisted as she stared at the words. As crazy as it seemed, it was obvious now that Lou *had* taken the children. And she wanted to destroy Fiona's marriage; to make sure there was no way back from this.

Nick may have cheated emotionally, but as hurt as she was, Fiona believed they could move past that. But if she told him about that night... She swallowed. He had always said he could deal with almost anything, but the one thing he couldn't take was if she was intimate with someone else. He'd been terribly hurt in the past, he'd said, and he needed to know he could trust the person he was sharing his life with. She'd solemnly sworn she would never betray him. She didn't remember all the finer details of what she'd done, but it could very well be enough to destroy their trust; their marriage.

She stared down at the phone, her mind flipping back to

that night. God, she wished it had never happened. It should never have happened. It never *would* have if she hadn't had so much to drink. She hadn't even been looking forward to going to the work party. It had been ages since she'd been out, and in desperation, she'd turned to Lou to ask her what to wear. Lou had taken one look at the few potential outfits she'd put together and shaken her head.

'Come with me,' she'd said, beckoning her into the bedroom. Fiona had followed, her eyes widening when she'd seen the huge closet full of clothes and shoes that Lou had in there. It was like being in a shop full of dreams, packed with garments in vivid colours made from expensive-looking fabrics.

'Wow,' she had breathed, reaching out to touch a spangled scarf. Lou always looked amazing, of course, but Fiona had had no idea she owned all of this. Where on earth did she wear it? When had she worn it?

Lou smiled. 'I know. It's a bit much, isn't it? I should donate some to charity and free up this space. I had a bit of a clothes habit when I was younger.'

A bit? Fiona nodded and smiled, thinking that was an understatement.

'But it does come in handy for times like this,' Lou went on, rifling through the closet. She selected a royal-blue midi dress with a nipped-in waist and a draped neckline and held it up against Fiona. 'This will look fantastic on you,' she said, and Fiona glanced in the mirror, her eyes widening in surprise. Lou was right. The blue brought out the deep blue of her eyes, and her skin looked more ivory than sickly white. And her hair, which had faded from glossy auburn to a greying ginger, actually looked a vibrant red again.

'Are you sure you don't mind me borrowing it?' she asked, running a hand over the silky fabric. She couldn't see the label, but she knew it was expensive.

Lou shook her head. 'Not at all. You can keep it, actually. I don't think I've even worn it! Must have got it on sale or something.' She rummaged again and came out with a pair of sparkly silver high-heeled sandals. 'These will look perfect with the dress if they fit. What size are you?' She glanced at Fiona's feet. 'Five?'

Fiona nodded, cringing as she thought of her toenails. It had been a very long time since she'd had a pedicure. 'Thank you so much,' she'd said, holding the clothes against her. 'I almost want to go now.'

Lou had put a hand on her arm. 'Enjoy it. Have a drink. Have a few! And a flirt or two. It will be good for you to get out. You deserve some male attention.' She laughed at the expression on Fiona's face. 'You *do*. I'm not saying you have to do anything, but just have fun. And if you're worried about the kids, they can stay here overnight, or Nick can come and get them when he's home.'

Fiona tilted her head now, Lou's words ringing in her ears. She'd definitely had a drink or two, and she'd definitely had a flirt – and attracted a man. Her heart sank as a thought filtered in. Had Lou been trying to encourage her to lose control? Had she wanted to destroy their marriage even then? Fiona had thought she'd been such a good friend, but...

God, if only she hadn't had all that tequila. If only she hadn't gone up to Teo's room for a nightcap. If only she hadn't closed her eyes for that one brief moment and sunk down onto his bed...

If only he hadn't chosen that moment to kiss her...

Guilt swarmed through her yet again. She hadn't wanted their harmless flirting to end with *that*. But one small thing had led to another, until... She sighed. Should she have known? Should she have walked away when he'd started complimenting her? Rejected his offer of a drink? She hadn't wanted to be rude, and if she was being honest, it felt so nice to be wanted; to be told how beautiful she was. To feel not like her, but more like Lou in these beautiful clothes.

She'd woken up in his room a few hours later, not even sure what exactly had happened. She didn't think she'd slept with him... had she? No, she was sure she hadn't. She hadn't even stayed the night; just taken an Uber home, had a shower and immersed herself in the daily grind, pulling the security blanket of domestic life around her. She'd thought she'd put the whole thing out of her mind until Lou had asked how the party was and the story had tumbled out. Lou had told her to forget about it, and Fiona had tried. She really had.

But now she had to tell Nick. She didn't have a choice. Maybe Lou could destroy their marriage, but Fiona couldn't let her hurt the kids. Tabitha's headband flashed into her mind, and she winced. If she hadn't already, that was.

Slowly, she climbed the stairs to the bedroom. She pushed open the door, and Nick glanced up from where he was hunched over his phone. Her eyes traced his familiar face as emotions flashed through her. They'd been together for years, and they'd built a life. It was a life she loved. She loved *him*, despite how far they'd drifted apart. Their world was busy and she enjoyed that, but by focusing only on the minutiae, they'd allowed the bigger picture of the love that had framed them to fall away, leaving them exposed and vulnerable.

And they'd both cracked.

Sadness and regret filtered into her. Why hadn't she done something sooner?

Why had she stood by and let it happen?

'I need to tell you something,' she began slowly, an echo of his earlier words to her. She glanced around the bedroom, knowing that in a second, the peaceful, warm nest they'd created together would be gone. But maybe it had disappeared long ago, without her even noticing.

'What?' Nick rubbed a hand through his hair, looking so pale and drawn.

She swivelled her phone towards him.

His brow furrowed as he read the message. 'It's Lou? Why is she texting you? She must have meant to send that to me.' He glanced up at her. 'I thought she didn't have her phone with her.'

'It's from a girl called Juniper,' Fiona said. 'She must be one of the kids in the car. Lou used her phone.' She bit her lip. Oh God. 'Nick... you remember that work party I went to a couple of months ago?'

His face was blank, and she dropped her eyes. Of course he didn't. He barely remembered what she did yesterday.

'When the kids slept over at Lou's?' she asked. 'On a school night?' She breathed in sharply as a shot of jealousy hit her. Had Lou been trying to get her out of the way so she could have Nick to herself? It seemed pretty likely now.

'Oh, yes,' he said, but she could see by his face that he still wasn't clear. It didn't matter, though. It had happened, and all that was important now was telling him and getting their children back as soon as possible.

'Well, I made a huge mistake that night.' She met his eyes, hating doing this. She never wanted to hurt him. 'I...' She swallowed, looking down again. She couldn't look at his face when she said the words. 'I had too much to drink,' she managed to get out. 'And I... well, I kissed someone. I don't think much else happened,' she added quickly, cringing as she realised how bad those words sounded. 'It didn't mean anything.' She still couldn't look up, couldn't bear to see the expression on his face. 'I was so drunk, and it... I'm sorry, Nick. So sorry.'

Silence fell, the only sound the ticking of the clock she hated and kept meaning to give to charity but never had. And then she heard a noise from Nick – something she'd never heard from him before. A groan of disbelief and pain, almost like he'd been wounded.

'You let me tell you how sorry I was for being friends with Lou – for a kiss I didn't even initiate, and that I stopped as soon as I could,' he said finally. 'And all the while you were sitting here knowing what you did and never even once thinking to tell me?'

'I didn't want to hurt you,' Fiona said. 'It meant nothing. The same way your kiss meant nothing.' She could hardly believe their marriage had come to this. Who *were* they?

'It's not the same,' Nick said, shaking his head. Her heart sank as she realised he could barely even bring himself to look at her. 'It's not the same at all. I didn't want to kiss her.' His face shifted as he said the words, and she wondered whether he was telling the truth; whether he even knew the truth. 'And I stopped it as soon as it happened.' He met her eyes now. 'Did you stop it? Did you want to kiss him?'

Fiona swallowed, and silence fell again.

'Exactly,' Nick said grimly. 'Was it just...' He breathed in, and she could see how vulnerable he was. God, she hated this. 'Was it just a kiss, or *was* it more?' The words were quiet, as if he had to force them from his very depths.

She held his gaze, her heart beating fast. What could she say? That she'd been so drunk it was all a blur? That she was almost certain they hadn't slept together, but as for anything else, well...

His face twisted. 'Right.' The word was coloured by his pain and anger, and an icy fear swept through her. Could they ever find their way back from this? 'You know what? I wish I hadn't pushed Lou away.'

Fiona sucked in air. He couldn't mean that.

'Not because I wanted to kiss her,' he said. 'But because if I had, I could have saved the kids from all of this. And as for us... I'm not sure there's anything left to save.' He shook his head

THE MOTHER NEXT DOOR 77

again. 'Text Lou. I'll call the police and let them know what's happened.' He didn't even wait for her to respond before picking up his phone and ringing the investigating officer in charge of the case, walking out of the room as he filled them in. It was like letting a stranger peek into the dark place where they hid their most painful secrets, but right now, Fiona would do anything to see the children.

She watched him go, feeling the picture of their life – their marriage – shatter into a million pieces. She'd been right to think this would ruin everything. She still knew her husband well, even if they were miles apart. But that was little consolation for the pain lodged inside. She didn't have time to think of that now, though. Her marriage might collapse, but she had to get her children back.

She picked up her phone from where he'd dropped it and started typing.

I told him about that night. Now please, PLEASE let the children go.

Then she sat back and waited.

THIRTEEN

ALISON

9.30 P.M.

Alison sat on the sofa, her eyes wide, staring at the heavy curtains. She'd been longing to change them for years – along with the hideous green-and-gold flocked wallpaper in the study. Funnily enough, that wallpaper was the height of fashion right now. Still, she hated it. The house had never felt like hers, despite the number of years she'd been here.

But while she might not love the house, she did love the life she lived inside it. Maybe she didn't deserve all she had, but she'd had to move forward somehow – she'd had to find a way to cope with what she'd done. She'd never been happier than when Gabby was born, and as she'd stared down at her daughter's sweet, innocent face, she'd vowed that nothing bad would happen to her. She'd promised to protect her; to use her new strength to keep her safe.

And now... now her daughter was out there without her. She prayed the kids weren't outside because rain was slicing through the air with a vengeance, and wind rattled the windows. Gabby might be fitter now, but could she use that strength to stand up for herself if she needed to? And even if she was strong, she didn't have her asthma medication with her. The exercise she'd been doing lately really helped, and she hadn't needed it as much, but what if she had an attack?

What if the river did burst its banks, and Gabby was nearby? Lou's car hadn't been found too far from where the river crossed the motorway, after all. Would Gabby be swept away or cut off from them?

Alison drew in a breath, once more batting away the feeling that justice would be served at last. This wasn't about the past. Even if Alison wasn't with Gabby, Lou was. That thought was the one thing keeping Alison from going completely crazy. The one thing stopping her from thinking that karma was out for her, after all.

Her mobile beeped, and she ran to grab it. Juniper! She'd saved the girl's number into her phone the day Gabby had showed her the bullying photo. Shaking with rage, she had called Juniper directly and told her to stop, then blocked the number from Gabby's phone. That had seemed to work – as far as she knew anyway. Why was Juniper texting her now? Were the kids all right? Was this a message from Gabby? Heart beating fast, she clicked it open.

It's Lou. I have your daughter. I'll return her when you tell the truth.

Alison stared at the phone, her mind spinning. What the hell? *Lou* had Gabby – she was the one keeping her from coming home? And what did she mean, 'tell the truth'? The truth about what? Alison didn't have any secrets – nothing besides... She winced. Nothing besides what she'd done to keep the gym afloat. Her mind flashed to Lou's expression when she'd told her about forging Greg's signature. She definitely hadn't approved. But what business was it of hers anyway?

Why would she want Alison to tell the truth about that – to the point where she'd taken Gabby to try to force her hand?

She must know that if the bank found out, they'd tell Alison to repay the money. There was no way Alison could do that. The gym would collapse without... She flinched as a thought hit. Without Lou's investment.

Had Lou been serious, after all? Did she want to invest so badly she'd do something like this?

Alison tilted her head, fear stirring inside as she remembered their conversation. It had seemed of little consequence at the time but loomed large in importance now. They'd been in the office, and she'd shared with Lou the fact that gym costs were rising on all fronts. Even though the membership was growing, the revenue wasn't enough any more. And then Lou had surprised her by offering to buy out 50 per cent of the business and become a partner.

Alison had stared. Did Lou even have that kind of money? It would definitely solve a problem, but... this gym was Alison's hideaway, the only place she felt completely comfortable; the only thing that belonged entirely to her. If Lou came on board, Alison had no doubt she'd want to redesign everything, from the simple, no-fuss way Alison had done it to a chichi place fit for the town's finest. And while that was no bad thing, it wasn't Alison. It wasn't the place she wanted.

'We can upgrade the café,' Lou was saying, as if she'd heard Alison's thoughts. 'Stock organic products, open a crèche with high-quality caregivers, redo the pool area and...' She stopped when Alison put a hand on her arm.

'That all sounds amazing,' she said carefully, not wanting to offend her friend. 'But don't you have your hands full with the kids and your own business?' Lou was always rushing around here, there and everywhere, talking non-stop about her projects. Alison honestly had no idea how she kept it all together.

Lou shrugged. 'I need something different. I'm ready for a new challenge.' She paused, leaning forward. 'Please, Alison. You need the money, I know you do. And this really could be amazing. Just think about it. Please.' She was smiling, but there was something strange in her eyes.

As much as Alison didn't want to offend her, she didn't want this place to belong to anyone but her. 'I'm sorry, Lou,' she said, 'I really am, but I'm not open to a partnership right now.'

Lou stared at her, then nodded and shrugged. 'That's a shame, but I understand. You want to keep it in the family.' She smiled even wider, as if trying to show it was okay, but still her eyes didn't look right. There was a hardness there that Alison hadn't seen before, and she felt the hairs bristle on the back of her neck. 'Well, good luck with it all. Let me know if you change your mind.'

'I won't change my mind,' Alison said. 'I'm sorry, but I won't.' She didn't want to leave Lou any room for the possibility.

'You might.' And with that, Lou had slung her gym bag over her shoulder and walked out of the room.

Alison blinked now, trying to get a grip on everything. *You might.* She shivered, remembering that hard look in Lou's eyes. Had she taken Gabby to force Alison to tell the truth about the remortgage, so the bank would cancel it, leaving her no choice but to accept Lou's offer or lose everything? Going to this extreme was hardly the ideal way to start a partnership, though. Who would want to work with someone who'd threatened their child?

Unless... Alison caught her breath. Maybe Lou didn't want a partnership; maybe she wanted everything. She'd said she was ready for a new challenge. With Alison unable to repay the money she'd taken, the gym would have to close; be sold to someone else. Maybe Lou was gunning to be that someone else.

Maybe she'd thought Alison would simply cave without getting the police involved, and she could swoop in to buy the business. And maybe she'd taken Juniper knowing that Gabby didn't get on with her and that her presence would make Alison even quicker to admit what she'd done. Alison jerked, wondering if Jasmine was in on all of this. Could that be why she hadn't sounded more worried: because Lou had told her what she was planning?

She shook her head. No, she was being ridiculous now, letting the past get the better of her for a second. Jasmine wouldn't call the police if she'd been in on it, unless... An image of the empty car at the side of the road flashed into her mind. Unless things somehow hadn't gone to plan and the kids *were* in danger now.

She sighed, wondering if she was going mad; if this was all some crazy joke. How could someone like Lou – someone who seemed so calm, so together – do this? But as hard as it was to believe, Lou *had* done this. Gabby wasn't in safe hands – in trusted hands – like Alison had told the police. Now Alison had to do whatever it took to get her back, even if it meant losing her business... and potentially her marriage. She had to tell Greg what she'd done, and then she'd call the bank.

'Greg?' She ran up the stairs to the snug, where he was watching news of the storm on TV. She'd never lied to him about anything. He trusted her with all his heart. How would he react when he learned she'd jeopardised something he held so dear?

He turned towards her. 'Is everything okay? Did the police find the kids? What's happened?'

Alison sat down beside him, touching his arm to calm the wild look in his eyes. 'The police haven't found anything. Not yet. But...' She handed him the mobile with the text on the screen. 'Lou sent me this just now.' She held her breath, watching him read it.

'I don't get it,' he said, looking up at her. His face had gone white now, the muscles pulling at his cheeks making it seem like he'd aged ten years in a minute. 'What does she want you to tell? And what does Gabby have to do with it?'

'It's not about Gabby,' Alison said, desperate now to reassure him. He looked like he was about to topple over. 'Not really. It's about the gym.'

'The gym?'

She scooted closer. 'You know how the business has been in a bit of a state lately,' she said. 'Well, I had to do something. So...' She stopped abruptly as Greg put his hand up.

'Ali, I know,' he said, and her brow furrowed.

'What do you mean?' There was no way he could have discovered what she had done. Was there?

'I know what you did – that you remortgaged the house.'

She stared. What the hell? How had he found out?

'You left your mobile here one day when you were out with Gabs. The bank called, and I picked up. There was a question about something on the remortgaging application, and since I was named, they asked if I could answer it so they could get on with the paperwork.'

Alison felt every muscle tense. Oh my God. Oh my *God*. 'Why didn't you tell me you knew?'

Greg held her gaze. 'Why didn't you ask me in the first place?'

She dropped her eyes. 'I was afraid you'd say no,' she said, plucking at a loose thread on the duvet. 'I know how much this house means to you.'

Greg put a hand on top of hers. 'I know how much *you* mean to me – and how much the gym means to you. This place...' He glanced around the room, sighing. 'This place never should have been mine. It was always supposed to be my younger stepsister's. She had some issues and was never able to hold down a full-time job, so my dad wanted to make sure she was cared for. Neither my sister nor I wanted it anyway. After my mum left, it never felt like home.'

Alison raised her eyebrows. She'd never heard this before. She'd known Greg had a stepsister, but she'd never met her. When Greg's father had remarried, Greg had already been at uni, and he hadn't ever lived with her. His father and step-mother had been killed in an accident a few years after Alison and Greg married, and she hadn't gone to the funeral. Neither Greg nor his sister – who was a couple years older than their stepsister and had been very close to her – had been able to reach her. They'd fallen out of touch years earlier.

'My dad left the house to her, like I said, but I couldn't track her down to let her know. Eventually, I hired a lawyer to help distribute the assets, with an insurance policy that if she was ever found, she could claim her share.' He shifted on the sofa. 'So legally the house belongs to me, but in a way it feels like I'm saving it for when she comes back. That's why I haven't wanted to change anything. It doesn't feel like it's mine. Yes, it's a great space and we are so lucky to have it. But what really matters is you.' He squeezed her hand. 'You – and Gabby. Without you both, this place is nothing. You're my rock, Alison. I've never met anyone as strong, as determined as you. And whatever you need, I will be there. I want to be your rock too. If you need me to pretend that I signed those papers myself, I'm more than happy to.'

Alison felt tears come to her eyes. A rock: strong and solid. That was how he saw her, and that was exactly how she wanted to be. Unmovable in the torrent. She wouldn't let anyone shift her, not like in the past. She *was* strong, and together they were even stronger. Together they could face anything, even a woman like Lou.

God, how had she got so lucky? That same old guilt, the same fear that it all would come crashing down, threaded into her, but she pushed it away. Karma would not triumph this time.

'Let me text Lou and tell her that I've told you,' she said, energy surging through her body once more. 'I won't say any more – the police can tell her she did all of this for nothing when they arrest her.' She shook her head. Arrest *Lou*, and all for the sake of owning the gym. It still seemed so unbelievable, but people did strange things somethings. Horrible things. She knew that from experience. 'She'd better have Gabby back here within the hour, or there's going to be hell to pay.'

It felt good to have power. Lou had thought she'd break her; break the gym. She couldn't have been more wrong. Alison grabbed the mobile and quickly texted her, then put the phone down again, awaiting the answering ping of a message.

'So tell me how Lou fits into all of this,' Greg said.

Alison quickly explained, and his eyebrows flew up. 'So you think she wanted the gym that badly?' he asked, echoing her own incredulity. 'Badly enough to do something like this?' His brow furrowed. 'Why wouldn't she just tell me or the bank herself?'

'I know it sounds crazy. It *is* crazy. But there's something...' She thought of the look in Lou's eyes that day; of the way Lou had said that Alison might change her mind, as if she knew something Alison didn't. 'There's something *off* about her. I can't quite put my finger on it, but it scared me.' Fear shot through her again as she thought of Gabby, alone somewhere without her medication.

Greg squeezed her hand. 'Well, now that you've told me everything and she knows you have, all of this will be over soon. It will be over, and we're not going to let someone like her bully us. Bullies only respond to strength, right?'

Alison nodded, thinking how she'd told Gabby that – told herself that – a million times.

'So let's call the police. Gabby will come home, and Lou

will face the consequences for what she tried to do to us.' He squeezed her hand again. 'She'll find out who's really in control. She picked the wrong people to mess with.'

Alison stared at him, love swelling inside. Now they just had to get Gabby home, and their little fortress would be complete.

Nothing would ever breach it again.

FOURTEEN

JASMINE

9.30 P.M.

Jasmine rubbed her fingers over her face. She could still feel the round red sites that had swollen from the injections, and she prayed that they'd be better soon. She couldn't look this bad when Juniper returned! Aidan had been so worried, but whatever had happened, Jasmine was sure Lou had everything in hand. The police would probably find them all in a diner somewhere, scoffing burgers and milkshakes, amazed that people had caused such a fuss. Aidan would be the one who'd be embarrassed then, praising her for staying so calm. In the meantime, at least she could tell him that she'd done something by contacting Alison to see if she'd heard anything – as well as sending the police Juniper's most flattering photo and lending them her hairbrush for a DNA sample. She hadn't been sitting around drinking like he'd accused her. But even if she had been drinking, this was hardly a usual situation. What mother didn't deserve a little comfort when her beloved daughter was missing?

Rain splattered against the window and wind banged the panes, and Jasmine winced as she gazed into the darkness. It was awful out there. Hopefully, Aidan would be home any minute with their daughter, and they'd put on their favourite Netflix show and snuggle up. She reached for the shot glass and had a quick one to tide her over until then.

'Juniper!' Her heart leapt as her daughter's name flashed up on her mobile. Oh thank God. She was okay. She had been right not to worry, after all. She clicked open the message and scanned it, her brow furrowing.

> It's Lou. I have your daughter. I'll return her when you tell the truth.

What in the actual *hell*? Jasmine read the message again, trying to understand the words. Lou had taken Juniper? *Lou?* She was keeping her away from home on purpose? But why? And what did she mean: *I'll return her when you tell the truth*? Jasmine didn't have any secrets, least of all from Lou. She glanced around the room, taking in the stylish decor they'd pored over for hours. For God's sake, they were the best of friends.

Yes, there'd been that one little incident where Lou had gone spare, but... Jasmine tilted her head, remembering Lou's words, that the truth had a way of coming out. She couldn't mean *that*, though, surely. What was there to tell anyway? Jasmine had had one drink and then chosen to drive, completely in control? Anyway, Lou had realised she'd overreacted. That comment about being a bad mother had been way over the top.

She stared at the screen, remembering that Lou had Alison's daughter too. Maybe this text was meant for Alison. Maybe Lou had sent it to the wrong person by mistake. God knows, Jasmine couldn't imagine what someone as wet as Alison could have done to cause Lou to flip out like this, but whatever it was, she was going to *kill* her for putting her daughter at risk. Anger surged through her as she brought up Alison's contact on the WhatsApp group. She was about to hit call when her mobile rang with an unknown number. Cautiously, she answered.

'Hello?' Her voice sounded loud in the empty space.

'It's Fiona. Fiona Bryson.'

The voice filtered through the handset, bringing a million memories with it. They might have kids at the same school, but just like with Alison, Jasmine hadn't spoken to Fiona for years. An image flashed through her mind of that first day in Year 7, when she'd been assigned the locker next to Fiona's. Fiona had shot her an admiring glance, and to Jasmine, it had felt like the sun after darkness. She'd basked in it, letting it buoy her up. That morning, she'd had to clean her mum up after she'd wet her trousers when she'd drunk too much the night before, and she felt like the scent of urine still clung to her. Fiona's gaze had righted her. Jasmine shot her a bright smile and started chattering away, loving how Fiona looked so stunned that she was talking to her.

Why the hell was the woman calling now? Had she heard that Juniper was missing and was ringing to offer commiserations and support? No, that would be very unlike Fiona. She never took any initiative on her own – or at least she never used to. An uncomfortable memory snaked into Jasmine's mind, and she shook her head to dislodge it.

'I'm ringing to let you know that I got a message from Lou,' Fiona said, her voice tight with tension. '"I have your children",' she read aloud. '"I'll return them when you tell the truth." It came from Juniper's phone, so that's how I know she has your daughter too. This whole thing is my fault, and I'm so sorry Juniper got caught up in it. Lou only wanted to take my kids in order to... Well, it doesn't matter. I don't know how Juniper ended up with them.'

Jasmine nodded, her earlier thoughts confirmed. She knew that message couldn't have been directed at her. Lou knew she had no secrets, and that one little incident was well behind them. God knows why the text had come through on her phone if it had been meant for Fiona, but obviously Lou wasn't thinking clearly right now. Maybe she'd sent it to a few contacts by accident.

'Anyway,' Fiona was continuing, 'I've texted the information she wanted, so she should return the children soon. I hope. Again, I'm so sorry.' Her voice cracked, and anger and irritation flooded through Jasmine.

'They'd better be back soon,' she said, her voice like a knife. 'Or you can bet I'll be taking action against you and your family, and whatever you did to cause this – whatever you did to put my daughter at risk. I'll make sure to get Alison in on it too. She's desperate to have Gabby back home.'

'Alison?' Fiona's tone was puzzled.

'Lou also has Gabby, Alison's daughter,' Jasmine said.

'Oh God. Well, I'm sure this will all be over soon.'

'Like I said, it'd better be.' Jasmine paused. 'Call me if you hear anything more.'

She hung up, then went upstairs to tidy her hair and put on some make-up. Juniper would be back any minute, and she'd no doubt be rattled by whatever had happened. Imagine Lou pulling a stunt like this to get back at someone. What on earth had Fiona done? But then Lou *was* a little extreme – that was obvious in her reaction to Jasmine that afternoon. Part of Jasmine couldn't help admiring her for such a gutsy manoeuvre tonight, even if she did want to kill her for involving Juniper.

She'd call Aidan now and tell him to come home. She'd tell him she'd found out what had happened, and that Juniper would be back soon. Then everything would return to normal.

It was only when she came back downstairs and picked up her drink that she realised the message she'd got had said *I have your daughter*. *Your daughter*, not *your children*, like Fiona had read out. Her message couldn't have been meant for Fiona, after all. Panic surged and she told herself to stay calm. Maybe she'd been right earlier when she'd thought it was for Alison. But Fiona had seemed certain she was the reason Lou had taken the children, so why would Lou be texting Alison?

Why would Lou be texting *her*?

Jasmine shook her head. Nothing made sense, but whatever was behind all of this, one thing she knew for sure: Lou had her daughter. She had her whole world, and Jasmine would do whatever she needed to keep her safe. She wasn't going to sit back and wait, like Aidan had silently accused her of.

Taking a deep breath, she picked up the phone to call the police.

FIFTEEN
FIONA
10.30 P.M.

Fiona clutched the phone, willing it to ring, to buzz, to vibrate... to do something. Something to show that Lou had released the twins now that she had told Nick everything and vice versa. Now that their marriage might be over.

She swallowed, pain ripping through her. Was Nick right that there was nothing left to save? Memories flooded into her brain: the moment she'd pledged to be his for ever, the honeymoon he'd booked as a surprise getaway when she'd thought they had no money left, those difficult first weeks with the twins when neither one of them had any idea what they were doing but, somehow, they managed to muddle through. He'd always been there for her... until he hadn't.

She tilted her head. When had that changed? When he'd gone back to the office and her life had been overtaken by all things baby? Later, when the kids had started school and she'd returned to work? When they'd moved out here, next door to Lou? Had their 'friendship' been going on for much longer than he'd said? How could she not have even noticed? Her heart sank as the realisation filtered in. She was so busy that she barely even noticed whether Nick was home or not. How could she expect to sense that he was leaning towards someone else, even if that person was right next door?

Maybe he was right. Maybe there was nothing left.

But she didn't have time to ponder that, she thought, shoving aside the pain. Right now, all she wanted was her children. Once they were safe in her arms again, she could face everything else – even Lou. God, she couldn't believe Alison and Jasmine's kids had been dragged into this too. Nick had said there were two other families, but she'd never for a second thought it might be them. Of all people, it was the two she was most eager to avoid.

An image flashed into her mind of herself at eleven, frizzy red hair and freckles, on her first day at the large, bustling comprehensive. She'd shrunk against the walls, wanting to fade from the corridors so that no older kids would bump into her. Then Jasmine had come striding through the door, with such confidence, as if she owned the place, despite only being a lowly Year 7. Even back then, before the beauty salon and the expensive clothes and everything else, she'd been beautiful, as if she'd dropped in from another planet, far from their awkward, gawky teen universe. Her blonde hair had fallen in perfect waves down her back, her school uniform fitted like it had been moulded to her body by an expert tailor, and she paraded down the corridor as if it was a catwalk, taking in the admiring glances from both younger and older students like they were her due.

She had opened up the locker beside Fiona's, chatting cheerfully as if they were best friends, even though it was the first time they'd spoken. Fiona had started smiling like an idiot before nodding and trying to rearrange her face into nonchalance, stunned that this beautiful girl wanted to talk to her. They'd stayed friends all through those first few years – even if Fiona sometimes secretly thought that it might be easier not to be friends with a girl who always liked to be front and centre; a girl who had no problem telling others exactly what she thought of them. Now that they *were* friends, though, it was easier to go along with whatever Jasmine said, although sometimes she'd feel bad for days afterwards.

And Alison... well, they might have hung out, but they hadn't really been friends. Their only connection to each other had been Jasmine, the glue that held them together. Just as suddenly as Jasmine had befriended Fiona, she'd started talking to Alison when Alison had joined their tutor group in Year 8. She'd been so quiet that Fiona didn't actually know her name for the first couple of weeks, but with Jasmine by her side, she started speaking up and gaining confidence. Fiona sometimes wondered if Jasmine only wanted to be with them because they did whatever she dictated, and not because she really liked them. But mostly, after feeling lonely and shy all through primary school, she was happy to finally have friends.

Everything had changed, though, in the blink of an eye.

Fiona's gut twisted and she shoved away thoughts of that terrible day. It was in the past, she told herself. They were years away from what had happened. They were different people, with different lives, and she couldn't let the memory swamp her. Not now. Not when there was something even bigger to deal with. Not when the children were missing.

Nick poked his head into the room, and Fiona looked up. His face was tense, and all warmth was gone from his eyes. 'It's half ten now. You haven't heard anything?'

She shook her head, and they both jumped as Nick's phone rang. He turned away and mumbled a few words, then spun towards her.

'The police are coming to update us,' he said in the foreign tone that sounded nothing like him. He glanced out the window, and she followed his gaze. It was too dark to see much, but she could hear the wind straining at the windows and the rain as it bounced on the panes. She shuddered, thinking of the twins out in that, and prayed they were all right. Her stomach clenched as she pictured the bloodstained headband. Could Lou have hurt Tabitha? If she was as angry as Nick had said – crazy enough to pull a stunt like this – they really didn't know her at all; she *was* the stranger Nick had glimpsed. What if she wasn't planning to return the kids? What if...

'The officer said it wasn't only us who received the message.' Nick's voice cut into her thoughts.

Fiona drew back. 'What? What do you mean?'

'The other families did too.' He paused. 'Both of the women anyway.'

Fiona swallowed. Alison and Jasmine had received the same message? Jasmine hadn't said anything about it when they'd spoken. But if this was about destroying Fiona and Nick's marriage – about Lou being upset because Nick had rejected her – then why text Alison and Jasmine?

Did Lou have something against them as well? Had she taken their children to force them to divulge ruinous secrets of their own?

She tilted her head, trying to make some sense of it all. She'd thought that Lou had only wanted Tim and Tabitha, but maybe the other children hadn't been there by accident. By the sounds of things, Lou had wanted them too. A chill went through her at the thought that this was bigger than her; than Nick. That maybe... She swallowed. What the hell was going on?

A knock on the door pulled her from her thoughts, and Nick strode over and yanked it open. The family liaison officer, Steph, nodded and came in, followed by Officer Gandhi. She took off her jacket and shook it out, grimacing at the water flying off it.

'How are you holding up?' she said in such a soft tone that Fiona felt the words wrap around her like a hug. Tears sprang to her eyes. This was exactly what she needed, a stark contrast to Nick's stony facade.

She nodded. 'We're... well, we're holding up as best we can.' She winced. *As best we can* didn't mean much at this point. 'Have you found anything more?'

Steph glanced at the other officer. 'Well, now that we know Lou has one of the children's phones with her, we've been able to use cell phone data to track down her general area.'

Fiona caught her breath. 'And?'

'It looks like she's deep in the forest,' Steph said, and Fiona covered her mouth. Oh, God. 'We're working on the assumption right now that the children are with her, although she hasn't responded to any of our attempts to reach out to her. Our search team is ready to go – smaller than usual, I'm afraid, because some of our people can't travel far right now due to the conditions. They're commencing the search as we speak, but the woodland is very dense, and in this wind and the dark, it may be slow going. Still, at least they'll be looking, and when conditions ease, we can move faster.' She touched Fiona's arm. 'I know it's hard, but I promise we're going to do everything we can to bring your children back safely.'

Fiona nodded, praying with every fibre of her being that the forecasters were wrong and the weather would let up soon. She tried not to think of the twins out there in the storm, injured and scared, hunkered down under a tree. At least they were together. Tim would do whatever he could to protect his sister, just like he always had. That was some comfort anyway.

'So let's talk about this message you received,' Officer Gandhi said. 'It's the same message as the other women got. From the same number, and at almost the same time. We've spoken with the families involved, and we know they each had a relationship with Lou Drayton. What we'd like to know is if there's something connecting all of you too. Something besides your individual relationships; some common event or past history that would lead Lou to take such actions.'

Nick was shaking his head. 'I don't even know those women, those families. Do you, Fiona?'

Fiona met his eyes, a million memories flooding through her head. She *had* known them, years ago, but not now. And Lou had nothing to do with that. She couldn't. No one knew what had happened. No one had seen. The truth of that day had been buried for ever. The words of the message flashed into her mind, and she pushed it away. Whatever truth Lou wanted them all to tell, it wasn't connected to their past at all. 'Only to see them at school,' she said. 'Nothing more.'

'All right.' The officer made a note of what they'd said, then took some photos of the message. He nodded towards Lou's house. 'We've got access to her home, and officers will be examining her laptop and any other electronic devices they find, as well as having a thorough search to see if we can find out her exact location, or what she might be planning. In the meantime, please let us know as soon as you hear anything – if you get another message, or a phone call... anything.' He stared hard at them. 'Telling us as soon as possible can make a huge difference. You gain nothing by sitting back and waiting, and everything by letting us do our job with all the relevant information.'

'I'll update you as soon as we have something to share,' Steph said. 'Like I said, hopefully by morning the storm will have broken, and we can really rally the troops. You have my number. Please call with any questions. Anything at all. That's what I'm here for.' Her eyes darted back and forth between Fiona and Nick, and Fiona wondered what she was thinking as she took in the distance between them. 'Lean on each other,' she said. 'You two are a team, and your children need that more than ever. They need you to be strong – to be there for them, now and when they come home. It's so easy to let the fear and uncertainty drive you apart; I've seen it happen more than once. But you need to stand together, believe me.' She turned and followed her colleague out the door.

Fiona swallowed and nodded, not daring to look at Nick to see how he'd taken Steph's words.

'What do you...' she started to say, but Nick had already walked away.

So much for standing together.

SIXTEEN
TABITHA
7 A.M.

The night seems to last for ever. Trees have been crashing down around us, the noise waking me up when I finally manage to drift off. My watch says it's almost seven, but the darkness makes it feel as if morning's far away. The space is even tighter with Lou and Juniper crammed in here, but at least the heat from their bodies warms it up. Thank goodness it's not *too* cold, or we'd really be in trouble. But the air is damp, and it feels like the chill is right inside my bones, as Mum would say. Tears come to my eyes as I think of Mum, waiting and worrying back at home. Lou asked us all for our parents' numbers so she could text them and let them know we're fine, but still.

I hope Dad is with her, and that they're okay. I bite my lip, remembering Tim's words about Dad and Lou kissing, and something twists inside me. Because even though I know it can't be true, some tiny, minuscule part of me thinks that maybe it's not as crazy as it sounds – not with Lou, but with someone else. Sometimes, Dad seems like a stranger in our family. He spends so much time at work that when he's home, it's as if he doesn't know how to talk to us. He doesn't really belong in the house, not like Mum.

Could he have decided he belongs somewhere else? *With someone else?*

We huddle together to try to keep warm, but Tim doesn't even look at me. He's furious that I let Lou in. I've never gone against what he tells me to do, and I guess this is a big one. But he's not right all the time, and we're already in enough trouble by following him. We should be grateful that Lou came after us – that she didn't leave us to go into the forest alone; that she wanted to make sure we're okay. If it wasn't for this crazy storm, I'm sure we'd be out of here by now.

Lou told us when she first came in that she'd called 999 and pinged them the location of this cabin, and they said they would come as soon as they could. I wasn't able to resist a triumphant glance at Tim when she said that, but he refused to meet my eyes. I love him, but he's never been able to admit when he's wrong – when I've done something right. Granted, he hasn't had much opportunity.

I pull the jumper closer around me and glance over at Lou. Her eyes are closed, and she's not moving. Her face is pale and her normally perfect dark hair a mess. I've never seen her so still; so quiet. If it wasn't for her steady breathing, I'd almost think she was... I cut myself off at the thought. Juniper is huddled in a corner on her own, and Gabby is leaning against Tim and me. I can tell by his breathing that Tim's awake, but of course he's not talking to me.

'Juniper!' he whispers, reaching out to kick her foot. Her eyes open, two black holes in the white hollow of her face, the blood drying in a dark patch on her head. I shudder. 'Do you have your mobile?'

Her eyes dart towards Lou, and something like terror flashes across her face. Why is she so afraid? A prickle of unease pokes a hole in my smug shield. Did *Lou* hurt Juniper? I push that crazy thought aside. It can't be Lou she's scared of, I tell myself. It must be something else.

But Juniper's next words only make me more apprehensive.

'I had it, but Lou took it,' she says, leaning forward so that she can whisper as quietly as possible. I can barely hear her over the howling wind outside.

'Why?' I ask before Tim can. There must be a reason. But that unease is growing inside, starting to smother my pride that I did something right. Maybe I didn't, after all. 'Why does she need your phone if she has hers?'

'She said she left it in the car when you all started running, and she wanted to stop you before you went too far into the woods.'

I nod, relief shooting through me. Of course.

'But then...' Juniper glances at Lou as she shifts in her sleep, 'when I asked for it back, she wouldn't give it to me. She said it's the one thing that will help rescuers find us, and that she needs to keep it safe.'

That makes sense, I think. Juniper would probably drain the battery, and then what would we be left with?

'I know Lou said that she texted our parents, but I wanted to talk to Mum and let her know we're okay,' Juniper continues. 'But Lou said it would take too much battery. And she got really angry when I tried to take the phone.'

I tilt my head, mulling over the words. I've never seen Lou angry, but that phone is the one thing connecting us to the outside world right now. Every bit of charge is important, and Juniper isn't exactly known for taking no for an answer. Lou probably had to get angry to show she meant business.

But Tim isn't having any of it. He's still raging at Lou, even though she's obviously just trying to keep us safe. 'We need to get that phone from her,' he says, speaking so low it's like he's talking to himself. 'She can't take it like that. She *shouldn't* take it like that.' He looks at me, but I don't give my answering nod. I know he wants me to think that he's right, especially after I went against him earlier. There's been a strange kind of power shift, and I can sense that he wants to restore it. He wants to be the one who takes control; who leads the way. That's why he's desperate to get the phone.

I meet his eyes and shake my head. We all want to talk to our parents. Gabby's been crying for her mum for the past few hours, and while I feel the same, at least I haven't been sobbing like her. But if we do get the phone, Juniper's going to go mad texting and calling everyone on her contacts list, and the battery will be dead. And then what we will do if we have a real emergency?

But Tim's staring back at me defiantly, and I can see how much he wants to do something. I admire that about him – how he acts while I sit back and watch. It's easy to be like that if you're with someone who does things for you before you can even make up your mind what to do. Tim's always been one step ahead of me, but not this time. I'm proud of myself for doing the right thing earlier, and I'm not going to let him mess it up for us now.

I drift into a daydream where everyone is patting me on the back when we're rescued, saying how brave I am and how my quick thinking is what saved us. Mum stares at me with admiration in her eyes, while Dad folds me into his arms and says he always knew I had it in me; that he knew I could do it. And...

I snap out of my reverie just in time to see Tim sliding the phone gingerly from Lou's jacket pocket and holding it up triumphantly. My heart drops, and anger surges through me. Why didn't I do something? I was so busy daydreaming that I didn't even notice him moving.

'I got it!' he mouths, waving it in the air.

Juniper immediately comes to life. 'Give it to me,' she says, scooting over and trying to wrestle it from his grasp.

But Tim shakes his head and holds it out of her reach. 'What's the password? Tell me what it is, and then I'll give it to you, okay? I want to check something.'

Juniper narrows her eyes, but she's so desperate that she tells him the four digits – 7777 – and sits back. Tim put in the numbers, and the screen comes to life. He clicks a few more buttons, and I watch with furrowed brow, my mind ticking over. What's he doing? He's wasting all this battery power so he can prove me wrong? Anger surges through me. Why can't he accept that I'm right – that Lou's trying to help? That she wants the best for us? He's taking this way too far, and I can't let him do it any longer. He could ruin everything.

While he's busy looking at the screen, his face creepy in the dim light, I slowly reach over and yank the phone from him. He gasps, but before he can do anything, I've nudged Lou awake. Her eyes fly open. Her chin comes up and she shakes herself, as if she doesn't know where she is.

'I have Juniper's phone,' I say, handing it over to her. 'Tim tried to take it, but I think it's best if you keep it. I know there's not much battery left, and we might need it to call the police.'

Lou nods. 'Thank you. That's very good thinking.' I expect her to give me one of her trademark hugs, but instead her face stays expressionless as she tucks the phone inside her shirt, then zips up her coat. She looks at Tim for a very long time, as if trying to read something there. He stares back, his face unreadable, and finally she glances away. 'Let's all try to get some sleep,' she says. 'Hopefully, in a few hours we'll be back home in our beds.' Her voice cracks and she clears her throat, then she moves so that she's leaning against the door, with her chin down and her eyes closed, shielding us from the storm outside.

Tim shoots me a furious look, as if he can't believe I did that. He shifts closer to me, and I can almost feel his anger. But I'm just as angry. He's not always right. He's *not*. And this time, I know beyond a shadow of any doubt that I am.

'Why did you do that?' he asks me. His voice is quiet but full of fury.

'You shouldn't have taken it,' I say through gritted teeth. 'I told you not to.'

He stares hard at me. 'She didn't call 999,' he says, and my eyebrows fly up.

'What do you mean?' I hiss.

'I mean, she never called 999,' he repeats. His words echo inside me, like rolling thunder. 'I checked the call log, and there's nothing there.'

'Well, maybe she texted,' I say, trying to keep the fear and doubt pushed down. Lou is here to help us. She is. She'd never hurt us.

But the fear and doubt balloon at Tim's next words. 'I checked there too.' He breathes in, and fear crosses his face. That's when I really start to get worried because he's never afraid. Not even when we set the shed on fire that time at Gran's by accident. 'There's nothing. Nothing but...' His voice trails off like he doesn't want to tell me, and I elbow him.

'But what?' I ask.

'There's a message she sent a few times, saying something like "I have the kids and I'll let them go when you tell everything."' He shakes his head. 'One of the numbers she sent it to is Mum's. And one was to Juniper's mum – she was in the contacts book.'

I stare at him, trying to take in what he's saying. Lou *meant* to take us? She wants to keep us here, in this cabin, until... until what? What does she want our mums to tell? What could be so important that she'd keep us away from them until they do?

My gut clenches, and I think I might be sick as it hits me. Tim was right. Lou isn't here to help. She's not here to rescue us, and... I swallow. I let her in. I let her inside this cabin with us. And I gave her back the phone. I not only brought her inside, but I ruined our one chance to get help.

I think of Juniper's hurt head, and panic surges through me as I remember her fearful look at Lou. But Lou wouldn't hurt us... would she? I glance over at her, trying to connect this new person with the laughing, caring woman I know. Her eyes open as if she senses me staring, and I pray to find a spark of familiarity. But instead, she gazes back like she doesn't recognise me either, and I shudder. For the first time, I'm really afraid. Not of the woods, and not of the storm. I'm afraid of her.

I sit back, the darkness ringing inside me. I was so certain of myself. I thought I was right, and I was determined to do something good. Instead, I've made things a million times worse. I should have listened to my brother, like always.

'It's okay,' Tim says, his voice kind as he pulls me closer. 'We'll be all right. I'll get us out of this. I promise.'

I nod, but the tears keep falling. It's not just about where we are now, or what might happen. It's about me. Because for once in my life, I did try to do something. And now... now I feel even smaller.

SEVENTEEN
FIONA
7 A.M.

Fiona sat in Tabitha's room, unable to stay in bed one minute longer. It was only 7 a.m., but she hadn't slept at all – not that she'd expected to when she'd come into her daughter's room to lie down. She'd wanted to be close to her children; to feel them around her, even if they weren't here. At least the twins had each other. They always wanted to be together, almost as if they couldn't exist on their own. Fiona had tried to split them up in Reception, thinking it would be good for each to gain some independence, but they'd both cried so much that she'd relented and had them put in the same class again. Even now, despite giving them separate rooms, she'd often come into Tim's room to find Tabitha curled into a ball at the foot of the bed, saying she'd had a bad dream. Tim had always been the one Tabitha turned to for comfort, and Fiona was never gladder of that than now.

Her head throbbed and her eyes felt like sandpaper, and she grabbed her mobile and went downstairs to make a cup of very strong coffee. It was the last thing her stomach needed right now, but she was desperate for something to help her get through the day; to help her bear this agonising fear and uncertainty. The search inside Lou's house had uncovered nothing.

The search outside hadn't found anything either. Steph had called to say that the team had made barely any headway, having to turn back after narrowly avoiding being crushed by a falling tree. Conditions were too risky to continue, but they'd vowed to start again once the wind weakened.

She peered towards the master bedroom, noticing light underneath the door. Was Nick awake? She'd gone into the bedroom last night and curled up next to him, but he'd continued staring at his phone. She'd felt even colder and emptier, and she'd got up again and gone to Tabitha's room.

The next couple of hours passed agonisingly slowly. Fiona prayed for the weather to break, but if anything, it was blowing stronger than ever. She couldn't bear to think of her kids out in that – if indeed that was where they still were. She chewed her lip. Maybe Lou had had a plan. Maybe she'd brought them somewhere warm and safe, with food and drink, heat and light. Maybe they were snuggled up in front of a TV somewhere, having the time of their lives and not even caring that they weren't at home.

Or maybe... She swallowed, not wanting to think of the alternative. She stared at the blank screen in front of her, recalling Steph's words earlier today that they hoped to find the children in the next few hours, but if not, they would appeal for information on social media and in the press. Nick had urged them to do that now, but Steph had said that with the storm, it was too dangerous to involve the public. It might look all right in town, but in a heavily forested area, it was a different story. The last thing they wanted was untrained people plunging into the woods, potentially getting into trouble themselves and distracting from the children's rescue.

Rescue. Fiona shook her head. Rescue from Lou, from the woman next door... from the woman she'd considered her best friend; the woman who'd wanted to be with her husband. But that wasn't the reason she'd taken Tim and Tabitha – at least not the only reason, since Alison and Jasmine had got the same text, and they knew nothing about the affair. Lou was obviously aware of their harmful secrets too. Why would she want to destroy them all? Fiona twisted the cushion in her lap, recalling the officer asking whether anything had happened between them and Lou, if anything connected them. She strained her mind, but the only thing connecting them was Lou herself – and the fact that their children went to the same school.

Maybe it was something to do with school. Maybe something had happened with Lou's two and the other kids. Lou always hated anything to do with bullying or intimidation, but would that be enough to hold the children against their will – to *hurt* them? Fiona shivered, thinking of Tabitha's bloody headband. Did Lou expect the parents to know what had happened, and that was why she'd sent those texts asking them to tell the truth? Did she hold the parents responsible too?

She raked her mind again for anything Tabitha and Tim might have told her, but she came up blank. Maybe Alison and Jasmine knew something?

Alison and Jasmine. Dread washed over her, and she got to her feet, shaking her head. Now wasn't the time to start falling backwards. This was the *present*, and the sooner she found out the real reason Lou had taken the children, the sooner the kids would be home safe and sound. The alternative didn't bear thinking about. She grabbed her mobile, the police officer's words ringing in her ears: the more information they had, the faster they could act. Even if that meant probing the two people she most wanted to forget, she would. She was certain neither one of them would want to hear from her either, but for the sake of their children, they'd need to work together. She felt shaky just thinking about it.

She'd start with Alison, and then call Jasmine. She'd ask them to come over. Despite the warnings to stay off the roads, she was sure they'd do anything to get their children to safety.

Anyway, so far all she could see outside was broken branches and leaves. They could talk, and hopefully they'd come up with something. Hopefully, they'd get their children back.

Then they could go back to forgetting each other once more.

Half an hour later, Fiona opened the door to let Alison in. Alison shrugged off her hood and removed her jacket, and Fiona motioned her over to the sofa. Every step was hesitant and jerky, as if she was deeply uncomfortable being here. Fiona felt just as awkward. It had been decades since they'd been alone together.

Her mind flashed back to the time Alison had invited both her and Jasmine over to her house for a sleepover. After the chaos of living with three stepbrothers, Fiona had found Alison's silent home unnerving. Her parents were busy working in their separate studies, and the two of them had sat in Alison's snug waiting for Jasmine to arrive and liven things up. When she was around, she made everything fun. She made *them* fun.

But Jasmine had never turned up, saying she had a funny stomach, and Fiona and Alison had passed a quiet night, watching a film Jasmine had been dying to see but that neither one of them was keen on. They'd barely spoken – Fiona had raked her mind to try to find something they could chat about – and they'd gone to bed early. She had left the next morning as soon as she could.

'Would you like some tea?' she asked now, thinking how strange all of this was. Looking at Alison was like staring into a funfair mirror that distorted everything. Alison had always been heavyset, but now she was like a professional athlete. Fiona could make out the contours of her muscles through her leggings, and her six-pack was visible under her slim-fitting track top. But even if her body was different, her face was remarkably the same: broad cheeks, dark eyes, and dark hair tugged back in the same ponytail she'd always had. Wrinkles pulled at the corner of her eyes, her forehead was lined now and the dark hair threaded with grey, but for an instant she was that same girl who used to orbit Jasmine the same way Fiona had back in secondary school.

The same girl who'd been part of such an awful event that they'd never been able to speak to each other again.

'I'd love some coffee, if you have any,' Alison said, cutting into her thoughts.

Fiona nodded and busied herself with the coffee machine. Upstairs, she could hear Nick on the phone asking for yet another update, and she swallowed. She'd told Nick that she'd asked Jasmine and Alison over to see if there was anything they were missing, hoping for a glimmer of warmth in response. But he'd nodded and turned back to his phone, telling her to let him know if they thought of anything. She'd half expected him to come down and talk to them himself, but he'd set up camp in the bedroom, claiming it as his own territory – his safe space away from her.

'Here you go,' she said, handing Alison the steaming cup. She noticed the other woman's hands trembling, and an image from long ago jolted through her. Alison had been shaking so much that the police had thought it wasn't only the cold and the wet; that they might need to take her in for shock. After what had happened, they were all in shock, but Alison... Fiona had wondered sometimes, when all was quiet and dark at night and the chaos of the day couldn't distract her any longer, how Alison managed to live with what she'd done. A huge house, a husband and daughter, a successful gym... She obviously *had* made a good life for herself; been able to push through the guilt and anger she must surely feel.

But then wasn't Fiona herself just as guilty? And didn't she manage to live with what she'd done too?

'How are you holding up?' she asked, repeating Steph's words, as they waited for Jasmine, who was taking her time, as usual. The two of them had always been waiting for her, it seemed. Some things never changed.

Alison sipped her coffee and met Fiona's eyes for the first time since she'd come through the door. 'I'm as okay as I can be,' she said. 'As anyone could be in this situation. What on earth was Lou thinking? I still can't believe it.' She rubbed her red eyes. 'Just worried about Gabby, since she doesn't have her asthma inhaler, and this weather' – they both looked outside, where the wind was howling and the trees were jerking back and forth like they were being shaken by an invisible hand – 'isn't likely to help.' She gulped, and Fiona could see her trying to steady herself. 'Thank God for my husband,' she said, and Fiona felt her gut clench, thinking of her own problems. 'He's been amazing through all of this, especially since...'

She stopped, and Fiona was about to ask her what she was going to say when there was a sharp rap at the door, and then another before Fiona could react to the first one. She hurried over and opened it. Jasmine pushed inside before she could even invite her in.

'It's awful out there,' she said, peeling off her coat and shaking out her hair.

Fiona tried not to stare at the red marks on her face. She wasn't up on the latest beauty treatments, but Jasmine had clearly had something done. Jasmine stared around the lounge with an expression of distaste, and Fiona felt a familiar feeling flare up inside of her, the feeling that she never measured up to Jasmine's high standards and that she never would; the uncertainty of not knowing what to do or what step to take. She drew in a breath as Jasmine settled onto the settee as if she was afraid of touching it. She wasn't a teen any longer. She was an adult with a life of her own. And she didn't need to measure up to

Jasmine now – instead, they needed each other if they wanted their children back.

'Oh, could I have a coffee?' Jasmine asked, spotting the mug in Alison's hand. 'I know I might look well rested, but I hardly slept at all last night. *God*.' Fiona thought she could see genuine emotion flashing across her face, although it was hard to tell with all the chemicals inside of it. 'I really hope Juniper's doing okay. I've no idea how she got caught up in all of this in the first place.' She looked over at Fiona. 'So, why are we here? Do you know something more about why Lou took the kids?' She shook back her hair. 'I have to say, I have no idea what on earth she's on about. Tell the truth? The truth about what? I don't have any secrets.'

Fiona swallowed. She *did* have secrets. They all did, even if it had nothing to do with this. 'When I first got the message, I thought it was about something I'd told Lou.' Her gut clenched as she pictured Nick's anguished face. 'I thought that if I told the truth, she'd let the children go.'

Alison nodded slowly. 'I thought the same thing.'

'But then I found out that you'd both received the same message.' Fiona gazed at the other two. They were watching her intently, and she waited for one of them to speak, but neither said a word. 'I don't think it's anything to do with us, at least not directly,' she continued. 'I think it must be something to do with the kids. Maybe something happened at school with all of them and Lou's children? That would explain why she didn't take her own two. Maybe she's trying to punish ours... punish us for what they've done.' She shook her head. 'I mean, it's extreme to do something like this, but Lou—'

'Gabby would never be involved in something like that. She'd never bully anyone,' Alison cut in. She glanced at Jasmine with a hardened expression. 'She knows only too well what it's like to be on the receiving end.'

'Don't blame Juniper,' Jasmine said. 'Gabby needs to toughen up.'

Alison stood, looming over Jasmine, and for the first time, Fiona realised how much taller she was. Somehow, it had always seemed like Jasmine was the bigger of the two. 'I believe your daughter has already done everything possible to make Gabby's life a living hell,' she said, her voice trembling. 'And I've been teaching her how to stand up for herself; to not take any more.' She looked down at Jasmine, and hatred flashed across her face. Her voice lowered. 'Gabby won't *ever* be as weak as I was that day.'

That day. The words echoed in the silent space, expanding until they pressed up against Fiona, sitting like a heavy weight on her chest. She froze, afraid to breathe; afraid to take it in. The years between them melted away, and for a second, it felt like they were the same three girls again.

Then Jasmine tossed her hair, and Fiona jerked back to the present. They weren't the same girls any longer – that was clear in how Alison had stood up to Jasmine. And they weren't here to talk about that past. They were here to get their children back.

'Juniper didn't think what she did was wrong,' Jasmine said, 'but she promised never to do it again. Besides, she loves Charina and Saish, and she loves Lou too. She wouldn't do anything to them.'

'Tabitha and Timothy wouldn't either,' Fiona said. Tim had always stuck up for the underdog, befriending the shy kids, and Tabitha *was* one of those shy kids. If it hadn't been for Tim, she might have felt as alone in primary school as Fiona had. Tabitha was so lucky to have her twin.

The room fell silent again, the three women staring at each other.

'Well, if no one has anything useful to say, I'm going home,' Jasmine said, standing up. 'I only came to see if you knew anything more. Clearly, you don't.' She brushed herself off, as if Fiona's settee had infected her, then grabbed her bag, put on her coat and left.

'I'd better go as well,' Alison said. 'Greg will be waiting at home. But please let me know if you think of anything.' She met Fiona's eyes, and Fiona could see her own worry and desperation reflected in them. 'I'll do anything to get my daughter back.'

Fiona nodded, despair swirling through her that they were no closer to finding out why Lou had taken the kids – and no closer to getting them home. Instead, all they'd done was argue. So much for working together. But when had they ever done that? They'd always followed the leader, Jasmine, and look where that had got them.

She watched through the rain as Alison's car pulled away, the silence inside now heavier than ever.

EIGHTEEN
FIONA
10 A.M.

Fiona turned the radio up, trying to drown out the sounds of the storm outside. Nick had come downstairs to give her another useless update: the weather was getting worse, and the police were doing everything they could besides physically searching for the children in the woods. Juniper's phone showed they were still there – or at least Juniper's phone was still there – and in desperation, the search team had tried to use drones to find them. The wind had whipped the drones out of the sky after only a few minutes. Fiona had gazed up at her husband, hoping for a bit of comfort, but he'd simply turned away and gone back to their room, slamming the door closed again.

She stared out at the driving rain, her mind ticking over through the haze of fear and fatigue. Jasmine and Alison seemed certain that whatever had caused Lou to act this way had nothing to do with the kids, but Fiona wasn't so sure. By the sounds of things, Juniper *had* been a bully – towards Gabby anyway. Could that have spread to Charina and Saish? Could Tim have tried to stop it and got involved somehow?

As much as she thought she knew Tabitha and Tim – as much as all parents believed they knew everything about their kids – no one knew better than her how children could keep terrible secrets. After all, what had her own parents really known about what had happened all those years ago? Nothing. They'd never in a million years have suspected what had gone on. Not that her mother had really been interested. All she'd wanted was for Fiona not to cause problems. Even now, retired and living in Spain, she barely seemed interested in her daughter's life.

Maybe she could talk to Lou's kids, Fiona thought now. If something had happened, they would be at the centre of it all. And while they might not tell her everything, she'd take whatever tiny clue they could give her. She picked up her mobile, then put it back down. This needed more than a simple phone call. This was something she had to do face to face.

She called up to Nick that she was going out, but he didn't even answer. Then she grabbed her car keys, shrugged on a mac and opened the front door. The wind lashed at her, tearing the hood from her head as she dashed to the car. The rain drummed on the roof so loudly so could hardly hear herself think. She swallowed, fear flooding through her. She was a nervous driver at the best of times, never mind in the middle of a storm. But she needed to do this, no matter the risk. For once, she wasn't going to sit back and simply let events unfold.

She started the engine and backed out, carefully easing around a fallen branch partially blocking the road. At least the streets were empty, but she had to grip the wheel tightly to stop the wind from pushing the car towards the middle of the road. She navigated across town to the neighbouring village where Krish lived. She'd dropped Charina and Saish at their father's one day as a favour to Lou, and he'd told her that he'd moved there after Lou had bought the house in Holmwood so that they could easily share custody of the children. Fiona remembered being impressed with how amicable everything seemed between them. She could hardly believe that two people who

got on that well would divorce. Lou's appeal for a fresh start had
obviously worked on all fronts.

Pain needled her as she pictured the woman she'd thought
had been her friend smiling into Nick's eyes, leaning closer,
trying to put her lips on his. How could she do that? How could
she laugh and joke with Fiona, day after day, while in the meantime she was making a play for her husband?

And why the *hell* had she taken the kids?

Hopefully, Fiona would soon be one step closer to finding
out. She pulled into the drive of the small bungalow nestled
amongst the trees in a cul-de-sac. Thank God she'd made it in
one piece. The lights were blazing, and sympathy swirled inside
her at the thought of what Lou's kids were going through. To
hear that their mother had disappeared taking other children
with her, putting herself and them in danger... that would be
terrible even if she was doing it for them. She shook her head as
she opened the car door and stepped out into the rain. Lou was
ruining her children's lives as well as her own. Those poor, poor
kids. What on earth had happened?

She pressed her finger against the buzzer, her hand slick
with rain. If possible, the wind was even stronger now, howling
around the treetops as if trying to rip them from the ground.
When Krish appeared, she took a step back in surprise at his
appearance. His hair was uncombed, he was wearing tracksuit
bottoms and a beat-up T-shirt, and he looked like he hadn't slept
in days. She ran a hand over her own hair, thinking she didn't
look any better. Her mind flashed back to the last time they'd
spoken, when Lou's car had been found by the side of the road.
God, had that only been yesterday? They both looked like
they'd aged a hundred years. She certainly felt like it.

'Have the police found something? What's happened?' His
voice was so panicked that Fiona put a hand on his arm to
calm him.

'Nothing's happened. Nothing more anyway,' she said.

'They didn't find anything in Lou's house last night, and I'm sure they told you that they still can't search for the children.' She turned to look behind her. 'It's wild out there.'

'Oh. Okay.' He drew in a breath, and she could see him visibly relax.

'Can I come in?'

'Of course.' He ushered her inside, past a room where Fiona caught a glimpse of Lou's two kids curled up on a sofa staring at their tablets.

'How are they doing?' she asked in a whisper, as he led her into the lounge. She settled on an armchair, thinking what a contrast this place was to Lou's immaculate lounge. Blankets were scattered around, pillows dotted the floor, and the coffee table was littered with mugs and plates.

Krish rubbed his eyes as he sat down across from her. 'I'm not going to lie. They're taking it pretty hard.'

'I can imagine,' Fiona responded. 'Did they say anything about why Lou might have done this?' Maybe they'd talked to Krish about what had happened.

'No, nothing.' He ran his hand through his hair again. 'I can't believe she would do this. It's so... so unlike her. I mean, she loves her neighbourhood. She loves her friends. And she loves her children.' He sighed. 'Because they *are* her children. No matter what, they really are.'

Fiona tilted her head. 'What do you mean?'

He stared at her. 'Well, you know that Charina and Saish aren't Lou's biological children, right? I had them with my first wife.'

'What?' Fiona's eyes popped. Lou had never said. Fiona had always thought the children were Lou's, and that was that. Lou had never given her any indication otherwise.

'My first wife left me after Saish was born, when Charina turned two.' Krish shook his head. 'She wasn't much of a mother before she left, and she wasn't one at all once she'd gone. She wanted nothing to do with the children – or me.' He held up his hands, as if he still couldn't believe it. 'I met Lou at the park one day. I was trying to change Saish's nappy, and Charina took off running, you know the way kids do at that age, without any clue where they're going. They just want to *run*.' A smile lit his face, making him look younger. 'She was heading for the main road, and I was screaming at her to stop, trying to chase after her, but there was no way I could make it in time. You can imagine how scared I was.'

The image flashed into Fiona's head, and she nodded.

'But then out of nowhere, Lou swept in. She'd been on the pavement, out for a walk, and she'd heard me screaming and seen Charina. She grabbed her right when she was about to step onto the road and carried her back to me. Charina was kicking and screaming, I was crying and trying to hold Saish, and all I could do was nod at Lou. I sank down onto the ground.' He paused. 'That day... I remember thinking it was all too much. That I couldn't do it. I couldn't be a single father. For God's sake, Charina had nearly died.'

He wiped a hand over his face, and Fiona could see his distress even now.

'But Lou... well, I don't know how, but she calmed me down. She sat beside me as the kids cried, and it was enough to know she was there. And when Charina stopped kicking off, Lou took her to the playground while I finally got myself together. It was getting dark, and she suggested we all hit McDonald's.' A smile played around his lips. 'I remember thinking she really didn't look the type who'd enjoy a Maccy's, but she was great with the kids and God knows I could have used an extra hand.' He met Fiona's eyes. 'It went from there. Lou was like an angel, really. She swooped in and rescued all of us. It wasn't just the kids – what had happened with my first wife had broken me, but I hadn't had the time to process that with everything the kids demanded. Lou helped me through everything. She helped me to see that my ex leaving was the best thing that could have happened.'

Fiona nodded. Lou was good at that; at making people see the other side.

'And then we fell in love, and that was that. She moved in. She might not have been the kids' biological mother, but she was their mum through and through. Everything was perfect.' His face twisted. 'For the most part.'

Fiona lifted an eyebrow. 'What happened?'

'Lou had... well, she had some issues that weren't really clear until we were living together. She loved the kids, but she couldn't have children of her own, and I don't think she was ever really able to accept that. She didn't have a lot of support around her either: no real family to speak of. She'd go through periods of depression, though that got better when I made her go to the doctor to get medication. But then she'd say she didn't need it, she was fine, and she'd start having mood swings.' He let out a breath. 'She'd take her medication again, stabilise, then go off it, and the cycle would continue.'

Fiona tilted her head, trying to take in his words. She'd never noticed anything wrong. Lou had always seemed one hundred per cent in control, more than anyone she knew. She swallowed, Nick's words echoing in her mind about how furious Lou had been when he'd rejected her advances; how it hadn't seemed like her. Fear shot through her, and a cold sweat drenched her. Maybe Lou wasn't stable right now. Maybe she *would* hurt the kids. Maybe she already had hurt Tabitha. Oh God.

Krish met her eyes, and she could see her own panic and confusion mirrored in his. 'I knew she struggled sometimes, but I never would have imagined something like this. I'd never have let the kids go to her if I thought she was in any way unsafe.'

Fiona nodded slowly. None of them had seen this coming. And never in a million years would she have guessed that

Charina and Saish were Lou's stepchildren; that Lou had only met Krish when the kids were babies. In all the time they'd spent together, she had never mentioned it.

But what did Fiona really know about her anyway? That she'd moved here after her divorce, that she'd set up a successful interior design business, that she had two children she doted on. Lou practically knew Fiona's whole history, but Fiona realised now that she knew little of Lou's past. Every time she'd asked something, Lou had smiled and said she'd moved here for a fresh start, and the past was better off behind them. Fiona had agreed wholeheartedly, but she knew better than anyone that you could never completely forget the past.

'I would have stayed with her if I could,' Krish said, rubbing his eyes. 'If she'd been with me, I could have stopped this happening, I know it. I always made sure she stayed on her meds.'

'So, why did you split up?' Fiona asked, before she could stop herself. It was none of her business, but she felt like she needed to know more about the woman she'd thought had been her friend.

Pain flashed across Krish's face, and he lowered his eyes. Clearly, despite the time that had passed, whatever had happened between them still hurt. 'We were out in London one night,' he said. 'It was one of those warm, sunny evenings where everyone was on the street, drinking. We were in Soho, on a terrace. It felt like we were on holiday.' His eyes took on a dreamy look. 'Things had been a little difficult between us – Lou had been going through one of her down times. But she'd started a new dose of medication, and she'd actually been the one to suggest going out. Everything was amazing until she went up to the bar to get some drinks. We were laughing and chatting, and it was just like old times.'

He went quiet, and Fiona could hear the kids' tablets bleeping in the other room. 'And then?' she asked.

me have a phone,' Charina said. 'Why are you asking? Do you think Mum took the kids because of something they did to us? She wouldn't do that.' She sounded so certain. 'I think something happened and she's trying to keep everyone safe.'

Fiona swallowed, thinking of the bloody headband and the texts they'd received. Oh, how she wished that were true.

'Thanks,' she said, turning away before they could see the tears in her eyes. They were so trusting; so caring. And they needed their mother, the same way her own children needed her now. She left the room and walked straight into Krish, who was listening outside the door.

'No luck, then,' he said, shaking his head. 'But I guess it doesn't really matter *why* she took them, does it? I mean, it's not going to get them back again.'

She met his eyes, realising he didn't know about the messages they'd received.

'Dad?' Charina called from the lounge, and Krish sighed.

'I'd better go see what they want. Let me know if you hear anything, okay?'

Fiona nodded, Krish's words echoing in her mind as she went out the door and into the rain. He was wrong. It *did* matter why Lou had taken them. And it *would* get them back if she could bloody well figure it out.

If it wasn't anything to do with the children, and it wasn't what had happened at the work do, then what was it? Fiona bit her lip, her mind churning. Yes, the three of them had a secret – one they'd buried for years; one they'd never told. But that had nothing to do with Lou, she reminded herself. It had nothing to do with the present.

Did it?

The sound of wind in the trees overhead reminded her of the rushing river water, and Alison's earlier words drifted into her mind. *That day.* Before she could fight it, she felt herself being dragged backwards by the river's current, engulfed by the memories she'd tried so hard to float above. The warmth of the day; the way the sun beat down on them, stinging their eyes, as the four of them hurried towards the river close to their school. Jasmine's laugh drifting back as she marched confidently forward; the scrape of fresh grass on bare skin. The scent of baking earth, and the screeching seagulls above, always on the lookout for dropped litter.

'I can't wait to jump in!' Jasmine had yelled, as they neared the gleaming water. Sometimes, there were crowds of kids there after school, but they'd had to wait for Jasmine to be released from her maths detention before heading home. Any kids who might have taken advantage of the unusually warm May day had already gone.

'I don't have my swimming cossie,' Fiona remembered saying, before cringing with embarrassment as Jasmine stripped off her school shirt and skirt and waded into the water. Clearly, Jasmine didn't have hers either. Why couldn't she just be cool? Alison was already plunging into the water, although she had her PE kit on anyway and could always change back into her uniform. Only Fiona and Mira hung back, watching awkwardly.

Fiona swallowed, glancing over at the other girl and trying not to stare at the large red birthmark stretching from her ear across her throat. Why on earth had Jasmine invited her? The only thing she liked about Mira was teasing her. She was always calling her 'the Curse' and mocking her birthmark; making fun of her weight and asking if the curse was stopping her from losing it. If someone who always made fun of Fiona had invited her out, she would never have said yes. In the silence, Mira's desperation to be liked hung heavy between them. Fiona recognised it instantly, and for some reason, it made her want to get away. She kicked off her socks and shoes, then gingerly waded in, watching as the current sucked at her ankles. God, it was cold... cold, and fast. It had rained a lot last week, and the river was higher than usual.

'Come on in, you two!' Jasmine was calling from where she and Alison were splashing each other. 'Stop being babies! A little cold water won't kill you, you know.'

Fiona was already freezing, her arms and legs prickled with gooseflesh. She took another step forward, wincing as the sharp pebbles bit into her feet, then looked back. 'Coming?'

Mira shook her head, her long dark hair flying out. 'I can't swim,' she said, staring at the rushing water in trepidation. Despite her words, though, she removed her shoes, placing them carefully on the riverbank and brushing the mud from them. 'They're my sister's,' she said, cheeks reddening as if she'd been caught out doing something uncool. 'She'll kill me if I get them dirty.'

'Okay.' Fiona shrugged, envy stabbing her as she watched Alison and Jasmine horsing around. She wanted to be with them – the three of them together, just like always. Annoyance flared when she thought of Mira beside her, and she plunged into the water, never minding that her skirt was soaked now and floating up around her legs. God, it was absolutely freezing, and Mira looked terrified. Something softened inside Fiona, and she beckoned the girl forward. Jasmine would never let her hear the end of it if she didn't go in. It was easier to do what she wanted.

'Come on,' she urged. 'One little step. You don't have to go all the way in. Stand by me.'

Mira took a step forward as Fiona watched and shivered. Then another, and another, until she was standing beside Fiona, with the water touching her thighs. Her jaw was clenched and her skin was pale, making the large purplish-red splotch on her neck even more vivid. Jasmine motioned for them both to go deeper. Fiona gingerly moved forward, the rushing water sucking at her legs. Behind her, she could hear Mira following.

'Here, take my hand.' Jasmine was approaching Mira now, stretching out a slender arm. 'Come on, get yourself under. Or can't you get birthmarks wet?' She grinned and narrowed her eyes, and Mira took another step.

'She can't...' Fiona wanted to say that Mira couldn't swim, but just as Mira was reaching out for Jasmine's hand, Alison pushed her and she tumbled forward, falling into the water and disappearing under the surface. Jasmine started laughing. Alison joined in, but fear rushed through Fiona as she lurched towards the place where Mira had gone under. 'She can't swim!' she shouted, not even feeling the rocks or the cold water now.

'Stop worrying,' Jasmine said, but a flash of fear went across her face. 'Fatties float, don't they? She's fine.' Even so, she stepped to where Mira had fallen, bending to rake her fingers through the water. Alison did the same, her own face contorted now with panic, all three of them scouring the river.

But Mira was gone. Fiona could remember those heart-stopping seconds with such a clarity that even in the midst of everything happening now, it almost felt like she was there at this very moment. The silence was deafening. The only thing she could hear was a voice in her head praying for Mira to come up again; praying that she was playing some kind of trick and that she would resurface any moment, even if playing tricks wasn't like her in the least. Fiona couldn't recall her ever even smiling – not that she would either if Jasmine was always picking on her. Why oh why had she come along today? All these thoughts raced through her head in those endless moments.

Finally, she and Alison staggered towards the riverbank as Jasmine continued searching. Alison got out her mobile, dialling 999 and telling the operator in a trembling voice what had happened. Sirens shrieked in the distance, and Jasmine clambered out of the river, grabbed her clothes and pulled them on.

'Listen,' she said, taking their arms. Fiona remembered standing there watching the water, her teeth chattering, arms and legs like ice even in the heat of the sun. Mira had to come out. She had to be okay. She had to. Jasmine gave her a little shake. 'Listen to me,' she repeated. 'We had nothing to do with this. No one saw us leave school together. We spotted Mira walking into the water on our way home. Then she fell and she never came up. We tried to find her, but we couldn't. That's what happened. That's it. Okay?'

Fiona and Alison had simply stared, neither of them able to say a word. Alison was so pale and shaky it looked like she was about to keel over.

'Anyway, I'm sure they'll find her,' Jasmine continued, slinging her satchel over her shoulder and doing up the last button on her shirt. 'They'll help her. She's probably floated off downstream and she'll just be a little cold. I'm sure she'll remember things the same way we do. Right, Alison?' She turned to their friend, who was standing there as silent as Fiona.

An emergency vehicle pulled up, and rescuers got out and raced over to them.

'Let me talk,' Jasmine said. 'If they ask you questions, stick to the story. Stick to the story and that will be it, okay?'

Fiona nodded, watching numbly as a rescuer plunged into the river, then pointed downstream to where water eddied in a cove created by the bend. Beside her, Jasmine was answering questions about how they'd been walking home and had seen Mira going into the water. They'd all tried to get her out, she explained, pointing to their wet clothes, but they hadn't been able to, and that was when they'd called 999. No, they hadn't been friends, but they did know each other from school.

The words flowed over and around Fiona like dark water, pulling and sucking at her as she watched the rescuers wade into the river and drag an object onto the bank... *Mira.*

The three of them stood motionless as the paramedics rushed over, performing CPR before bundling her into the ambulance and screeching off with the siren blaring.

'Oh my God,' Alison said, over and over, before Jasmine told her sharply to shut up.

A man with a kind face approached them, and Fiona wanted to tell him not to be kind – that they didn't deserve it, not at all. That they'd done this to Mira. They were responsible. But she could barely even speak.

'I'm sure you're wondering how your friend is doing,' he began. 'She's taken in a lot of water and hasn't been breathing for some time, but we've managed to revive her. She's in a very serious state, but your quick action in calling us may have saved her. Good work, girls.' He patted Jasmine's arm, and she smiled up at him, and it was all Fiona could do not to be sick.

They finally left the riverbank and went their separate ways home. Fiona had stood under the hot shower for ages, but it couldn't warm her insides. Because of them, Mira had almost died. She still *might* die. Fiona shouldn't have encouraged her in. She should have told Jasmine sooner that she couldn't swim. She should have done something to stop her. She should have, but she hadn't. And Alison... She swallowed, bile burning her throat as she pictured how she'd shoved Mira and she'd fallen into the water.

How she'd never come up.

Fiona had tried to miss school the next day by saying she was ill, but her mum had told her she'd be fine and asked her to please go – she had big plans to have the book club over, and she didn't want anyone else in the house. Fiona had gone in a daze. Everyone had heard about Mira, and Jasmine was lapping up her new heroine status. Fiona wondered what would happen when Mira came back. Because she would, of course. She had to get better; there was no other option. Would she tell the truth? Or would she be too scared to say what had really happened?

The weeks went on, though, and Mira didn't come back. Without her, everything returned to normal; everything but

NINETEEN

JASMINE

Jasmine navigated the deserted roads back towards her house, every bit of her dying for a drink. Of course she didn't *need* one, but today was hardly a usual day. And she hated the reminder that she'd once been friends with people she wouldn't be caught dead talking to now. Going to Fiona's had brought her back to the days when she didn't have nice clothes or nice things... when the only thing she did have was power over losers who were desperate to hang onto her.

Why the hell had she agreed to meet with Fiona and Alison in the first place? Yes, she'd wanted to do everything she could to get Juniper back, and sure, she'd jumped at the chance to show Aidan she did care – he'd left to drive the streets again the second it had got light; he hadn't even come to bed last night. But if that useless family liaison officer and her sidekick couldn't come up with anything on Lou, then the three of them were hardly going to be able to. She'd sat there for ages last night answering the police's questions, offering them the most expensive coffee even after Steph told her that maybe she needed some herself. The way the woman had looked at her had made her blood boil, as if *she* was the one who was going to hurt her daughter. If anyone should be held accountable, it should be the police. They were the ones doing nothing. They couldn't even brave a storm to find lost children, for God's sake. Why the hell would you be on a search-and-rescue team if you were such a pussy in the first place?

She never should have agreed to go to Fiona's. She grimaced, picturing that godawful sofa. Fiona looked exactly the same: a plain-Jane version of her former self, with nondescript lanky locks, knitted jumper and faded jeans. As for Alison, Jasmine did have to give her some credit for effort. She wasn't the same overweight moon-faced girl, but her body was way too muscly to resemble anything attractive, and she could do with a good facial-hair remover. At least she'd rediscovered her cheekbones.

But for Alison to bring up that day... Well, she *had* been weak. She was the one who had pushed Mira into the water in the first place, and if she hadn't wanted to, she could have said no. It wasn't Jasmine's fault Mira had drowned, the same way it wasn't Juniper's fault that Gabby had been bullied. Victim mentality, like Lou had said. Jasmine shook her head, thinking of Lou. *She* was anything but a victim.

She pressed on the accelerator as a memory of the day at the river filled her mind. It had been so sunny, the first proper summer weather of the year. And she'd had such a crap day, with Mrs Richards calling home to speak to her mother about something – Jasmine couldn't even remember what now. Ah yes, she thought, her cheeks burning with shame, even though it was years later. The money was due for the class trip, money Jasmine knew her mum didn't have; money she'd been trying to save up only to discover her mother had found the secret stash and spent it all on booze. She could still remember the way Mrs Richards had looked at her when she'd come back to the class-room after that phone call: pityingly, as if she knew there was a problem. She could only imagine the state of her mother when she'd answered the phone.

She'd torn out of the classroom with Alison and Fiona hot on her heels, desperate to do something to shed the day; to show she wasn't the daughter of a poor drunk woman but someone else: someone daring, someone with power. She'd told them they were all going swimming, hoping the boys from the upper years would still be there to eye her perfect body and make admiring catcalls as she got in the water. That would make her feel better.

They'd just left the school and were cutting across the back car park when they saw Mira leaning against the wall. Jasmine didn't know Mira well – she was in her tutor group with Mrs Richards, but they hadn't talked much. If she was being honest, she'd been kind of grossed out by the huge red birthmark that stretched across Mira's neck to the top of her chin, making snide remarks here and there about it that Mira couldn't hear but that made everyone else laugh. Mira's family had money, though – everyone knew she lived in a huge house on the outskirts of town – so she was fair game as far as Jasmine was concerned. If you were rich, nothing else mattered.

The three of them were passing her when Mira reached out to touch Jasmine on the shoulder. 'Hey,' she said tentatively. 'I heard Mrs Richards talking to you. If you need some cash for the trip, I can lend it to you, no problem.'

'I don't need cash,' Jasmine said, conscious of Alison and Fiona's eyes on her. 'What gave you that stupid idea?'

Mira bit her lip. 'Oh, sorry. I thought I heard Mrs Richards say that your mum needed to pay the money now.'

Jasmine's cheeks burned. 'My mum has the money. I've no idea what the hell you're talking about. The curse must have affected your brain.' Anger surged inside as she stared at Mira. How dare she say something like that in front of Fiona and Alison? How dare she say something like that full stop? No one at school knew where Jasmine lived; knew that she had to make weekly visits to the food bank and prop her mother up in line to get her benefits cheque. No one knew how she had to stretch to make every pound last as long as she could, or how she'd go without lunch, not because she was watching her weight or had amazing willpower, like Fiona always admired, but because there was no food at home and no money to buy anything from the cafeteria at school. She had tried so hard to hide all of that from everyone, and now this nobody could ruin everything in one fell swoop. She could understand Mira being jealous of her, but trying to humiliate her was going way too far.

She stared at the girl, rage growing as she took in her clean, tailored blazer and neatly creased skirt, and the black designer shoes Jasmine had been eyeing up for months, knowing she'd never be able to buy them in a million years. Fury exploded inside her. Suddenly, a gem of an idea came to her, and she smiled.

'Hey, would you like to come swimming with us? We're off to the river for a quick dip.'

Happiness mixed with surprise flashed across Mira's face. 'Sure,' she said, falling into step beside Alison and Fiona. 'I was supposed to wait for my sister, but she can catch me up.'

Jasmine marched ahead, anger growing with every step. She'd get Mira in the water and push her under, then tell Alison to hide her stuff, throw those shoes in the river... or something like that. She was desperate now to show Mira who really had the power, money or not.

But things hadn't turned out the way she'd planned, not at all. She'd only wanted to embarrass Mira, not for her to end up in a coma and die. But really, she thought now as she stopped at a red light at an empty junction, if Mira couldn't swim, then why the hell had she got into the water in the first place?

The light turned green and she pulled away, remembering how she'd watched Mira fall after she'd signalled Alison to shove her – and how she hadn't come up again. At first, she'd thought Mira had been joking. She'd been about to ask Fiona to grab her things from the riverbank and chuck them in. But then... well, then it was obvious it wasn't a joke, after all, and Alison and Fiona had called 999. Jasmine had waded from the water a few minutes later, shielding her eyes from the glare, only managing to make out the silhouette of a girl leaning on her bicycle, watching from across the meadow.

Fear had shot through her as she recalled Mira's words that her sister would catch her up. Was this Mira's sister? How much had she seen? Jasmine blinked against the sun, and when she opened her eyes, the girl was gone. She had shaken her head, wondering if she'd really seen someone or if it had been the light playing tricks.

She'd tried to find Mira's sister in school over the next few days to get a sense of what she might have seen, but she hadn't been there. Then the family moved to London to be close to Mira in her care home, and eventually Jasmine's worries had disappeared. If she'd known something, she would have spoken up by now. The blurry girl on the bike hadn't disappeared, though: she'd haunted Jasmine's dreams for months after the accident – haunted her still, usually when she'd had too much to drink. She'd told herself that the girl wasn't real, and that Alison and Fiona would keep their mouths shut. And Mira, well... if Mira recovered, she'd think of a way to keep her quiet. She had to. She couldn't let her ruin all her hopes and dreams. They were the only things she had.

Then Mira had died. When Alison had told her the news, Jasmine had felt herself split in two. One part was mired in regret and anger, wishing she'd never seen Mira in the car park that day, never invited her along, never had a mother who couldn't even afford a school trip. But the other part felt free, still able to kick past all the detritus and destruction of her life and reach for the surface. Because even though Mira was dead, it meant that Jasmine was safe. She could continue trying to escape from her mother and the poverty she'd been born into. No one would ever jeopardise that.

The split that had formed when Mira died had sealed itself over long ago, regret and anger locked deep inside where they could no longer touch her. Sure, she wished it hadn't happened. She was sorry it had, but the only thing she could do was focus on achieving the perfect life – being the perfect person – she'd always wanted. She'd done just that, and she wouldn't let herself be pulled backwards again.

She rubbed at her eyes, feeling the weight of the hangover now pressing against her head, then stared into the distance, where the wind was whipping the trees on the horizon. The turn for her house came up, but she drove past. She didn't want to go home, back to pacing around the place, alone without Juniper. What she needed was a good blow-dry and facial to make her feel balanced again – make her feel *herself*. With no one going out in the storm, she'd decided late last night to close the salon today. She'd take some me-time now in her own little sanctuary.

Then she could face the world once more, with the present firmly in place.

TWENTY
ALISON
10 A.M.

Alison drove home through the empty streets, the strong wind buffeting the sides of her car. Her mobile rang on the seat beside her, and she glanced down. It was Greg, probably wondering why she hadn't returned by now. He hadn't wanted her to leave, but she'd told him that meeting Fiona and Alison might help get Gabby back home quicker – she'd prayed it would anyway. The night had seemed eternal, with Greg blaring the news for the latest weather forecast interspersed with her ringing Steph for any new information. When Steph had told them they'd pulled the searchers until conditions improved, Greg had collapsed on the bed with his head in his hands, saying he couldn't bear to think of Gabby out there in the wind and rain. He'd turned and clutched onto her, as if she was the only thing keeping him afloat.

The muscles in her forearms strained as she struggled to keep the car on the road, and she swallowed, thinking of Gabby. Please God, let her daughter get through this without needing her inhaler. She'd be fine, she tried to reassure herself. She'd been building up stamina at the gym every day, running further and further. She had to be all right. Alison couldn't bear to think of the alternative.

And you're fine, too, she told herself as she gripped the steering wheel, even though inside she felt shaky and fearful. Seeing Jasmine had brought back memories of the girl she had been... the one who'd towered over her friend physically but still let herself be bossed around; the one who'd tried desperately to find Mira after she'd pushed her into the water at Jasmine's bidding. Even now she could feel the panic and disbelief as the rushing current carried Mira away.

Looking back, Alison didn't know how she'd made it through that time. That day had ripped her apart, taking away the friends she'd relied on as well as any fledgling sense of self-worth and happiness. She'd plodded through every hour like a shadow, the guilt eating her up inside. One day, at the start of the long summer holiday, when she couldn't take it any more, she'd gone on a train to north London, where the teachers had told her Mira was still in a coma. Alison had to say she was sorry, and then maybe she'd feel better. Then maybe she could look at herself in the mirror again.

She'd only travelled to London once or twice a year, and the city was strange and foreign to her, but she had to do this. Somehow, she managed to find her way through the warren of Tube tunnels to Mira's long-term care facility, steeling herself to enter the uninviting brick building that looked like it hadn't been painted since the 1970s. She opened the door and went to the receptionist behind the counter, who was staring into her cup of tea as if she could read her future there. The whole place was deathly silent.

'Um, hi,' Alison said timidly, her voice echoing around the foyer. 'I'm here to visit someone?' She bit her lip, wondering for the millionth time what Mira would look like. Would she have tubes down her throat, like you saw in movies? Had she lost a lot of weight? Would her hair still be long, or would someone have cut it short? Would it just look like she was sleeping?

The woman met her eyes, shoving her bright red hair off her forehead. 'Visiting hours are tonight from six until eight,' she said in a bored voice, as if reading from a script. 'You can come back then.'

Panic surged through Alison. She couldn't stay in London until then. She was meant to be at the gym right now, and her mother would be picking her up before supper. There was no way she could explain her absence. Ever since the incident, the only place she went was the gym. She was more alone than she'd ever been, but that was okay. She deserved it after what she'd done. But maybe this – saying sorry – would go a little way towards making up for it. It was all she could think of to do.

'I can't,' she said, her voice shaking. 'I need to see her. Please.'

The woman must have spotted the desperation in her eyes because she put down her cup of tea and sighed. 'What's the name?' she asked.

'Mira,' Alison whispered. She hadn't spoken Mira's name since the accident, and it felt strange in her mouth. 'Mira Penrose.'

'Right, then. Let me have a look. Maybe I can get you in.' The woman clacked on the keyboard, and Alison held her breath. She had to see her. She couldn't bear any more of this guilt.

The woman's face softened as she looked up at Alison. 'Are you a friend? Family?' she asked kindly.

'Friend,' Alison said, dread stirring inside at the woman's sympathetic expression. Was something wrong? 'I'm a friend from school.' She swallowed back the bile burning her throat. She wasn't a friend. She was anything but. She'd almost killed Mira.

The woman reached out a hand. 'I'm sorry,' she said in that

same kind voice, so at odds with her earlier strident tones. 'You're too late, I'm afraid.'

Alison stared, her mind whirling. Why was she sorry? What did she mean, 'too late'? Mira wasn't... Her stomach clenched, and the bile rose again. Mira was okay. She was alive.

'Mira Penrose—'

'No.' Alison shook her head so hard her neck hurt. She wouldn't let the woman finish. She couldn't. She raced past the reception desk and down the corridor, looking at the names on each door. Mira had to be here. She had to be. She ran up the stairs and down another corridor, names flashing in front of her eyes. Finally, Mira's name came into view, and she slumped against the wall, her heart pounding as relief poured through her. Thank God. Thank God, thank God. Mira was here.

But she froze when she went inside the room. Because even though Mira's name was still on the door, the room was stripped bare of her presence. All that remained was a withered bouquet of flowers in the corner of the room, their life drained away the same way the life had drained from Mira.

Alison stood in the middle of the space as it swung around her. She'd killed someone. She'd taken Mira's life away. Just when she'd thought she couldn't stand any more guilt, it was worse than ever. She was about to flee from the room – from the crushing weight of the pain – when a cleaner appeared.

'You friend or family?' The woman reached into the bag hanging off her trolley and fished out a folded piece of paper. 'This was with the flowers. I don't know if it's important. Maybe someone wants it.'

Alison blinked at the scrap of paper in her hand, trying to make out the scrawl. There were several lines written on it, and she covered her mouth as the words came into focus. Three names: *Jasmine, Alison, Fiona*. Over and over, as if someone was trying to drill them into their head. As if someone was making sure they would never forget them.

Jasmine, Alison, Fiona. She stared at the names, trying to take them in. What did it mean? Why was it here? Had Mira regained consciousness and written this down before she died? It seemed unlikely, and it didn't look like Mira's writing, but then she'd hardly have the stable script of a healthy teen now.

Maybe someone else had written this? Someone Mira had told the truth to?

Someone who *knew* the truth about that day?

Alison had slipped the paper into her pocket, feeling it burn next to her skin. In a daze, she made her way to the train and went home. She crawled under the covers and told her mum she was ill, then went to sleep. It was as if her body had to shut down because it was all too much. When she awoke in the morning, her mum had done her laundry. Heart pounding, Alison scrabbled in the pocket of her jeans, where she'd shoved the paper. It was still there, a wrinkled ball, and when she unwound it, it was blank – like the slate had been wiped clean. She'd torn it apart and put it in the toilet, then flushed, as if she could get rid of it.

In the wake of what she'd learned – Mira's death – somehow the piece of paper stayed buried in a corner of her mind. She'd never told Fiona or Jasmine about it, even when she'd texted to tell them of Mira's death, tears streaming down her face so she could barely type. Fiona didn't respond, but Jasmine did, to say she was sorry, but at least they knew their secret was safe. Alison had simply read the message, then blocked the number. She never wanted to see Jasmine again – she was more sure of that than she was of anything. She never wanted to see anything that reminded her of that day or what she'd done – including her own reflection.

In the years since, she'd done everything possible to transform herself. Her mum had been thrilled to see her take an interest in her appearance, buying her her first gym membership. She'd never said anything, but Alison could see her relief that her daughter had a place where she could fit in. She would spend hours exercising, urging herself to do twenty more bench presses; to jog five miles more. But try as she might, nothing she did would ever change what had happened. All she could do was make sure she was strong enough not to let it happen again, to her or her loved ones.

And now the past had reared up, like she had always dreaded it would. Because no matter what Jasmine or Fiona believed about why Lou had taken the kids, Alison knew there was every possibility that someone else knew what had happened that day. That was the most likely connection between them. She'd sat on the sofa, praying there was something else; praying she was wrong. Maybe Jasmine or Fiona knew something. Maybe the past *was* buried for ever. But when they hadn't been able to think of anything, Alison knew she had to be right. Head spinning, she'd left Fiona's house barely recognising the words trickling from her mouth. All she could see was that note with their three names.

But even though she might never be able to change the past, she had changed herself. She wasn't fearful now of Jasmine's impatience or disdain. She didn't need anyone's approval. She wasn't afraid, and it was time now to use her strength to keep her child safe; to keep her family together. If the searchers weren't brave enough to look for the kids in the storm, then she would. She wasn't going to hang around while the wind got stronger and the river higher. She'd find them, and she'd bring her daughter home, no matter the cost. She'd protect her, like she'd vowed.

She swung the car around and started towards the motorway and the spot where she'd first seen Lou's car. She'd never forget the horror of coming across the empty vehicle with the doors open, all the things inside and no sign of Lou or the children. She rubbed her eyes as she pulled over to the side of the road and parked up. God, was that only yesterday?

She yanked on the handbrake and grabbed her phone, texting Greg to say she'd be back soon. No way could she say what she was really doing. He'd be frantic with worry, even more than he already was. The motorway was shockingly quiet; people had heeded the police's request to stay in. She swallowed, glancing out at the swaying branches with leaves and other bits of debris flying through the air. *Were* the kids really out there in this? Where on earth could Lou have taken them from here without a car?

She tilted her head as a thought snuck in. If you made it across this huge swathe of forest, around a lake in the middle and then up an incline, you came to a car park close to a National Trust lookout. Could she have parked another car there, maybe, and ditched the Range Rover here to throw them all off the scent? But why would she leave all their things?

None of this made sense, Alison thought as she left the shelter of the car and headed into the gale. But even if she didn't find the kids, maybe she would find something in the woods to point her in the right direction. She pulled her mac closer around her body and put up the hood, securing it firmly under her chin even as rain trickled down her back. The wind pulled at her and water lashed against her face, but the only thing she could feel was the determination and strength surging through her muscles. It felt like she'd been training for ever for this very moment. She gazed out from the motorway and into the dense, dark forest.

Then she took a deep breath and plunged in.

TWENTY-ONE

TABITHA

10 A.M.

The wind is trying to tear down this cabin, rattling the windows and thumping the door, even though Lou is sitting with her back against it. I cringe as I hear another tree falling, but I'm not sure where I'd rather be: in here with Lou or out there.

I look at her now, her chin tucked into her jumper, and I shiver. I still can't believe she took us. I can't believe she might have hurt Juniper. And I can't believe she hasn't let the police know where we are – and that Tim was right. Tim was right, and I was wrong, and now I've ruined any chance we had of getting out of here. The police could have been on their way right now if it wasn't for me.

It's so strange to think the police need to rescue us from *Lou*. She's my friend. I know she is. She loves me. It's not just laughing and TikTok; over the years, she's taught me to ride a bike, make scrambled eggs, helped me with my maths...

'Lou.' Before I can stop myself, I reach out and nudge her with my foot, and she lifts her head. 'Please can we go home now? Please?'

She sighs, and for a second I think she's going to say yes. 'It depends on your mum,' she says. She glances around the room. 'It depends on all your mums.'

I stare, trying once more to make out the soft, laughing Lou I know under the hard expression that's come over her. 'My mum wouldn't hurt anyone,' I say. 'I don't know what happened, but I know that for sure.' I do too. Mum is so gentle, so calm. She's always watching out to make sure we're all okay, cleaning up after everyone. I can't even imagine her yelling, let alone doing something worse.

But Lou lets out a strange laugh, then closes her eyes. 'Sometimes, silence is the worst pain of all,' she says, and since I don't even know what she means, I have no idea what to say next.

Instead, I turn to look at Juniper, in the corner furthest away from Lou. Her lips are so pale it's like they're blended into her face, and her eyes look vacant. Her hair is matted to her head with blood, and she's shaking with cold. And Gabby... she's stopped crying, but she's definitely not okay. Her breath is coming in rasping gasps, as if there's something clogging her lungs. She said she needs her inhaler, but she doesn't have it. She grabbed it from the car and put it in her pocket before getting out, but it must have fallen somewhere in the woods.

I draw my knees up to my chest, Gabby's rasps growing louder. Whatever Mum needs to do to get us out of here, she'd better do it fast.

Fiona sat in the car outside Krish's house, watching the water run down the windscreen and trying not to think that the kids were out in this, scared and praying to come home soon. She had to figure out what Lou wanted, but *how*? She started the engine and backed out of the drive, hoping an idea would come to her. A gust of wind shook the car, and she winced. She had to think of something fast.

She drove towards home, deciding to take the motorway that looped around the town rather than the narrow roads that could be blocked by fallen trees. The windscreen wipers were barely keeping up with the rain, and she slowed to a crawl, holding her breath as she crossed the bridge over the swollen river. She exhaled slowly and pressed down on the accelerator, praying the water didn't get any higher – praying the children were safely out of the river's reach. The wipers pushed the curtain of rain aside, and she squinted. What was that? A shape was slowly moving down the hard shoulder, bent under the force of the weather. It looked... Her heart leapt. Was that a woman?

Could it be Lou?

Wrenching the wheel, she pulled over and rolled to a stop behind the figure, who had now turned towards her. With the water running down the windscreen, she still couldn't make out if it was Lou or not. If it was, what was she doing here alone? Where were the children? She glanced at the dark mass of trees stretching out by the side of the motorway. Surely, they couldn't be in there all on their own. *Please.*

She turned off the engine and got out of the car. She squinted against the driving rain as the figure moved closer, her heart lurching as the face came into focus.

'Alison.' She sighed, not sure how she felt. Relieved that Lou hadn't abandoned the children alone in the woods, but disappointed that she wasn't any nearer to finding her – or the kids. 'What are you doing here?'

Alison came closer. She was absolutely soaking, her hair plastered to her face. Her face was white and her lips were blue, but she moved steadily, as if nothing – not even the wind – would knock her down. She shook her head, emotion pulling at her features. 'I was trying to find Gabby, but I couldn't get far enough into the woods. It's no wonder the search was called off. I nearly got hit by a falling branch.'

Fiona took her arm and propelled her into the car, then turned on the engine and blasted the heat. Alison's face regained some colour, and she turned to face Fiona.

'I think this is about what happened that day.' She swallowed. 'What we... what I did. And I couldn't let Gabby be harmed by my actions.'

Fiona shifted in her seat as Alison echoed her earlier thoughts. For a split second, she wondered if she could be right. Then she reminded herself again that it couldn't be that. Like Fiona, Alison was grabbing at any possibility that might connect them; might get their children back. 'I had the same thought, actually,' she said softly. 'But there's no way anyone could know. The school told us Mira was in a coma, right? She couldn't have said anything. I know we want to get our kids back, but we need to focus on what makes sense. And Mira...' The name seemed to fill the small space, no matter how quietly she said it. 'Well, it can't be that.'

Alison swallowed, her eyes locked on Fiona's. 'There was a note.'

'A note?' What was Alison talking about?

She nodded. 'When I went to visit Mira... when I found out she was...' Her voice cracked. 'A cleaner found a note. And...'

Fiona's throat tightened. 'And what?'

'It had our names on it. That was all. Just Jasmine, Alison, Fiona. Over and over again.' Alison breathed in. 'I couldn't tell if it was Mira's handwriting or someone else's, but she must have come to. Maybe she wrote it, and someone saw it – her family, maybe, or another person at the hospital. Maybe she told someone else. But however those names got there, someone *could* know.'

Fiona held her gaze, trying to take it in. A note, in Mira's room. A note with names – three names. The names of the people who had killed her. Her heart beat so fast that she felt light-headed, and sweat broke out once more. There was a chance that what had happened wasn't a secret between the three of them like they'd thought. There was a chance that someone else knew. The dark thing they'd kept quiet for decades... someone knew. Oh God.

'Lou must know,' Alison continued, her voice ringing with desperation. 'That's why she took our kids. It has to be.'

Fiona stared, her mind whirring as she tried to fit everything together. Could Alison be right? Could Lou be the one who'd found that note – or who'd written it? Could she be Mira's sister? She swallowed as the thought tightened around her. Had she been living next to Fiona all this time, smiling and laughing while all the while knowing what Fiona had done – all the while planning to somehow force the truth into the light?

No, surely not, she thought once more. It was too much, like something from a horror film. But... Lou had taken their children. She'd sent them all the same message demanding the truth. And at the moment, none of them could think of any other reason why she would target them, and only them.

The three who had been listed on that note.

Was it possible?

'I can't let Gabby suffer because of something I did.' Alison's stare bored through Fiona. 'So there's only one thing left to do. We need to tell the truth about Mira. About what we did to her. We need to tell the police, and then our children will be safe.'

Her voice shook with intensity, and Fiona tilted her head. Was that really the only thing they could do? But what if they were wrong? There was a possibility Lou knew the truth, but what if she didn't? What if they told the police what had happened that day and Lou still didn't release the children? What if she hadn't written or read that note and wasn't connected to Mira, after all? They were all culpable. They'd all be found guilty. Their families would be destroyed, and God knows hers was broken enough right now.

She put a hand on Alison's arm, stunned to feel the strength beneath it. It was so hard to reconcile the chubby, pliable girl she remembered with this determined, strong woman. Alison had changed so much. She wasn't the same girl who'd let Jasmine boss her around. But Fiona... Her heart dropped at the realisation that the past few decades hadn't changed her at all. She *was* still that girl who'd rather keep her head down, tidy away any errant emotions and go along with things, like her mum had asked of her all those years ago. But it hadn't worked, had it? Not with helping Mira, and not with Nick. She'd tidied away everything so much that she hadn't even noticed her marriage was falling apart.

She stared at Alison, picturing her children, bloodied and

cold, out in the woods with Lou standing over them. Then she pictured them going through life without her, bearing the pain and shame of having a mother in prison, and her gut twisted. As much as she wanted her kids back, she couldn't let Alison destroy their lives, not without knowing more – not without at least trying to find out who Lou really was and whether she could know the truth about that day.

She couldn't shrink away any longer; trail behind whoever charged forward. She had to change, too, for her kids and for her family. She thought of how she'd called Alison and Jasmine in the first place, and how she'd gone to Krish's despite Jasmine rubbishing her idea that it might be something to do with the kids. Maybe, just maybe, she *had* already started to change without even realising.

'If you're right, we need to come forward.' Dread rose at the thought of all that would entail, but she'd do it in a heartbeat if it meant getting her children back safe and sound. 'But if you're wrong, well...' She met Alison's eyes, thinking that if anyone would suffer the consequences, it would be her. 'It could be disastrous for our families.' She watched as Alison absorbed her words. 'We need to try to find some link between Lou and Mira first, before we say anything. And Jasmine will probably want evidence too,' she added, thinking there was no 'probably' about it. Jasmine would definitely want proof before exploding her whole world. Fiona didn't doubt she would say whatever she needed to, though, if she had to. A mother would do anything to protect her child, no matter how self-obsessed she might seem.

'But how long will that take?' Alison asked. 'Gabby's out there without her inhaler. I don't have time to waste.'

Fiona nodded slowly, thinking of the bloody headband. Alison was right: they didn't have time. Whatever they decided, they needed to act quickly.

She paused, an idea hitting. 'If we can get into Lou's house, maybe we can find something. The police have already searched there, but they wouldn't have looked for what we want to know. Maybe Lou's a relative of Mira, or perhaps she visited the care home when Mira was there. Maybe... maybe she was in there herself.' Her mind flashed back to Krish's words about how Lou had periods of instability, and how she'd been on medication. Could she have been a fellow patient? Anyone could have seen that note, after all. 'Then we can be sure about going to the police, and everything that will happen afterwards. And if we don't find anything, we can talk about what to do next.' Her stomach twisted at the thought of the risk they'd be taking either way if they found no clear answers.

She held her breath as Alison nodded.

'I don't have a key, but...' Fiona bit her lip, thinking how strange it was that she had given Lou an extra key to hang onto in case of emergency, but Lou had never done the same. Had she been trying to hide something? Fiona had thought nothing of it at the time, but... 'I can ask Krish for his, I guess, unless you have one?'

'I don't, but let's not waste time going back to Krish's. I bet I can figure out a way to get inside,' Alison said. 'Come on, let's go. I can come back and get my car later. The sooner we find out if I'm right, the better.'

Ten minutes later, they were standing outside Lou's house. It was strange to be here looking in. Her place had always seemed so open, so light... just like Lou herself. Now they both seemed the exact opposite.

'So, what are we going to do?' Fiona asked, her teeth chattering as the wind whipped around them. Alison didn't even seem to notice as she examined the bay window at the front. Fiona glanced nervously around them. To all intents and purposes, they were breaking into a house. The last thing they needed was to explain everything to the police before they figured out exactly who Lou was.

'Let's go to the back,' Alison said, her jaw set. Fiona followed her around the side, pausing to gaze up at her own house looming over Lou's smaller one. She'd never noticed how much taller it was. Somehow Lou's had always seemed so much more desirable than her own. Pain hit her as she realised that Nick had felt the same.

'Right, here.' Alison wedged her fingers under a sash window by the back door, sliding it up and down with force until there was a big enough space to get through. 'You're smaller than me. You should be able to fit through.'

Sucking in her stomach, Fiona eased her head and chest through the window. Alison grabbed her legs, and in another few seconds she'd landed in a heap on the floor. She got to her feet, breathing in the fresh, clean smell of Lou's place as memories flooded through her mind: when Lou had first moved in and invited her over for drinks. When their kids were playing with water balloons in the back garden and Lou had grabbed one and soaked her. When Lou had listened to her pouring out her heart about Nick and how sorry she was about what she'd done... She blinked, the golden images shattering into a million sharp shards. Had that all been fake? Was it simply a way to get back at Fiona for the part she had played in Mira's death... to get revenge by taking the very thing most dear to her heart: her children? Why now, though, and why did Lou care so much? Who *was* she? It was still so hard to wrap her head around it all.

Now, hopefully, they were about to find out.

Fiona unlocked the back door. She let Alison inside, then flicked on the lights. The usually pristine place was a mess from the police search, with cushions upended and papers strewn across every surface. She resisted the urge to tidy up, thinking that at least it would make their search easier.

Alison sloughed off her jacket and hung it up, then

slipped off her shoes. Fiona did the same, thinking how strange it was that they were worried about sullying the carpet of a woman who had taken their children. Lou's presence was strong in this house, and being here without her felt wrong.

But they needed to do this, she reminded herself. Lou had taken their children and put them in danger. And before their whole lives imploded, they needed to try and work out exactly who she was.

'Right. Where should we start?' she asked, her voice echoing in the empty house.

'I'll check the lounge. You take the bedrooms,' Alison said, and Fiona nodded and padded down the hallway.

The kids' rooms were tidy, and it looked like they'd taken most of their things with them to Krish's. Sadness flooded in as Fiona realised that they'd never live here again... never have Lou as the mother they'd come to know and love. Once this was over, she'd be jailed for her actions, regardless of her reasons. Fear shot through her as she realised the true depth of Lou's anger and emotion. If this was about Mira, they must have been very close. By the sounds of things, her death had had a devastating impact on Lou's life. Maybe it was one of the reasons why she'd been so depressed.

She went into Lou's bedroom, unease creeping over her as she stood in the middle of the room. Had Nick been in here? Surely not, given what he'd said, but she couldn't help picturing the two of them beside the bed, with Lou leaning in to try to kiss him. Was all of that because she'd wanted to get back at Fiona, or had it actually been genuine? Even if it hadn't been real on Lou's side, though, the connection had been important to Nick. Fiona pushed aside the hurt and pain when she thought of her husband, forcing herself to focus on the task at hand. After rifling through the bedside table, looking under the bed and combing through the wardrobe, though, she found nothing. No pictures, no letters, nothing to suggest a hint of connection to the past, let alone to Mira.

She left the bedroom and went into the kitchen at the same time Alison was leaving the lounge. 'Anything?' Alison asked, and Fiona shook her head.

'Are there any other places she could be storing stuff?' Alison asked. 'I mean, there's nothing here.'

Fiona shook her head again before an image popped into her mind. There was a tiny skylight she could see from the bedroom that overlooked Lou's house. She remembered asking Lou once what was there, and Lou had said it was a loft space that the previous owner had converted into an office, but that it made her claustrophobic, so she'd simply closed it off.

'There is a loft,' she said. 'I'm not sure how to get up there, though. I've never been.'

'Let's have a look.' Alison padded slowly down the corridor, squinting up in the dim light, then pointed at a small square recess in the ceiling. 'Bingo.' She went to the corner of the kitchen and grabbed a broom, then pushed the square up. A flap came down and a metal ladder unfurled. 'Come on.' She grasped the ladder and disappeared into the space.

Fiona managed to haul herself upwards, cursing her lack of strength. The ladder felt rickety, and she heaved a sigh of relief as she dragged her body onto the cold floor of the loft.

'God, it's freezing.' She got to her feet, thinking she could totally understand why Lou didn't want to work in here. The skylight let in grey light, but the space still felt dark and closed in. She gazed up at the sky, seeing the hulk of her house looming over.

'Is there anything here?' She glanced at Alison, realising she'd gone quiet. She was hunched over a box in the corner, with the flaps open, staring inside. 'What is it?' Her heart stuttered at the expression on Alison's face. What had she found?

But Alison didn't answer. Instead, she slowly backed away,

her face white, and Fiona moved forward and gazed into the box. She squinted. What was it? There was something dark in the corner, and she leaned in. Then it hit her, and she tumbled backwards as if she'd been struck.

It was a pair of shoes. Black shoes, glossy in the dim light... glossy except for mud coating the soles. She recognised them instantly. These were the shoes Mira had been wearing; the shoes she'd worn for the very last time that day. They'd belonged to her sister. And they were here in Lou's things.

That meant... Fiona swallowed as the darkness grew within. That had to mean Lou was Mira's sister. The same sister Fiona had been so relieved not to face all those years ago. She'd been beside her, closer than she'd ever thought possible, and she'd never even known. But how could she? They didn't really look alike: Mira had been heavyset, with a round face, while Lou was slender, with sculpted features. That didn't mean anything, though: Fiona's own twins barely looked like brother and sister.

Fiona didn't know how old Lou was – she could be either younger or older than Mira. Probably older, if she'd lent Mira the shoes. They must have been very close if she would go to this extreme. She drew in a breath, remembering once more how Lou had been on medication. Was it to deal with the traumatic death of her sister? Krish's words about why they'd broken up rang in her mind: she hadn't wanted to be with someone who could be so violent. In light of her past, it made sense now.

It *all* made sense. Lou was Mira's sister, and she knew what had happened that day. That was why she'd taken the kids. That was the truth she wanted them to tell.

'Lou is Mira's sister,' Fiona said, turning to look at Alison. She was in the corner of the room, as far away from the shoes as she could get. Her face was still pale, drained of any expression. It was like she was in shock.

'I remember her taking those shoes off,' Fiona continued. 'I remember her saying they were her sister's.' She paused, her mind spinning. 'She must have regained consciousness enough to write that note – or to tell someone; tell Lou. However Lou found out, though, at least we know that you're right. This *is* about that day. We need to tell the police what really happened.' Emotions buffeted her like the wind outside: relief that they'd worked out what would bring their kids to safety, but despair and pain at the havoc it would wreak. She might have saved the kids physically, but this would cause them all emotional destruction.

She glanced over at Alison, expecting her to agree, but Alison was still frozen. Her presence – which had filled the space with her strength; her solid form – was weak now, almost as if she'd shrunk. For an instant, Fiona's mind flashed back to that girl who'd watched the water, waiting for Mira to reappear. She had the same vacant look now.

'Yes,' Alison echoed weakly. 'We need to say what really happened.'

They both stared into the box, neither one of them wanting to touch the shoes, as if by making contact, they would be reliving that terrible day. In a way, they *were* reliving that day. They had to – for their children. Fiona closed her eyes for a second, a strange peace filtering in alongside the pain. Finally, she wouldn't have to keep moving, keep tidying, keep doing all she could to make sure everything stayed buried. Finally, she could stop and be still, for the first time in years.

She reached into the box and picked up the shoes, noticing Alison trembling. She reached out a hand to steady her, but Alison shrank away. Fiona could understand. None of this was easy, but it needed to be done.

'Let's go,' she said, cradling the shoes with one hand and easing herself down the ladder. She heard Alison coming after her, then following her through the darkened house. She closed the door behind them, and led the way through the rain back to her own house, thinking how strange it was that she was now the one completely in charge. Alison seemed to have faded away as soon as she'd seen those shoes.

Inside, she grabbed her phone, biting her lip. Should they call the police now and tell them the truth, or should they wait to talk to Jasmine first? Lou had wanted all three of them to confess. They had all played a part, and this was something they had to do together. Fiona had no idea how Lou would check that they'd each told the truth before releasing the kids, but they couldn't risk her hearing that two of them had confessed and not the third. They couldn't risk any complications. Not now – not when they were so close.

'Let's call Jasmine.' She took a deep breath. 'I'll get her to come here, and we'll show her the shoes. And then... then together we can call the police. We can say what really happened that day to Mira, and Lou will let the children go.' *Please God, she would let them go.*

It would all be over soon, she told herself. This terrible ordeal... her marriage... her life as she knew it. She would pay a very high price, but she wouldn't hesitate to save her loved ones.

She'd just never thought her children – her family – would pay such a heavy price too.

TWENTY-THREE

TABITHA

11.30 A.M.

It feels like we've been stuck inside this hut for ever. We're all hungry and thirsty. Juniper has asked Lou a million times if she has any water or food, and each time Lou shakes her head and checks the phone. Each time, I will her to text or call someone, to do anything to get us out of here – or to say that our mums have done whatever she needs them to in order to let us go. Then everything will be fine. Everything will go back to normal. Mum, Dad, Tim and I together in our house, warm and cosy, for ever and ever. But each time, her face only twists. She puts the phone back into the front of her jumper and sinks into herself, as if she's turning off a switch. And no matter how turned off she is, no one can get that phone again without her noticing.

A tear drips down my cheek, and I swipe it away. This is all my fault. If I'd never let Lou in... if I'd never given back the phone... God! We could be home, warm and dry, by now. I lift my head to peek out the tiny window. The woods look ferocious, like some sort of monster about to devour us. I wouldn't go out there if you paid me. But... I glance around the cramped space, taking in Juniper staring at the wall. Tim's beside her, slumped over with his eyes closed, like he knows it's all over and he's defeated. And Gabby... My heart clutches. Her chest is rising and falling, and her lips are a strange pale colour. She's making that wheezing noise, even louder than before. 'Gabby, are you okay?' I hiss.

She nods. 'Fine,' she whispers, like she doesn't want to use up too much air. 'I just really need my inhaler. I'll be okay, though.'

I nod, but despite Gabby's brave words, she doesn't look fine – far from it. And while I don't know much about asthma, I do know that things can get bad, especially out here in the cold. She needs help, and I'm not sure how much longer we can wait. I swallow, wondering what to do. I've already made so many mistakes that I really don't want to make another.

'Tim?' I prod his leg, and his eyes fly open as he turns towards me. 'Gabby's having an asthma attack. We have to wake Lou and ask if we can retrace our steps to find her inhaler.'

Tim stares at me like I'm an idiot, not that I can blame him. 'Retrace our steps?' he asks. 'There's no way I can remember how we got here, and Lou's hardly going to let us out.' He looks at Gabby. 'You'll be okay, right? I mean, you're not going to die or anything?' He grins to take the sting from his words, but my stomach still clenches.

Gabby nods and closes her eyes, but it's clear that she's anything but comfortable. 'I'm sure I'll be better in a bit,' she rasps.

'We need to tell Lou,' I say, the worry lodged inside me like a cold, hard lump. 'We can't wait and see what happens. We need to get out of here.'

Tim stares at me in that same way. 'We all need to get out of here, Tabs. But we need to play this right.' His words make it clear that I *haven't* played it right, not that I need a reminder. 'Waking Lou up to tell her Gabby's not well could give her the extra bit of information she needs to force our mums to do whatever it is she's asking. And it must be something bad, or they would have already done it.' He shakes his head. 'We have to stay strong – for them. Gabby said she'd be fine, didn't she? Lou doesn't have to know. The police will come for us, or we can make a break for it when the storm stops. Okay?'

I nod. He's probably right. No, he *is* right. I need to listen – I can't make another mistake. Watching Gabby's chest heave up and down, guilt sweeps over me as I realise that my mistakes might cost some of us more than others.

But I really hope not.

Alison followed Fiona inside, numbly going straight to the place on the sofa she'd sat before. It felt so strange that after years of not seeing her childhood friends, this was the second time she'd been inside one of their homes.

She cleared her throat, trying to think of what to say in the silence. She could hardly conjure any thoughts, let alone words. Seeing Jasmine had reminded her of the weak girl she'd once been, but she'd told herself she'd changed. Then she'd spotted the shoes, and it had struck her again that no matter how much she had changed, she couldn't undo her actions. A tidal wave of guilt and pain had engulfed her, washing away all the strength she'd worked so hard to gain.

How could she have pushed Mira? How could she have listened to Jasmine and never once spoken up? How could she have been so *weak*? She closed her eyes, feeling exactly like she had that day: flabby and worthless, as if her clothes were too tight even now.

That day, her PE top had bitten into her neck and her shorts kept riding up to show way too much of her chubby legs. She'd longed to be like Jasmine, who always made her school uniform look like something off the catwalk – or even Fiona, who was skinny without trying. She'd been hot and sweaty, but when Jasmine had finally come out from her detention and mentioned swimming in the river, taking off her clothes in public was the last thing Alison had wanted. You didn't argue with Jasmine, though, and she was in a strop over something the teacher had said, so she and Fiona had followed along, as usual.

Sometimes, Alison wondered why someone as pretty as Jasmine wanted to be friends with them and not the group of blonde-haired identikit girls who basically ran the school, but she didn't dare ask. Before Jasmine had decided to be her friend, she'd had practically no one to hang around with apart from the kids who took refuge in the French room with the teacher who was nice enough to realise they had nowhere else to go. Moving to a new school at the start of Year 8, when all the kids had already formed their own little groups, had been awful.

But when Jasmine had asked her one day if she could break into her locker after the lock had broken, and Alison had managed to prise it open, all that had changed, and they'd been friends ever since. Alison felt like an ogre next to Jasmine's slender form, but she was just happy to have friends, even if she wasn't about to spill her innermost thoughts for fear Jasmine might use them against her one day. She'd seen her do that to Fiona when she'd said she was too shy to try out for drama. Jasmine had stuck her name down on the sheet and poor Fiona had nearly died when the drama teacher called her up to audition. She'd done it, though, even though her face had been flaming.

They'd been going through the car park when Mira had tagged along for some reason – Alison had heard her say something, but she'd been too busy trying to tug down her shorts to hear it clearly. And then they'd gone into the river. No way was Alison stripping, so she'd simply plunged in, loving the feel of the water against her hot skin. Even now she could feel that delicious coolness settling into her bones. She'd closed her eyes, and for a second, everything was right.

And then Jasmine's voice cut into her consciousness, yelling at Mira to get in and making fun of her birthmark. Mira's face had tightened, and she'd taken a step forward, and then Jasmine had told Alison to shove her under. Alison had thought it had all been a bit of fun, so she'd done it – she'd been so desperate to avoid Jasmine making fun of her. Anyway, didn't everyone know how to swim?

Mira went under the water, and time seemed to slow as they frantically searched. Alison lurched out to the bank and grabbed her mobile, calling 999. As she told the operator where they were, her eyes focused on Mira's shoes, resting neatly at the top of the bank. She picked them up, then took them down to the edge of the river. It was the least she could do for when Mira came out. At least she'd have shoes to wear when she clambered up the bank.

But she never came out. She never wore those shoes again. Alison had caused her death by pushing her under, and no matter how much she tried to fortify herself against that, she could never, ever forget it. She closed her eyes, Lou's face coming into her head. All that time they'd spent together at the gym, all the chatting and laughing... All that time, Lou had known her darkest secret. God, she must have hated her. Alison had killed her sister. No wonder she wanted revenge.

A knock sounded at the door, and Fiona stood up. 'That must be Jasmine.'

Alison's eyes widened as Jasmine came in. Her hair was even more perfect than a few hours before, tumbling gracefully in waves over her shoulders. Had she actually gone to have her hair done, in the midst of all that was happening? How on earth could she do that? Fiona's face twisted as she took in her appearance, and Alison knew she was thinking the same thing. *Unbelievable.*

'It's brutal out there,' Jasmine said, settling beside Alison. 'So, what did you two want to talk to me about? You said it was urgent. Did you find out anything more about why Lou took the kids?' Her expression said it couldn't have been anything to do with her.

Fiona picked up Mira's shoes and held them out. Jasmine's face stayed the same, but Alison could see by the look in her eyes that she knew what they were. She knew who they belonged to.

'Where did you get those?' she asked. Her voice was calm, but her hand was shaking as she smoothed back her hair.

'Alison and I found them in Lou's loft,' Fiona began. She glanced at Alison, expecting her to chime in, but Alison couldn't even muster a nod. Her muscles were so weak she could barely move. 'I remember Mira saying they belonged to her sister.'

She paused, and Alison kept her eyes on Jasmine, her face still unchanged. She must have nerves of steel, she thought.

'We think Lou is Mira's sister, and that somehow she knows what happened. It's not about the kids. It's about us and what we did that day. And now she wants us to tell the truth.' Fiona breathed in. 'The truth about Mira's death.'

The words hung heavy in the air, and all three women sat in silence as they let them sink in.

'I know it sounds crazy,' Fiona continued, when no one spoke. 'The thought had crossed my mind, but I convinced myself I was just spooked. And then Alison told me...' She looked at Alison again.

'Alison told you what?' Jasmine's voice was so sharp that Alison flinched.

'There was a note,' she mumbled. 'When I went to see Mira in that care home, everything else had been cleared away from her room, but there was a note with our names on it.' She could see the scrawled writing clear as day, even now.

'What?' Jasmine's jaw dropped. 'And you never told us?' Her voice rose, and she cleared her throat. 'I mean, not that it affects any of us as much as you, of course. You *were* the one who pushed her in.'

Alison dropped her head, gulping in air. 'I did,' she whispered. 'I pushed her.' Another wave of guilt and blame swept over her, and she felt herself sinking into the darkness she'd tried so hard to keep at bay.

'So with the note, the shoes and the fact that she targeted us three, we know now what we need to do to get our children back.' Fiona's voice rang out loud and determined in the room. 'We need to say what part we played – and we need to be honest, finally. Alison may have been the one to push her, but we all had a hand in what happened. Lou obviously knows that.'

She paused, clearly waiting for Jasmine to agree, but there was only silence.

'This is for our children,' she continued, even louder. 'And yes, there will be consequences for us. But Alison agrees we need to do it, and we need to do it quickly. Right, Alison?'

Alison tried to respond that yes, of course they needed to – she'd do anything to get Gabby back – but her voice wouldn't obey. She was dropping deeper now, twisting and turning as the blackness closed in. It was all she could do to keep breathing.

But Jasmine was just sitting there too. Had she even heard Fiona? Alison wondered. Surely, she didn't need more proof. She glanced at her sideways. It was impossible to read what she was thinking from her face... or was that the Botox?

'Why don't I call the police?' Fiona said. 'I'll get Steph and the other officer to come over, or we can tell them over the phone if we want to be even faster. We can tell them what happened, and why Lou took the kids. We—'

'Stop.' Jasmine's voice erupted from her like a bullet from a gun, slicing through Fiona's soft one. 'Just *stop*. No one's calling the police. No one's saying anything.'

Alison blinked. What was Jasmine talking about? They *had* to call the police. They had to tell the truth. They needed their children home again. She struggled to fight her way to the surface, to force a sound from her throat, but instead she stayed trapped in the darkness. Fear and frustration filtered into her. She had to speak up now for her daughter. She had to.

'But we are,' Fiona said softly, and Alison gulped in relief. Thank goodness for Fiona. 'We need to do this if we want the kids back. I know it's hard, but we have to.'

Jasmine turned to look at her, and Fiona drew back. 'Do you know what this will do to us if we tell the police what happened? Have you even thought about that?'

'Yes, of course,' Fiona said, her voice strong and steady. 'That's why I wanted to be sure before we said anything. The police will have questions to ask us, and it's not going to be easy.'

Alison could feel her throat tightening as she pictured Greg's response to the fact that she was the one who'd pushed Mira to her death. Because ultimately, she *was* responsible. What would he think when he found out the truth? Would he be there for her like he'd promised?

'Not going to be easy?' Jasmine snorted. 'If the truth comes out, Alison could be in prison for years. She pushed Mira in. I'm no lawyer, but that sounds like manslaughter to me.'

Alison swallowed. *Manslaughter?* Oh God. Would she actually go to prison? What would her daughter do without her? Gabby had always been so close to her; she needed her. Alison had known there would be consequences, like Fiona had said, but she'd been so desperate to get her daughter back that she hadn't stopped to think them through. She hadn't needed to: anything that happened to her was worth it for Gabby's safe return. She'd never imagined that her daughter would suffer from those consequences too, though. Guilt crashed over her again, the undertow dragging her further into the depths.

'People will never look at us the same way again.' Jasmine glanced at Alison. 'And even if we're lucky and we don't go to jail, imagine how this will affect our business if it gets out. You can forget about keeping your gym members. No one will want to come to a murderer's place.'

Her words engulfed Alison, looming larger and louder as they flooded her consciousness. *A murderer's place.* That was what she was, and Jasmine was right. Her business would fail, taking the house with it. Even if Greg didn't love it the way she'd thought, it was still their home. It was the only home Gabby had known, and now she would have to leave.

'But our kids could be in danger,' Fiona said, desperation in her voice. 'We have to think about them. I can't bear to even picture them out there in the woods. I can't—'

Jasmine put a hand on her arm. 'The kids will be fine. Of course they will. Don't you see?' She paused, and her grip tightened. 'If all Lou wants is for us to tell what happened that day, she's not crazy or unhinged... She doesn't want to hurt anyone.'

Fiona jerked towards her. 'Didn't the police tell you?' she said, her voice high. 'They found Tabitha's headband. It was covered in blood.'

Covered in blood? Oh my God. Alison sucked in air, and even Jasmine looked shocked.

'She probably bumped her head on something,' Jasmine said, her face settling back into its calm expression. 'You know how kids bleed. Or Lou is trying to scare us.' She waved a hand breezily in the air. 'I reckon they're all fine, and she's waiting for a text from us or the police that we've said what happened. And if it's just a waiting game, then as soon as the storm is over, they'll be found safe and sound. After all, the police know the area they're in, thanks to Juniper's phone.' She tilted her head. 'I don't know about you, but I'm not going to jeopardise my family's future if they're going to be found soon anyway.'

Alison felt the weight of those words press in on her. That

was exactly what would happen if they told the truth: she would jeopardise her family's future – and not only jeopardise it. In her case, she was certain to destroy it. She'd pledged to protect Gabby, and now she was about to tear her life apart.

'You don't know that,' Fiona said. 'I'm not willing to wait, and Alison isn't either. Gabby might need her inhaler, and Tabitha is clearly injured. And if the two of us tell the police what really happened, they're going to talk to you too.'

'No one is going to tell the police anything,' Jasmine repeated, almost in a snarl. 'Nothing about Mira, and nothing about that day.'

Fiona looked at Alison, and then back at Jasmine. 'I am. And Alison will too,' she said in a strong tone. She glanced at Alison once more, likely hoping for support, but even if Alison had been able to speak, she wasn't certain what to say. Every inch of her wanted her daughter back as soon as possible, but did she want to dismantle Gabby's whole world in the process? Did she even *need* to do that? Her gaze swept from Jasmine to Fiona. It felt like she was drifting, unmoored from anything solid as her certainty faded away.

Jasmine got to her feet. 'If you dare say a word to the police,' she hissed, 'I'll tell them *you* were the one who suggested Mira go into the water.'

'What?' Fiona drew in her breath. 'That was you. It was all your idea.'

Jasmine took a step closer, her head tilted to the side. 'Now that I think about it, neither Alison nor I went into the river until after Mira went under.'

Fiona shook her head. 'You know that's not—'

'Weren't you the one who pushed her in, then held her down? Didn't you say she deserved a good dunking?'

Fiona's eyes widened. '*What?* I never pushed her or held her down. I never touched her.'

'Isn't that right, Alison?' Jasmine said, and they both turned to face her. Her mind flipped back to that dreadful day, and how Jasmine had looked at both of them and told them to be quiet, just like now. Alison *had* kept quiet, and, somehow, she'd found a way to live – to build a life she loved. She'd listened to Jasmine then, grateful for someone to tell her what to do; to give her a way out of this when the shock and fear wouldn't let her think clearly.

Now she was in the grip of guilt and blame again, spinning madly in competing currents. Maybe Jasmine was right. Maybe Alison should listen to her once more. She knew how much Jasmine loved Juniper. She would never risk her daughter's life unless she truly believed what she was saying. And Gabby was more than likely fine. She would be okay. The police would probably find the kids in the next few hours, once the storm died down, and nothing about the past ever need be mentioned. Her family would be safe. Her daughter's life – her future; her happiness – would be safe.

Or would it? Was she risking more by waiting?

Who was right, Fiona or Jasmine?

'I... I...' She churned from one decision to the other, unable to latch onto something to drag her to shore; to give her a second to catch her breath. Glancing up at the two women, standing taut and determined as if ready for battle, she felt even more helpless. They were so strong, so certain, while she was so weak she couldn't even *speak*, even when she'd wanted to. And now she had no idea what to say. Something inside her gave way, and she felt herself sinking further as her remaining air ran out.

'So.' Jasmine faced Fiona triumphantly. 'Feel free to go ahead and tell the police what happened – your version of events. But Alison and I have a different story, and who do you think they'll believe? And if it's just you who reveals what happened that day, do you think Lou will release only your children? She's hardly going to let them give away where they've been hiding. Are you willing to risk your whole life – to maybe even go to prison and not see your children anyway – for something that won't get your kids back in the end?'

Fiona held her gaze. Even as she struggled to breathe, Alison had to admire Jasmine's logic and cunning.

Jasmine nodded, as if Fiona's silence was consent. 'We're all in this together. So let's let the police do their thing. By the end of the day, I know the children will be back with us. They'll be back, and we never need mention this again.' She stared at the shoes on the counter, then grabbed her handbag and swept out of the house.

Fiona turned to look at Alison. 'Alison, please. We can't wait for the police to find them. What about Gabby's asthma? What about the storm? We don't know how much longer it will be until they can resume the search. We need Lou to bring them back now.'

But Alison couldn't answer. She could barely even make out Fiona's words. The world around her felt muffled and blurred, like she was gazing up at everything from the bottom of the sea. As if in slow motion, she dragged herself to her feet and walked out into the rain. Drops ran down her face, a reminder that no matter where she fled to, she could never outrun the water. It had washed away the strength she'd built up; the strength she'd thought would help her protect her family. It hadn't, though. Not even close. It had crumbled easily when the sweeping waves of the past rushed over her.

She wasn't strong. Not for her, not for Mira and not for her child.

She hadn't changed, no matter how different her reflection was. She was nothing.

Just like she'd always been.

TWENTY-FIVE

JASMINE

Jasmine drove back towards her house on the other side of town, checking her phone to see if Aidan had got in touch. He hadn't, but that was okay. He was probably still out searching. But she had everything under control. She *did*. Okay, so she'd struggled to keep calm when Alison and Fiona had shown her the shoes. For a split second, they'd brought her back to a place of desire and desperation. She remembered so clearly how much she'd wanted them; how angry she'd felt when Mira had asked if she needed money... how Mira had almost ruined everything. But then she had swallowed, reminding herself that she had everything she needed now. And while the shoes showed that Lou did have some connection to Mira, they didn't prove she knew anything. She was safe.

Then Fiona had said that the shoes belonged to Mira's sister, and that *Lou* was Mira's sister. Jasmine's world had trembled as she remembered Mira saying her sister would catch them up, and how she had seen the girl on the bicycle waiting on the bank. She'd taken a deep breath, telling herself over and over that the girl wasn't real. And even if she had been real – even if she had been Mira's sister – she hadn't seen anything... she hadn't seen everything. If she knew what had happened, she would have said something. Wouldn't she?

But then Alison had told her about the note with their three names. Neither she nor Fiona knew how Mira could have written it if she'd been unconscious, but Jasmine knew. Mira hadn't written it – her sister had. *Lou* had. She did know. Lou's words that day Jasmine had dropped off the kids scrolled through her head, and she shivered. *These things have a way of coming out. The sooner you tell the truth, the better for everyone.* She knew, and she wanted the past blown wide open.

Jasmine couldn't let that happen. She couldn't. If the truth about what had happened that day came to the surface, it wasn't only the past that would be blown apart. It was the present too – the life she'd always wanted; the life she'd managed to achieve. Because Fiona hadn't caused Mira's death, of course. And no matter what she believed, it hadn't been Alison either.

It had been Jasmine.

She'd only held Mira down for a few seconds. It couldn't have been any longer, because then Fiona or Alison would have noticed. They'd been busy calling 999, though, so they hadn't been looking towards the river. They hadn't seen Mira come to the surface again, gasping for air and locking eyes with Jasmine. They hadn't seen how she'd clutched at her, desperately clinging on.

Something about her fearful grip had made Jasmine snap. It was the same way her mother would cling to her when she'd had too much to drink, asking her over and over again if she'd been a good mother. Jasmine would tell her yes, even though she couldn't be much worse. She'd shoved down the anger then, but somehow it had bubbled back up and engulfed her now, and Mira's face had morphed into her mother's. Jasmine had pushed her under the water once more, wanting her to be gone.

And then she was. Mira was dead, and no one had seen what had really happened... at least that was what she'd thought until now. But how much did Lou really know? Had she seen Jasmine hold Mira under? How much of the truth did she expect Jasmine to reveal? If Jasmine didn't tell her everything, would she release Juniper?

Jasmine pulled into the empty driveway and sat in the car for a minute, gazing at the house in front of her. It was all she'd ever dreamed of. When she'd first walked in, she'd stood in the lounge and breathed in the smell of *new*: of fresh paint, new carpet, pristine fabric unsullied by any touch. It was a far cry from the black mould and smell of rot that sat heavy in the air of her mother's bedsit. She had been dying to escape all of that, and she had. Finally, she had.

But Juniper... She swallowed, getting out of the car and hurrying into the house. Juniper didn't have that resilience. She'd grown up cushioned, wrapped in layers of softness and comfort that Jasmine and Aidan had given her – softness and comfort that would be ripped away if the truth came out. *Manslaughter*. The word floated into her head, and she winced. Jasmine had run from the shame and embarrassment of her mum her whole life, and she couldn't bear for her daughter do the same. She couldn't bear to be that mother. She *wasn't* a bad mother.

She had to be strong now. If she wanted Juniper to have the life she deserved – the mother she deserved – she had to stay the course and keep quiet. She had to make sure Alison and Fiona did too. Like she'd told them, Lou wouldn't hurt the kids. Whatever had happened to Tabitha must have been an accident. Lou wanted to punish the parents, not the children, and if they waited it out, the police would find the kids before long. She thought of Juniper huddled in the cold, wet woods, and she shuddered before pushing away the image. She couldn't let fear rule her now; ruin her daughter's life. She might be taking a gamble that the truth would never come out, but that gamble was worth everything. Her *daughter* was worth everything.

She looked up at the sky, glowering down at her as the rain lashed against her face. Then she went inside, into the house that the woman who was trying to ruin everything had helped make the place of her dreams. God, she'd thought Lou had been her friend, when all along... She stared at the lounge, as if it was tainted now. She'd thought she'd escaped the past, but she'd never have guessed it had been waiting to ambush her where she'd sought shelter. Before she could stop herself, she grabbed a mirror Lou had chosen and smashed it to the floor. It shattered on the hard tile, pieces of glass skittering around her.

Jasmine stood in the centre of the room, letting out a cry of rage. She may have let Lou into her life, but she wasn't going to let her destroy it.

No matter what she'd done.

TWENTY-SIX
TABITHA
12:30 P.M.

Gabby's gasps are getting louder, and her face is whiter than ever. I hate watching this. I hate seeing how her chest is moving up and down like someone is pushing in on it and then letting go. It's awful, and even though she says she's fine and it's been much worse, I can't imagine she's feeling okay. She's *not* okay. And if I'm being honest, I'm not sure Juniper is either. Her face is so pale, and she's even been sick a few times. With that big wound on her head, she might have a concussion. I've tried to keep her from going to sleep like they say on all those medical shows, but I fell asleep myself, and when I woke up, she was still sleeping. I'm almost afraid to check to see if I can wake her up again.

I look over at my brother. He's asleep along with everyone else, including Lou. Apart from me, only Gabby is awake, alone in her struggle to drawn in enough air. It must be almost lunchtime, and I'm starving and thirsty, but there's nothing to eat or drink. Outside, the storm still sounds bad, the rain thumping on the roof. How can they come for us when it's like this? And how long will it last? We'll be fine without food and water for a bit, and Juniper will probably be okay for a while, but Gabby needs her medicine. No matter what Tim said – no matter what Gabby said – she's not getting better.

I bite my lip, my mind whirring. I made some terrible mistakes, like letting Lou in and giving her back the phone. I can't let my mistakes kill Gabby. I can't be the reason she died. It might sound dramatic, but if she gets worse, she *could* die. And despite what Tim says, I can't sit here and watch it happen. I need to do something.

I tilt my head. Gabby dropped her inhaler somewhere between here and the car. For all she knows, it could be right outside this cabin! If I can get out of here and have a quick look, I might be able to find it. I push aside the idea that it could be anywhere in the woods, and that I only have the vaguest notion where the car is right now and the pathway that we took. Maybe I won't find it, but at least I will have tried. Whatever the consequences, they can't be worse than Gabby dying.

But... My stomach twists as fear grips me. Can I really go out there alone? Can I do it without Lou catching me? What if it makes her angry and she does something to hurt the rest of the kids? What if I get lost? It's one thing to be in the middle of the storm in this hut with Tim and everyone else, and another to be wandering around in the woods on my own.

I turn to look at my brother, still fast asleep. He's always been there. I've always leaned on him, except for today, and look how that went. But even though I'm about to go against what he said yet again, I know I need to do this – for Gabby, for me. I don't even have to ask him; I know it myself. No second-guessing, no uncertainty. I feel it in my heart so strongly that despite my fear, I can't stop.

My pulse is racing, but I pull my coat more tightly around me and get to my feet. Gabby raises her eyebrows but no one else seems to notice I'm moving, and I put a finger to my lips to tell her to keep quiet. Lou's leg is outstretched, blocking the door, and as I try to ease over it, her eyes fly open. *Shit.*

'What is it?' she asks, her voice like gravel, as if she hasn't used it for years.

'Um...' My mind whirs as my heart races. Think. *Think*. 'I need to use the toilet,' I say, my voice shaking. I still can't believe I'm afraid of her. I barely even recognise her, even though she looks exactly the same. Something has changed.

'Okay.' She stands slowly, like she's aged a million years. 'I'll take you outside.'

Tim stirs and meets my eyes as she scrapes open the door, and I try to telegraph my plan before turning to follow her. She grips my arm with a deathly strength, and I wince. 'Sorry,' she says, noticing my expression, 'but I'm going to stay with you. Let's go over there, behind the tree.'

She's going to stay with me? What will she do when she finds out I don't really need to go? The wind tears at us as we step forward, and I scan the ground frantically, hoping I can spot Gabby's inhaler without having to get away. But it's impossible to see much as Lou hauls me across the sodden forest floor.

Then she stumbles over a root and crashes heavily to the ground, still holding onto my arm. I manage to stop myself falling just in time. I jerk to get away, but she's still holding me tightly.

'Shit,' I hear her murmur, then follow her gaze to where Juniper's phone has tumbled from her shirt and is lying underneath a prickly bush. My eyes widen. Can I get it? She swipes for it, but with one hand holding onto me, she can't reach it. I feel her fingers relax their grip, and I tear myself away and lunge for the phone, scooping it up before she gets to me. And then I'm running through the forest, desperate to escape. I don't care where I'm going. It doesn't matter now. Gabby will be fine – we will be safe. I have the phone. A rare feeling of triumph sweeps through me, and even though I'm freezing cold and soaked through, I can't help smiling.

Lou crashes after me, but I'm running faster. I plunge

deeper into the trees, veering wildly towards where I think the motorway is. If I can keep going – keep increasing the distance between us, keep changing direction, keeping moving and not stopping – she won't find me. This storm is my friend now, wiping away any trace of footprints and making listening out for noises impossible.

When I've covered enough distance and I'm sure Lou's not behind me, I get out the phone and turn it on, smiling again as it comes to life. This is it. I've done it. I *can* do something good. I'll text Mum quickly to let her know we're okay but that Gabby needs help, then I'll call 999. I put in Mum's number and start typing, gasping as a message flashes up on the screen that there's only 2 per cent battery left.

We need help fast, I type. *We*

The screen starts fading, and I frantically jab at the send button just as it goes black.

I keep walking, but this time I'm not smiling. I'm alone in the woods, and I don't even know if my message went through. I don't know where I am, and I've practically zero chance now of finding Gabby's inhaler. I draw my jumper closer and force myself to keep plodding forward.

It's better to sit down if you're lost, I remember telling Tim what feels like for ever ago. But I can't sit. I *won't* sit. I managed to get away. I'm our only chance for the others to get out of here.

I'm not going to let them down. I'm not going to let *me* down.

Not this time.

TWENTY-SEVEN

FIONA

12.30 P.M.

Fiona stayed glued to the sofa after Alison and Jasmine left, unable to muster the strength to move. She'd taken a step forward – a step towards change – by not letting Alison charge ahead without proof of a link between Lou and Mira. She'd taken another step when she'd told Jasmine what they needed to do to get their children back; when she'd stood up to her. But in the end, it had all come to nothing. Jasmine was the one with the power, and all Fiona could do was stand by and stay quiet.

Jasmine was right: if only Fiona confessed to her part in Mira's death, Lou was unlikely to release just Tabitha and Tim. They knew too much; they could help the police put an end to all of this before she was ready. And if she only heard from Fiona, would she think the other two were refusing to own up? Would that heighten her anger, possibly putting them all in danger, like Fiona had thought earlier? Fiona would be ruining her whole life – potentially sent to prison for manslaughter – while risking the children's safety.

And if she lied? If she sent a text to Lou saying they'd all confessed? That might placate Lou for a bit – until she discov-

THE MOTHER NEXT DOOR

ered that only Fiona had owned up. Because of course she wasn't going to let the children go until she'd checked that the truth – the whole truth, as she believed it – had come out, maybe by calling the police to see what they knew. What would be the point in all of this otherwise?

How could Alison have sat there and nodded along with Jasmine's plan? Ever since she'd seen the shoes, it was like she'd disappeared. Fiona could understand her guilt and pain. Alison had been the one to push Mira, after all. Was that why she'd kept quiet? Because she had the most to lose? She'd been happy to tell the truth before they'd talked to Jasmine, though. What had changed?

And how much did Lou even know? Did she know that Alison had pushed Mira? That Fiona had stood by and watched? About Jasmine's terrible taunts? Or did she just have the three names, unaware of their individual actions?

What exactly did she want from them?

Fiona let out a cry of frustration and got to her feet, frantically yanking out all the pots and pans from the kitchen cabinets. She grabbed a cloth and started wiping them down, working until her arms ached and sweat beaded on her brow, waiting for the moment when the anger and frustration would ease. But the longer she worked, the more her emotions expanded, until she threw the cloth in the sink and stood silent, vibrating with tension.

Outside, the rain continued, although it seemed like the wind might have died down slightly – or was that wishful thinking? Nick had come downstairs to tell her that the looming threats of flash floods and the river bursting its banks were looking more and more likely. She shook her head, thinking of Jasmine's instruction to 'let the police do their thing'. How could she even say that? Right now, the most the police could do was continue to patrol the town, keeping an eye out for anything unusual. Steph had rung to say that the searchers were still on standby, waiting for the storm to ease before they could enter the woods. All they could do now was hope for the weather to improve.

Her phone bleeped and she grabbed it, eyebrows rising when she saw Juniper's name come up on the screen. Was this another message from Lou? Fingers shaking, Fiona clicked it open.

We need help fast. We

The message stopped abruptly, and Fiona's hand flew to her mouth. The kids needed help. They needed help, and they needed it now. She jabbed at the phone, desperate to reach them, but the call refused to connect. Over and over she tried, her heart pounding and fear pouring through her. Was it Tabitha? Her head wound? Or was Gabby having an asthma attack? Was it something to do with the rising river; the floods? It could be any of them. It could be all of them. Even if the police *could* start searching the woods right now, they wouldn't be able to reach the children quickly enough. Only one person could help, if she wanted to: Lou.

Fiona put down the phone, a sudden determination sweeping over her. The past had reared up again, the stain she thought she'd covered reappearing, larger and darker than ever. But this time she wasn't going to try to bury it – she wasn't going to bury herself in her efforts to suppress it. She didn't know if that was possible now anyway. She thought of her relief when she'd realised the truth was out at last, and how she'd been ready to speak up and face the consequences – ready to act for her children. Because this was about more than her... or Alison or Jasmine, or their businesses, or how people saw them. This was about the dearest things to them. And no matter what

Jasmine threatened now, she couldn't sit back and try to scrub reality away. Not when her kids' lives depended on it. She had to do something.

But what?

She picked up the mobile, remembering Alison sitting there so vacantly as Jasmine's triumphant voice rang through the room. Alison *had* been eager to tell the truth before talking to Jasmine. Fiona knew she was terrified about her daughter; worried about Gabby being out in the woods on her own, possibly without her inhaler. Once she found out about this message, Fiona was sure she'd agree they had to act now. And if she could get Alison on her side, then Jasmine would have to come on board too.

And then... then she would tell her husband – tell the police – everything. And regardless of what happened afterwards, at least their children would be safe.

Fiona punched in Alison's number. As she paced back and forth, she prayed that she'd be able to convince her. That she would get through to her and break the spell that had fallen over Alison ever since she'd seen the shoes. That she could get her to see that no matter what had happened in the past, this was what was important now. Her daughter. Their children. Nothing else.

But the phone just rang and rang before clicking through to voicemail. Fiona hung up, staring at the handset in disbelief. Why the hell wasn't Alison answering? Her daughter was in danger, and she wasn't even picking up the phone.

She continued pacing, unable to sit. She couldn't rest while the kids were out there. If Alison wasn't answering, she'd have to call Jasmine. She bit her lip. Would this message be enough? Would it force her to act? What if it wasn't?

She tilted her head as an idea filtered in. Maybe she could tell Jasmine that Alison had agreed to tell the truth; to tell the police what had happened. They could band together, using Jasmine's plan against her. Okay, so it was risky saying that Alison was on her side when she hadn't yet reached her, but she was sure Alison would agree. And if Fiona couldn't get in touch with her, then hopefully Jasmine couldn't either.

She tapped in Jasmine's number, thinking that for the first time ever, she was the one in charge. It had taken her children being threatened, but finally, after all this time, she was going to be in control.

'Fiona.' Jasmine's smooth voice came on the line, and Fiona felt her determination strengthen.

'I got a message from Juniper's phone that they need help fast,' she said. 'It could be Gabby needing her meds, it could be Tabitha, it could be any one of our kids. We can't wait for the storm to stop and the police to search. We don't have that luxury now.'

She waited for Jasmine to say something, but there was only silence.

'Alison and I have decided to tell the police exactly what went on – what really happened that day,' Fiona said quickly. There was no time to waste. 'But you're right: we're in this together. Lou's not likely to release any of the kids until we all come clean, and with Alison and me telling the truth, there's no point you pretending any differently.' She swallowed. 'Whatever happens to us... well, this is for our kids. Come over as soon as you can. Alison's on her way. The family liaison officer will meet us here, and then we'll text Lou to say we've admitted our part in Mira's death. And then... then we will have our children back.'

'All right,' Jasmine said, and Fiona felt a rush of relief mixed with a kind of pride. She'd done it. She hadn't given in or stood silently by, biting her lip as she held back guilt or fear. Finally, she was doing something right. 'I'll be there in five minutes. Wait for me to arrive.'

Fiona nodded and hung up. It had been easier than she'd thought to bring Jasmine on board. If only she'd been more forceful sooner... She shook her head, breathing through the guilt. She couldn't bring back Mira, but she could help bring back the kids.

Now she just had to find Alison.

TWENTY-EIGHT

JASMINE

1 P.M.

Jasmine's hands shook as she put her phone down. What the hell was happening? She'd been so certain she had everything under control, but now it was all falling apart. Fiona must have told Alison about the message that the kids needed help, and that had been enough to make her crumble. A thread of fear curled into her, and she swallowed. Was Juniper okay? Did they really need help, or was it another tactic from Lou? *Would* she hurt the kids? Despite what she'd told Fiona, and herself, Jasmine had to admit she really wasn't sure. She'd thought she'd known Lou, but she hadn't at all.

But there *had* to be another way besides going to the police. There had to be! Because even if Alison and Fiona didn't know the whole story, there was every chance that Lou might. And if Lou didn't release the kids, would Alison and Fiona wonder if there was more that wasn't being said? Would Lou tell them there was a truth to do with Jasmine that still hadn't come out?

And if she didn't, would she do something worse? Something to Juniper this time – if she hadn't already?

God! She was dying for a drink. It might only be midday,

but she needed something to calm her nerves; to help her to think. There had to be a way out of this. There had to be something she could do... something to stop Fiona and Alison – fast. She hurried to the drinks cabinet at the side of the room, grabbed a glass and poured herself a liberal slug of vodka. She had a quick shot, and then another. She was pouring a third when Aidan walked through the front door. She plunked it down quickly.

'I've just got off the phone with Steph,' he said, taking off his jacket. 'She said the wind is finally starting to drop, and according to the radar, it looks like the worst of the storm is over. She's hopeful they'll be able to get the drones in the air again and send in searchers in the next hour.' His face was whiter than she'd ever seen it, and fatigue pulled at his eyes. He was wearing a ripped T-shirt she hadn't seen before, and for the first time she could remember, stubble poked through his perfect dimpled chin. As she stared at him, he seemed to symbolise the loss of control she was feeling; as if everything, including him, was coming apart at the seams.

'Are you drinking?' His eyes widened as he spotted the shot glass on the sideboard. 'And...' his gaze swept over her, 'did you have your *hair* done?' His voice rose in shock. 'Our daughter is missing. She's being held somewhere, out there in the worst storm for years. I've been driving the streets for hours looking for her. And you went to the salon?' She could see the disgust on his face, and it made her feel even more out of control than ever.

He shook his head. 'I came back to make sure you were okay. But I can see now that you're fine.' His lip curled. 'I can't even look at you,' he muttered, turning away from her. 'You're...' He drew himself together. 'I can't do this now. Let's get Juniper back, and then we need to talk.' And with that, he grabbed his jacket and went out the door.

Jasmine mouth dropped open in disbelief. What did he mean, he couldn't even look at her? Why did they need to talk? She spun around, trying to focus on something – on anything – to anchor herself. But the room swung around her, and she felt herself sway. It wasn't only the alcohol, she knew. It was her world. Everything was tilting madly. And somehow, she had to steady it. She had to make it right: for her, for her marriage, for Juniper. She was only drinking because of this whole mad Lou thing. And Aidan was only being like this because of that too. Once she fixed that, everything would be okay again. She'd show him she could drink less... because she didn't need alcohol, not really. They would go back to being the perfect family with the perfect house and the perfect daughter.

But how? How could she fix this? What could she do? Alison and Fiona were waiting for her, itching to tell the police what had happened; itching for her to join them in what they thought was the truth. They were willing to trade their lives for their children, but they didn't understand that their kids would never be able to escape the shame of what they'd done. By trying to save them, they'd be ruining everything.

She had to stop them. Somehow, she had to convince them to keep quiet and stay strong – to hang in there now that the police were about to start searching. She didn't know what she'd say, but she'd always been able to sway them in the past. She would do the same now.

She grabbed the keys and rushed to the car, pressing the pedal to the floor. The road wavered in front of her, but she gripped the steering wheel and took deep breaths. It would be fine, she told herself as she raced across town towards Fiona's. She passed the secondary school and the river. The rain had petered to a drizzle, and a low haze hung over the marshland, the mist drifting like ghostly fingers. She watched it move, squinting against the shifting white. It formed and re-formed, the droplets of water coming together to make the silhouette of a girl on a bike, standing on the riverbank, gazing in the direction of the water. Jasmine stared, sure she must be imagining things, but when she blinked to clear her vision, the girl was still there.

That was the last thing she saw before the sharp shriek of metal on metal filled her ears, and everything went black.

TWENTY-NINE
ALISON
1 P.M.

Alison curled up on the sofa. Across the room, her phone was ringing, but she hadn't the energy to answer. She hadn't even the energy to remove her wet clothes, sodden and cold from the walk to her car from Fiona's. She was tired, so tired. What had been the point of all that training; of trying to make herself stronger? In the end, all those changes she'd thought she'd made had been swept away. She shifted on the sofa, pain gripping her. She shouldn't have had a child. She shouldn't have had a *family*. She'd known about the note. She'd known all of this might come back one day, and now it had. Now it had, and she hadn't been able to stop it touching their lives. Her own daughter was out there in a ferocious storm because of her.

Gabby's face floated into her mind, the image so vivid that for a second it was almost like she was right here. Alison reached out a hand to touch her, feeling something other than guilt and shame for the first time since she'd seen Mira's shoes. Love vibrated inside of her, so strongly that she sat up, peering above the surface of the darkness that had closed over her.

'Hey, honey.' Greg came down the stairs and folded her into his arms. 'Are you all right? Is this about the flood?'

She jerked towards him, every muscle now taut. 'The flood?'

'It was just on the news,' he said. 'The storm is moving on, but the river is so high that it's burst its banks and flooded the motorway. They're saying there could be other localised flooding too.'

Alison stared into his eyes, his words echoing in her head. The river was gathering power, erupting from where it had been neatly contained and sweeping away anything in its path. It was a mirror of what had happened inside of her, the emotions bursting from where they'd been dammed up for years, destroying all her defences and returning her to the past.

But it hadn't been able to wash away everything, she realised now, Gabby's face filling her mind's eye once more. The dark waters couldn't touch the love she had for her daughter. That had nothing to do with strength, and nothing to do with resilience. She hadn't needed to build it up or anchor it in place. It was knitted into every single part of her; into her soul. And somewhere deep inside, she felt that love buoy her up again, propel her forward. The river might have destroyed her, but she wouldn't – she couldn't – let it destroy her child.

She stared into Greg's eyes, energy flooding through her once more. She would keep her vow to her daughter. She would keep her safe.

She'd go to the police and confess what she'd done, then tell Jasmine that she'd finally told the truth. With Alison taking the blame, Jasmine's part in the whole thing would be minimised, and she shouldn't baulk too much at admitting what had happened. After all, she hadn't even touched Mira. With all three of them on board, Lou would release the kids. Gabby would be safe. And then... well, maybe Alison would be charged. Maybe her marriage would fall apart; her business close. But the one thing she knew would remain unchanged was her love for her daughter.

'I have to tell you something,' she said slowly, looking at Greg. 'I did something... something awful when I was younger.' The guilt grasped her in its fist, squeezing hard, and she let it. She had no defences left, but it didn't matter. Nothing mattered but Gabby. 'Something I never told anyone about; something no one knows except Fiona and Alison.' She paused. 'And Lou. We think that's why Lou took the kids.'

Greg's eyebrows flew up, but he didn't say anything.

'Lou wants us to admit what happened. And...' she swallowed, 'it's going to change our lives.' Pain ripped through her. It would do more than change them. It would tear them apart. But at least she could save Gabby.

He held her close. 'Look, whatever you did can't be that bad, I'm sure. I know you, inside out. I'll be here for you no matter what. I love you.'

Alison let herself relax against him – to feel his warmth and comfort one last time – before pulling away. He didn't know her inside out, not like he thought. He didn't know the secret that had been at the core of her; that had the power to ruin everything. He wanted to be there for her, but he had no idea who she really was, and what she'd done.

'I need to go now,' she said, her stomach twisting at the thought that the next time she saw him, he would be unable to look at her the same way. 'I need to talk to the police.' She turned to grab her keys, but he took her arm.

'Wait,' he said, his eyes concerned. 'Can you slow down? Tell me a bit more. What did you do? What was it?'

'I killed someone.' The words fell like a hammer, and Greg's eyes widened. She hadn't meant to tell him so bluntly, but she couldn't keep the words in any longer. 'I killed a girl, back when I was in high school. She... she drowned, in a river.' She drew in a breath. 'Mira, her name was. Mira Penrose.'

His mouth dropped open, but no words came out. She stood for a second watching the emotions cross his face. Then, before he could say anything, she fled from the house. Tears blinded her, and she could barely see as she got into the car. She dashed them from her eyes, pulling out her phone and leaving a message for Steph that she was on her way in to the station.

The last thing she saw as she drove away was Greg standing on the porch still staring at her, as if saying goodbye for the very last time.

THIRTY

FIONA

1 P.M.

Fiona circled the room as she waited for Jasmine, frantically dialling Alison over and over. Where on earth was she? She had hoped both women would get here before Steph, the family liaison officer, arrived. It felt important that the three of them were in the same room when they finally released the truth. Besides, Fiona wanted to make sure that Jasmine *did* tell the truth about what had happened that day, and that she didn't try to weasel out of the part she'd played. If Lou knew everything, Jasmine's attempts would only stall things.

She glanced up at the ceiling, Nick's footsteps thudding above her as he paced back and forth. She'd been so desperate to reach Alison that she hadn't yet told him about the latest text, but she had to now. She had to tell him everything. She put the phone down and took a breath.

'Nick?' she called, her voice echoing through the empty house.

He came down the stairs. He looked awful, with bloodshot eyes and messy hair, holding himself tightly as if afraid to emerge from his sanctuary. Fiona stared at him, thinking how awkward he appeared in their house after what had happened between them. He'd thought this place could be the home of their dreams. Instead, everything had fallen apart.

And now their lives were about to be completely destroyed.

'What's happening? I heard you on the phone asking for Steph to come.' His eyes were wild.

Fiona turned to face him, this man she'd thought she knew so well... this man who'd thought he knew her, but who had no idea about the horrific thing that was embedded so deeply within her, tainting her past and her present no matter how much she tried to ignore it.

It was time to confess.

'Nick, sit down.'

His face went even paler, and he collapsed onto the sofa. She settled into a chair across from him. 'I got a message from Juniper's phone saying they needed help. I don't know what that means exactly, but we don't have time to waste.'

Nick's eyes widened. 'They need help? We have to do something. We need to find them now!'

Fiona looked out the window, surprised to see that it had stopped raining and the trees were still. 'Even if the searchers can go into the woods now, it's going to take a while to reach the kids. But there is something we can do. Something *I* can do.' She paused, feeling Nick's gaze burning into her.

'I need to tell you something,' she began for the second time that day. 'Something that happened when I was younger.' Fear went through her as she stared at him. He would be the first person she'd ever told. What would he say? Would he turn away like he had before? Would he believe she could do something like that; be the kind of person who could play a part in a child's death? Would he realise she was no longer that person?

Because she wasn't. She *had* changed. It had taken her children going missing – and a ghost from the past – to force her, but she had. And no matter the consequences, she wasn't going back to being the sort of person who kept her gaze lowered, finding safety in minutiae while much bigger things – even damaging things, like almost cheating on her husband – happened around her; happened *to* her. Now she could see the bigger picture, and even though it was infinitely scarier, she had to act for her family.

'Oh.' Nick relaxed against the sofa. 'I thought this had something to do with the kids.'

'It does.' She bit her lip, wondering where to start. 'Nick, when I was in high school, a girl called Mira died in the river. She drowned.'

'Okay...' His brow furrowed, and she could see him wondering about the connection.

'The police thought that no one was there at the time, but they were wrong. I was there. Me, Alison and Jasmine.'

Nick tilted his head. 'You, Alison and Jasmine? The same... the same mothers whose children Lou took?'

Fiona nodded. 'Yes.' She glanced down. 'And we think – well, we know – that Lou did this because of what happened with Mira. To get us to say what really happened. You see...' She shook her head, the old guilt and pain flaring. God, this was hard. The words had been locked away so tightly. 'Mira couldn't swim. We didn't know that at the time. And we were teasing her. She had this terrible birthmark, and Jasmine was making fun of it, saying it stopped her swimming. I encouraged her to get in the water, then Alison pushed her under. She... she never came up.' Her voice was a whisper.

Silence swirled in the room, and finally she dared to meet Nick's eyes. 'And you never told anyone?' His voice was incredulous, his eyes full of horror.

'No. When the ambulance came, we told them we'd seen her go under and we tried to save her.' She paused, thinking back to those horrible moments. 'She died in hospital after being in a coma. She never regained consciousness.' She shifted on the chair. 'That's what we thought anyway. But she must have come to at some point and told someone what really happened. We think that someone was Lou.'

Nick was staring at her, trying to put the pieces together. 'Lou?'

She nodded. 'Alison and I managed to get into her house earlier, and—'

'You broke into her house?' She could see him attempting to equate the action with the woman she used to be, and she nodded.

'We think Lou is her sister. We found some shoes in her loft, the same ones Mira was wearing the day at the river. She told me back then they belonged to her sister. When we saw them, everything started to make sense. Why all three of us got that text. The truth she wants us to tell.'

Nick was shaking his head. 'Sense? None of this makes sense. How could Lou be so close to us all this time and none of us knew who she really was? Did she move here just to do this... this crazy plan? Spending years getting to know us, only to take our children to force you to tell the truth?' His voice rose in disbelief. 'If she knows the truth, why doesn't she just tell the police herself?'

'I don't know.' Fiona shrugged. 'Maybe she doesn't know everything, or she's afraid the police won't believe her. I'm not sure.'

'I mean, to do something like this...' He rubbed a hand through his hair. 'She's ruined her own life now. She'll go to prison.' He turned to face her. 'She told me she didn't have a sister,' he said.

Fiona's gut clenched. 'I guess that's because Mira is dead.'

'Mira is dead.' He repeated the words, holding her gaze as

he tried to take it in. 'And Steph is coming so you can tell her about your involvement in all of this. And then what? How will Lou know you've come clean? And what will that mean for you?' He paused. 'This seems so crazy. I can't get my head around it.'

'Jasmine's on her way, and I'm trying to reach Alison. We'll talk to Steph and then text Lou on Juniper's phone.' She breathed out. 'I'll ask Steph to call Lou and verify what we said. And then...' Happiness rushed through her at the thought of gathering Tabitha and Tim in her arms; of tucking them into bed, warm and cosy, and watching them sleep. No matter what happened afterwards, it would be worth it. She bit her lip, thinking of Tabitha's headband and the last text she'd received, that they needed help. Please God, let them be okay. 'I'm not sure what will happen after that. I guess the police will want to talk to us more. We might... we might be charged.' She swallowed. 'I don't really know, but none of that matters if it means Lou lets the kids go.'

Nick nodded, his face serious. 'But how do you know she will let them go?' he asked. 'I mean, if she's crazy enough to do this, then maybe she's crazy enough to...' His face twisted.

Fear shot through her, and instantly her body tensed again. Nick had voiced her worst fears. Lou *had* to release them. She had to. 'I don't know,' she said slowly. 'But we have to try.'

There was a knock on the door, and Nick got to his feet. 'Do you want me to stay? Or do you want to talk to Steph yourselves?'

Fiona stood too, staring at her husband. She'd let him shield her for so long from the reality of what she had done. She'd hidden inside his love and the life they'd created. She *did* love him, but now she could see that by using their marriage as a place to cower, she'd been too afraid to let it grow and change; too fearful to address any problems or issues lest she lose that shield. If she ever wanted a chance of repairing her marriage, she couldn't use it that way any longer.

And she was ready now: ready to move out from his cover. Ready to step up and face things heads on, even if it was more than difficult.

Ready to tell Lou how sorry she was, like she should have done years ago.

'I think this is something we need to do alone, just the three of us,' she said.

'Okay.' He nodded. 'Let me know if you need me.' For a second, it felt like a bit of the ice had melted. Then he turned and went up the stairs.

'So I'm guessing you heard about the flooding, and you'd like an update,' Steph said as she bustled inside, taking off her hat and coat and slinging them on a chair before Fiona could even offer to hang them up. 'The good news is that the children are far from the flooding on the motorway,' she went on. 'The river is very high and still rising, so the situation is fluid, but it shouldn't affect their area. Our search team is heading into the woods as we speak, and we hope to reach the part we believe the children are located in an hour or two. Now that the wind has died down, we'll be able to get our drones and a helicopter into the air as well. The brush is quite thick in places, which can be tricky, but we will be doing everything we can to find them. If we struggle to spot them, we'll put out a child rescue alert on social media and with local media.'

Her words flowed over Fiona, and she nodded. All of this was great, but it would take time. And right now, they didn't have time. She glanced at the door. God, where the hell was Jasmine? What was taking so long? Steph had got here quickly; the roads seemed fine. And why wasn't Alison answering her bloody phone?

'That's brilliant,' she said, swallowing. 'But I didn't ask you here for an update. We have something to tell you. Give it a minute, and Jasmine will be here. Alison should be on her way shortly too.'

Steph cocked her head, her eyes suddenly narrowing. 'Something to tell me? What do you mean?'

'Soon,' Fiona said, glancing at the door again. 'We'll tell you everything soon.'

THIRTY-ONE

TABITHA

1.30 P.M.

I'm not sure I can walk another step. My legs ache, and I'm so cold that every muscle is a block of ice. It's like a nightmare where you need to run, but despite all your efforts, you only move an inch.

But I can't stop trying. I need to keep going for Gabby. I need to find the motorway and get a car to stop, as soon as I can. An image of Gabby's pale face and blue lips comes into my mind, and fear goes through me. Has she got worse? How long can she last? Has Lou gone back to the cabin now – are they all still there, or has she dragged them off somewhere else now that I've escaped? The questions fly through my mind as I force my legs to move, one after the other, stepping over rocks and fallen branches.

I gaze up at the sky. Thankfully it's stopped raining, even though I still feel as wet as ever. The wind has stopped too, and the sky is starting to clear. The grey isn't as heavy as it was before, as if someone is gradually lifting the lid to let the light in. I need to do the same now. I need to let the light in for Gabby... and for Juniper and Tim. Strength and determination go through me, and I clutch onto them as I move my legs faster.

Everyone's depending on me now. I can save Gabby. I can save everyone.

The only problem is that I have no idea where I'm going. Am I headed further into the woods or towards the motorway? Maybe somewhere back towards town? I've been walking for a while now, so I should be close to the road if I was going in that direction. I pause for a minute, holding my breath. A soft whoosh filters into my ears, the sound of... Happiness rushes through me. Of a road! That sounds like cars! I listen again, but there's only silence this time, so I charge towards where I thought I heard the sound, praying I'm right. Another whoosh comes, sounding louder, and my heart picks up pace. I must be heading in the right direction. I have to be.

I step over another branch, moving faster and faster as the sounds get louder. It's as if the closer I am, the more energy I have. Finally, I see a break in the treeline, light filtering through as the branches thin, and I step out of the forest.

I'm standing at the edge of the road.

I start to smile. I've done it. I've found my way out. But... I swallow, looking left and right. This doesn't look like the motorway. It's a smaller road that I don't recognise. There aren't any signs, either, so I have no idea which direction I should even start walking in.

I'm debating what to do when I hear a sound, the far-off whoosh of a car approaching. Then I see it cresting the hill and coming towards me, and I step out onto the road as far as I dare, my heart in my throat as I wave my hands in the air. *Please stop, please stop*, I repeat over and over as I stretch my hands up towards the grey sky, trying to make myself as big as possible while not getting run over.

Relief floods through me when the car puts its indicator on and pulls over to the side of the road. Yes! It's stopping!

I run towards it, my breath tearing at my lungs. God, I'm tired. But this will be over soon, I tell myself. Soon I'll see Mum and Dad. They'll be so proud. Neither of them thought I could do this. Then again, I didn't think I could either.

'Are you okay?' A woman with kind eyes peers at me through the window, and I feel tears come to my own eyes. 'Are you here on your own? What are you doing out in the storm?'

'I need help,' I say. The words barely emerge, and I realise how dry my throat is and how much it hurts. I try to clear it. 'I need help.' My voice is louder this time. 'Please, call 999. Tell them who I am. Tabitha Bryson. They've been looking for me.' A tear runs down my cheek, and I swipe it away. I have to stay strong. I have to tell everything. 'They've been looking for me and my friends, and one of them is in danger.'

The woman nods. Without asking any more questions, she takes out her phone and punches in the number, then pulls back out onto the road. I sink down in the passenger seat and listen as she speaks, the car speeding down the motorway. My eyes widen as I take in the flooded meadows on either side of us, and the huge stretch of water looming ahead, as if the motorway has turned into a lake. Too late, the woman slams on the brakes and the car begins to skid, then spins like a fairground ride.

The last thing I see before I screw my eyes shut is a torrent of water rushing towards us.

THIRTY-TWO

JASMINE

1.30 P.M.

Jasmine slowly opened her eyes, a metallic taste in her mouth. She spat, feeling like she was chewing on something. Horror flooded through her when she realised it was glass, and that the metallic taste was blood. Groaning, she managed to undo her seat belt and slowly open the car door. She gasped as pain pummelled her. What the hell had happened?

She groaned again as the memory seeped in. She'd been on her way to convince Alison and Fiona not to talk to the police when she'd thought she'd seen... she'd thought she'd seen... She blinked, swiping blood from her face as she squinted at a figure on the riverbank.

It wasn't the girl on the bicycle. She was gone. And in her place was... No, it couldn't be.

Was it *Lou*?

Jasmine staggered to her feet. Maybe she didn't need to talk to Alison and Fiona, after all. Maybe all she needed was to get to Lou and find out how much she knew about her part in everything. If she could do that, maybe she could minimise whatever Alison and Fiona were telling Steph right now. They didn't know the real truth anyway. The pain was almost unbearable, but she forced herself forward. She had to talk to Lou. She had to. She *could* fix this.

She blinked again, and the figure disappeared. For a second Jasmine wondered if her mind was playing tricks on her. It couldn't really be Lou, could it? What would she be doing here? And where were the kids? Panic gripped her as she glanced down at the rushing river, higher and faster because of the storm. The usual gently lazy waters were turbulent, and broken branches and debris rushed by. The kids... No. Lou might have taken them, but she'd never do *that*. For one second, she thought she saw Mira streaming by in those waters, but then she told herself that of course it couldn't be. She was in shock from the accident.

But there *was* someone there, just along the riverbank, and it did look like Lou. She wasn't imagining it. Slowly, Jasmine dragged herself across the grassy field and over to the bank. She lifted a hand in the air, wincing again at the pain that shot through her.

'Lou.' The word came out in a raspy whisper. That small movement of her mouth caused the tiny bits of glass lodged in her lips and tongue to cut deeper. She could taste blood again.

Lou carried on along the bank, not even looking towards Jasmine. Where was she going?

'Lou!' Her voice came out louder this time, and Lou turned to face her. Jasmine hobbled towards her as fast as she could, holding her side, her heart beating fast. Finally. Finally, she was going to talk to her. It had only been a day since Lou had disappeared with the children, but it felt like for ever.

Lou stood still at the side of the river, her eyes widening as she looked at Jasmine. 'What the hell happened?'

Jasmine put a hand to her face. She must look a sight with all the blood, but surely it couldn't be that bad. Lou was staring at her as if she was a monster. She tilted her head. Well, given what Lou might know, it made sense, she guessed. But she wasn't a monster. She wasn't. Yes, in that moment she'd wanted Mira to suffer. But she hadn't wanted her to *die*.

'So, who are you really?' She tried to make her voice as assertive and confident as always. But it seemed to trickle from her, like she was turning off the tap of who she used to be and returning once more to that girl from the bedsit who went to food banks. '*Are* you Mira's sister?'

Lou let out a snort. 'What, you don't recognise me? Then again, you never really knew me, did you.' Her eyes burned through Jasmine. 'But I know you. I know everything.'

Jasmine's gut clenched, and she felt her legs weaken. So the girl on the bike had been real that day, after all. She'd been real, and she was Mira's sister.

'What do you want?' she asked, her voice shaking. 'What do you want from me? Tell me and I'll give it to you.' She spat out a piece of glass. 'Just... just give me Juniper back again. Give me Juniper, and I'll give you anything.'

'What I want, you can't give me. But this...' Lou's face twisted as she ran her eyes over Jasmine again, 'this is something anyway. This, and people knowing what you did – what really happened. You tried to hide it for so long. You all did. I think you actually forgot.' She shook her head hard, her hair flying out around her.

'I want you to tell the truth,' she went on. 'I want to hear you say what happened; that you *do* remember what happened. The whole truth: that Mira reached out to you even after she went under. That...' she let out a breath, 'you saw her struggle when no one else did, and you didn't help. You held her under. You let her drown. The fear you must have felt when you realised Juniper was missing... your perfect face... that's nothing compared to what you did to Mira. *Nothing.*'

Jasmine touched her face once more, panic shooting through her when she felt the glass and blood. It could be fixed, she told herself. It could. All of this could. But even as she tried to convince herself, the fear and doubt were growing.

She crossed the space between them as quickly as she could and grabbed Lou's arm. 'Please,' she said, her voice shaky and thready. Her heart was beating so fast, and she was in so much pain that she didn't know how much longer she could stay on her feet. 'Don't hurt Juniper. I did it, okay? I didn't help Mira. I held her under. And I'm sorry. I didn't mean for her to die. Just give me back my daughter. *Please.*'

But Lou shook her off and stepped away, and Jasmine's mind flashed back to that day in the river when Mira had reached out for help, and she'd pushed her under.

And as she stared into Lou's eyes, she knew she was going under too.

THIRTY-THREE

ALISON

1.30 P.M.

Alison swung the car onto a shortcut to the motorway and the police station. Soon the police would know the truth about how Mira had died. Alison's life as she knew it would be over, just as surely as Mira's was. She sighed, glancing towards the long meadow that sloped down to the river. If only she could turn back time. If only she'd never listened to Jasmine; never wanted to be her friend. Everything could have been so different. Everything...

She blinked as the wreckage of a vehicle came into sight on the side of the road. It had smashed into a guard rail, the bonnet crunched like an accordion and the windscreen shattered. 'Wait!' she said, the word squeaking out of her. That was Jasmine's car!

She screeched to a halt and dashed out of her own car and over to the wreckage. The driver's door was open, and Jasmine's bag and jacket were still inside, but there was no sign of Jasmine herself. Alison shivered, thinking this was like finding Lou's Range Rover, with all the kids' things yet no children to be seen.

Where could she have gone? She glanced at the car door

handle, where there was a smear of blood. By the looks of things, she was injured too.

She gazed across the field towards the river. This very spot was where the nightmare had begun. This was where Mira had drowned. Was it a coincidence that Jasmine had crashed here?

A flash of movement caught her eye, and she noticed two figures standing by the bank. She squinted, making out a sheath of blonde hair. Jasmine. And was that... Adrenaline shot through her. Was that *Lou*? But what was she doing here? Were the kids here too?

Gabby. Heart pounding, Alison ran towards the river, praying to spot her, but all she could see was Jasmine and Lou. She was about to call out and ask where the kids were when she heard something that made her stop.

'Mira reached out to you even after she went under,' Lou was saying, shaking her head. 'You saw her struggle when no one else did, and you didn't help. You held her under. You let her drown.'

Alison's mouth dropped open and she took a step back. What? Mira had come up again after Alison had pushed her? She'd reached out to Jasmine, but Jasmine hadn't helped?

Jasmine had held her under?

Mira had died because of *Jasmine*?

Rage and pain circled inside her as she watched Jasmine clutch at Lou's arm, then Lou shake her off. How could Jasmine have let her believe all this time that she was the one responsible? How could you do that to someone... someone who was supposed to be your friend? Jasmine knew how much Alison had suffered. She knew how distraught and upset she had been. For God's sake, she hadn't been able to go to school for weeks afterwards. Her parents had forced her to see a counsellor, and even then she hadn't been able to tell the truth – or at least the truth as she'd believed it. She'd thought she'd killed someone. She'd lived with the burden for years, and it had shaped everything she'd done. Even the new person she thought she'd become had been because of that, a futile attempt to escape the past. It hadn't been real. Nothing she'd believed had.

'It was you,' she said now, and both Jasmine and Lou swung around. Alison drew back in shock at Jasmine's face. It was covered in blood, gaping wounds still oozing. In the midst of the crimson, Jasmine's blue eyes looked even bluer, as if she was a creature from somewhere else... someone not of this world. In a way, she wasn't. Anyone with a heart couldn't have done what she did.

'It was you who killed Mira,' Alison continued. 'It wasn't just me. You held her under. You let her die.' Anger surged through her, fuelling the strength of her muscles once more, and she took a step forward, revulsion mingling with the fury inside. How could she ever have felt she was nothing next to someone like Jasmine? The rage erupted, and for one instant, every bit of her longed to push Jasmine down the riverbank... down into the rushing waters below, the waters that had changed everything.

But that would make her just as bad, wouldn't it? For the first time, as Alison stared at the woman in front of her, shaking and covered in blood, Jasmine seemed so small – so weak. And Alison realised that she wasn't the strong, confident woman everyone thought. She *was* weak: desperately clinging onto her position of power then, and all her material goods now. In a flash of clarity, Alison could see why Jasmine had chosen her and Fiona to be friends. It was because they were easy to subdue; to boss around. With them, her status would never be challenged.

It would be so easy to use the strength in her body to shove Jasmine down the bank, but she knew now that real strength wasn't physical. You could be the strongest person in the world, the most beautiful person in the world, and still be weak. Real strength – strength that could never be washed away – was found inside, in the love for the people you held dear. Alison had that in spades.

She turned away from Jasmine and towards Lou, fear flashing through her when she saw the fury there. Where were the kids? What had she done to them? But before she could say a word, Lou stepped closer. 'Jasmine didn't help when Mira reached out, that's true. But you pushed her. You were the one who made her go under in the first place, weren't you?'

Alison nodded. 'Yes. I was. And I've regretted it every day since, I really have. I'm so, so sorry, Lou. More than you'll ever know.' She breathed in, knowing she could never compensate Lou for the part she'd played in hurting her sister, but hoping that her words could mean something – enough, even, to set Gabby free. 'But please, let the kids go. They didn't do anything wrong. They don't deserve this.'

'Mira didn't deserve to have her life taken away either,' Lou said in the same strange, cold voice, and panic gripped Alison. Life taken away *either*? She glanced down at the rushing waters, her heart beating fast. Lou wouldn't do that to the children, would she?

Lou looked at her with an expression of disgust and rage. 'If Mira had lived, you wouldn't have half of what you have now. Not your husband, not your house. You don't deserve Greg, and you don't deserve that house.'

Alison shook her head. The way Lou was talking, it was as if she knew Greg; knew the house. But she'd never met him, and had never been to their home. What was she talking about?

'The house you're living in now,' Lou said, her face twisting, 'that's where Mira grew up. She was supposed to have it when she got older, but then...' She glanced towards the river.

Alison stared at her, trying to figure out what she meant. *That's where Mira grew up... supposed to have it.* She tilted her head, straining to remember the conversation with Greg when she'd told him about forging his signature on the remortgage papers. He hadn't minded so much, not because he loved the house, but because... She swallowed. Because the house was supposed to have been his stepsister's.

Could Mira have been his stepsister? But... no. It wasn't possible. Lou must be mistaken.

'It couldn't have been Mira's.' She shouted to be heard over the roar of a helicopter. 'Greg's stepsister was supposed to have the house. And she's alive. She's not dead.'

'Mira didn't die,' Lou said in a hard tone, and Alison took a step back. *What?* 'At least not that day in the river. Not in the care home either. It took years until she finally faded away. But every day she lived was torture.'

Alison blinked. Mira hadn't passed away in the care home? But what about the bare room she'd seen; the receptionist telling her she was too late? She shook her head again, struggling to take it in. She'd been so certain Mira had died that day. Was it possible she'd been wrong?

Was it possible that Mira was related to Greg?

She remembered Greg saying that his stepsister had had some issues, and that they'd lost touch. Maybe they'd lost touch because she'd died; maybe that was why they hadn't been able to find her to claim her inheritance. Maybe... She swayed as she realised that she might have built her whole world in the house of the woman whose life she'd played a part in stealing.

But how did Lou know all of this? Who was she? She couldn't be Mira's sister, as they'd believed. Greg had only had one stepsister.

And what *had* happened to Mira in the end? How had she really died?

She stared hard into Lou's eyes, her mind spinning. There was something... something floating out of reach; a hint of an idea that she couldn't grasp.

Slowly, as if she was watching from far away, the thought came into focus, and she froze.

Fiona sat on the sofa, anxiously jerking her gaze between the door and her mobile. Where on earth was Jasmine, and why wasn't Alison picking up? Beside her, Steph was making noises about how much she had to do; that she couldn't wait any longer. Fiona bit her lip. Should she just tell her?

A phone bleeped, and Fiona sighed with relief, only for her heart to drop when she realised it was Steph's.

'Sorry, one minute.' Steph dug it out of her pocket and scanned the screen. 'More flooding. Not to worry, though – it's a local road on the other side of the forest from where the kids are, and it shouldn't affect our efforts. There's also a message that Alison is on her way to the station?' She looked hard at Fiona. 'Aren't we waiting for her here?'

Fiona raised her eyebrows. Alison was on her way to the station? What for? 'Oh, she must have got confused and thought I meant to meet there.'

'Well, why don't we go in together?' Steph said, getting up. 'I can give you a lift or you can take your car – whatever's easiest. Dispatch say that as long as you follow any detours they've set up, the roads through town should be safe now that the wind has dropped.'

'I'll take my car.' Fiona lurched to her feet, thinking she could make a call from there to tell Jasmine of the change in plans. Where *was* she anyway? She thought of Nick in the bedroom, the radio still blaring, and started up the stairs to tell him where she was going. 'I'll meet you there,' she said, turning to see Steph lift a hand and go out the door.

A few minutes later, Fiona got into her car and started down the street. The road was busier now as people emerged, and as she eased around a fire crew removing a fallen tree from the road, her low-fuel warning light came on. Her heart sank. Now of all times! She turned onto a side road towards the nearest filling station, praying it was open. The road passed by her old secondary school, and in the distance, she could see the river snaking through the meadow. She was trying so hard not to look at it that she almost missed the bright red Mini at the side of road, its hood crumpled up against the guard rail.

Her eyes widened as a thought hit. Jasmine had a bright red car exactly like this. Fiona remembered how annoyed other parents got when she parked up on the double yellows in front of the school, yakking on her phone and blocking the road for everyone behind her. Was this her car? Could this be why she'd never made it to Fiona's?

Fiona pulled over, her heart pounding. She got out of her car, relief pouring through her when she noticed the driver's seat was empty. At least whoever had been involved in this crash wasn't too badly injured. She peered in at the passenger seat. That was Jasmine's bag. Fiona wasn't really into designers, but even she knew an expensive handbag when she saw one. This was definitely Jasmine's Mini.

She moved back. So where was Jasmine? She swept her gaze around the meadows, eyes widening when she spotted three figures by the river. Her heart lurched as they came into focus.

It was Jasmine and Alison... and *Lou*.

Lou! Did that mean the kids were there too? She raced towards the river, muscles aching as she urged them across the sodden ground.

Over the noise of the rushing water and gusting wind, she could make out the faint sound of voices. As she got closer, she heard something that stopped her in her tracks: Lou, saying that Mira had reached out to Jasmine after she'd been pushed in, but that Jasmine hadn't helped her.

She'd done the very opposite. She'd held her under.

Fiona's mouth fell open. A few feet away, Alison recoiled as if someone had struck her. Mira had come up after Alison pushed her, and Jasmine hadn't helped? She'd held her under the water instead? How could she do that? Alison moved towards Jasmine, looking like she was going to shove her into the river, and Fiona held her breath. But just as she was about to cry out for her to stop, Alison turned back towards Lou, as if Jasmine wasn't worth her time any longer.

Fiona moved closer, trying to make out more of their words. Lou was saying something about how Alison had taken Mira's home – taken away the very place she'd grown up in. Fiona tilted her head as a memory flooded in; a memory of when they'd been walking to the river that fateful day so long ago now. Mira had asked her if she wanted to go back to her house after swimming. Fiona couldn't remember where she'd lived, but she did remember Mira saying that her stepbrother was home from uni. Could that stepbrother have become Alison's husband? Could Alison now be living in Mira's childhood home? What a cruel twist of fate that would be. But how could Alison not know?

A helicopter swooped over them and towards the forest, the

noise blocking out whatever Alison and Lou were saying. Fiona looked up as it buzzed overhead, praying it would spot the kids.

The helicopter disappeared into the distance, and the two women were now quiet. The silence seemed to stretch on for ever, twisting and turning around them like the bends of the river. 'But it can't be,' Alison said finally. 'It can't.'

Fiona tilted her head. What was she talking about?

'It can't,' Alison was repeating, over and over, as if trying to convince herself. 'Mira is dead, right? You said so. You *did*. She's dead.' The words fell like heavy weights in the air.

Lou stepped forward now, her presence larger than ever, as if she'd solidified herself. 'You're right,' she said. 'Mira *is* dead. She died because she had to. She couldn't bear to live, thinking about what had happened to her... thinking that people had hated her so much – thought she was so ugly – that she was better off dead. She spent most of those first few weeks in a coma, but sometimes she would wake. Sometimes, she would speak those three names. Three names she wrote down, over and over, so she would never forget.'

Fiona stood still, cemented to the ground. She couldn't move. She had to hear this.

'When she left the care home, she was nothing. It was all she could do to breathe every day and try to make it from one minute to the next. And then, after years of this half-life, she decided to do the only thing she could: to die. But not to kill herself, because that would be letting those girls win. She would become someone else. Someone with a new name and no ties to the past. Someone confident; someone beautiful. Someone with no birthmarks and nothing to weigh her down.'

Lou paused, and the rushing water seemed even louder. Then she threw back her hair, and for the first time, Fiona could see a very faint stretch of rough skin on her neck where count- less laser sessions must have removed the birthmark. Lou had been so proud of her hair, always wearing it down to frame her beautiful face, that Fiona had never even noticed.

She lifted her chin. 'Mira became me.'

Fiona gasped, and Lou turned to meet her eyes. All of a sudden, she knew beyond a shadow of a doubt. Lou *was* Mira. That was how she knew everything. That was how she had the shoes.

And that was why she was willing to implode her whole life to do this to them. Because it hadn't happened to someone she cared about; a member of her family.

It had happened to her.

Fiona continued staring into Lou's – Mira's – eyes. Something had shifted in them... something that let Fiona see the girl she'd been; the girl they'd all believed was dead. Jasmine looked at her too, and Fiona tried not to cringe as she took in her ruined face. She was barely recognisable as the woman she had seen only hours earlier.

Alison was slowly shaking her head. 'They never said you were dead,' she said, the words ebbing out of her as if she was caught in a current of past memories. 'They told me you were gone; that I was too late. The room was empty, and I... I thought...' She breathed in. 'I found the names,' she said. 'The names on a piece of paper. That was all that was left.'

'You *were* too late,' Mira said. 'You are now too. Because there's nothing you can do to make this better. What happened that day... I tried to escape it, but I never could. Changing how I looked, how I acted, cutting ties with everything from my past, moving abroad, trying to build a new life. I even changed my *name*. But I couldn't run from the nightmares. I couldn't run from the knowledge that people had tried to kill me.' Her face hardened. 'It affected everything. My health, my marriage... it even stopped me having children because how could I take the risk that I'd pass my birthmark on to them and they'd face the very same problem?' She let out a breath. 'I had nothing left of my old life, and I couldn't have a new one. I was trapped. I was trapped, and yet you three – the people who'd done that to me – were off having your own brilliant lives.'

She turned to Alison. 'You'd even taken my home. My family.' She shook her head. 'I always wanted brothers and sisters. When Mum remarried, finally I had them. I didn't know Greg well because he was already off at uni. But my sister – stepsister – was only a couple of years older than me. I adored her.' She smiled, a wistful look coming into her eyes. 'She was exactly what I wanted to be: beautiful, kind. She knew how to dress and how to get people to like her. I really looked up to her, but I was recuperating for so long that by the time I was well, she'd left home. I'd lost her, like I did everything else.' Her eyes narrowed. 'When I realised that you were living in my house, I knew I had to do something. I didn't know what exactly, but that was when I decided to move back to Holmwood. To get close to you all and ruin your lives the same way you ruined mine.'

'But I didn't know,' Alison said. 'I didn't know Greg was your stepbrother and that was supposed to be your house. How could I?'

'And then to find out what you'd done with the mortgage for your own personal gain, without even telling him...'

Alison winced, and Fiona wondered what all that was about.

Mira turned to Jasmine. 'And you, with your perfect face, perfect husband, perfect daughter. Acting like you'd never in a million years do anything wrong. Like you were someone everyone should look up to.' Her lip curled. 'Now your outside mirrors your inside.'

Jasmine tried to speak, but nothing came out.

'And you, Fiona.' Mira turned to look at her again, and Fiona held her gaze. She needed to hear this. She needed to face everything head on. 'I wouldn't have gone into the river in the first place if it hadn't been for you. I was terrified of the water, and even Jasmine's insults wouldn't have got me in there, as much as I wanted to be a part of your little group.'

She paused, and Fiona held her breath.

'But you...' Mira swallowed, as if she was trying to keep hold of the emotion threatening to overtake her, 'you were *nice* – or so I thought. I knew Jasmine could be cruel. I knew it and I accepted it. I realised that if I wanted to be her friend, I'd have to handle the odd remark or two. But you never said anything unkind to anyone – to me.' She paused, and Fiona thought once more of that moment when Mira had invited her over. 'And so when you told me to get into the water, I did. I trusted you.'

Fiona flinched, but she didn't look away.

'I've realised that not being unkind doesn't mean that someone's nice. It doesn't mean they like you. All it means is that they don't care enough to do something; to say something. You didn't even care to find out where your husband was all those nights he was with me.'

Fiona blinked, taking in the words. Mira was right that she hadn't done anything, but she *had* cared. She'd cared, but she'd been too afraid to face reality.

Mira stepped back, as if she couldn't bear to be close to Fiona. 'None of you deserve your lives. None of you deserve your children. You had something I never would. Something you all took away from me. And I wanted...' she swallowed again, 'I wanted you to feel what it was like when something was taken away from you. Something dear. The thing you care about most of all... or at least that you should.' She looked out to the water. 'I wanted you to feel the fear and the panic, along with ruining your lives when the truth came out about what you did. To have people look at you with disgust, the same way they looked at me.'

'I'm sorry,' Fiona said, staring at her. 'I'm so sorry.' It didn't change things, but what else could she say? Mira was right. She should have done something to stop what was happening.

'The kids weren't supposed to get lost in the woods,' Mira said, still staring down at the water. 'They weren't supposed to run from the car. No one was supposed to get hurt, but things don't always go to plan, do they?' She shook her head, and fear flared inside Fiona. Where were they now? What had happened to them?

'You might be sorry, but it's not enough.' Mira looked at Jasmine with her face torn to shreds; at Alison, whose worry was etched even deeper on her face with each passing moment. 'None of this is enough. I thought it would be, but it isn't. It isn't, and I can't do this any longer.'

She started down the bank towards the rushing water. Fiona moved forward, trying to grab onto her, but Mira was too fast.

'Wait!' Alison called, as she reached the edge. 'Where is Gabby? Where are the kids? What do you mean, no one was supposed to get hurt? Are they okay? You have to tell us! *Please.*' But the wind tossed away her voice, and Mira just turned and stared, then waded into the river.

Fiona scrambled down the bank after her. She couldn't let this happen; couldn't let Mira disappear under the water again. Not this time. 'Mira!' she shouted. 'Don't go any further. Please, stop!'

But Mira didn't stop. The water rose higher and higher, swallowing her up, like she was vanishing in front of their very eyes. As they watched, the strong current pulled her off her feet.

'Call 999!' Fiona shouted to Jasmine, panic gripping her as she watched Mira go under.

Alison hurried towards her, and the two of them plunged into the water, struggling to stay stable as the ice-cold river pulled and sucked at their feet. Branches and other debris rushed by, and Alison grabbed Fiona's hand to steady them both. Linked together, the river couldn't knock them down. 'We have to find her,' Fiona said. 'We have to.'

Alison nodded. Still holding hands, they raked through the

shallow water, unable to go any further than knee height. Debris crashed into them, and every step was painful. After a few minutes, Alison turned to face her.

'I think she's gone,' she said quietly, in a grim echo of the past. 'And the river is way too fast for either of us to go deeper. We could end up getting swept away too.'

Fiona nodded, pain and grief sitting heavy on her. Alison was right. Mira really was gone. The river was like something alive, something that had been starved and was eager to consume anything in its path. It had taken Mira's life years ago – and theirs, too, whether they'd realised it at the time or not. She prayed with all her heart that it hadn't taken the children.

'Wait.' She squinted at something that was bobbing in an eddy near the bank, held back from the rushing current by debris. 'What's that?' As she waded towards it and picked it up, she could feel the blood draining from her face. 'It's Tabitha's shoe,' she said, her voice trembling. 'Her *shoe*.' She met Alison's eyes. 'Do you think...'

Alison shook her head, but Fiona could see she was making the same horrific connection. Mira's shoes had been left on the bank the day she'd almost drowned. And now... now they'd found Tabitha's shoe. Horror exploded inside her, and Jasmine's scream as she saw what Fiona was holding was like an echo of her own desperate fear.

It was too late for Mira now. Fiona didn't think there was any way she could survive the river this time. She didn't *want* to survive the river this time.

But was it too late for the children?

Sirens cut through the air, and she sank to the ground.

THIRTY-FIVE
ALISON
3 P.M.

Alison sat in the police station, feeling numb. Divers and searchers were doing all they could, but they hadn't found Lou's body... or anything else, thank goodness. The children had to be okay, she thought. They couldn't be in the river. After all that had happened, there had to be a light in this darkness.

She breathed in, still unable to believe everything she'd uncovered. Lou was Mira. Mira was alive. And not just that, but she was Greg's stepsister – a stepsister he hadn't seen for decades. How did he feel now, knowing what Alison had done? Not to someone he hadn't known, but to his stepsister, who had taken his child because of his wife's actions? Even if Mira hadn't drowned as they'd believed, what they'd done had ruined her life – and ultimately caused her death. How could he *not* look at her differently?

She glanced over to where Nick and Greg were sitting on the opposite side of the room. Neither of them was speaking, each lost in his own thoughts. Greg had put his arms limply around her when he'd come in. She'd told him that Mira was Lou, and that she was now presumed dead. His face had gone white. Across the room, Fiona and Nick had been talking in low tones, but Alison hadn't been able to make out anything. She had bitten her lip, remembering what Lou – Mira – had said about Fiona's husband and her. God, none of them had had any idea who she really was.

She looked up at the clock, willing it to both slow down and go faster. Steph had said that searchers were approaching the children's location now. But were the children even there, or had Lou... She swallowed, thinking of Tabitha's shoe bobbing gently in an eddy near the bank. Jasmine's scream had gone right through her.

Jasmine. She shuddered, thinking of the moment earlier that afternoon when Jasmine had turned around on the river-bank and Alison had seen her face. It had been a mess, covered in blood, with glass embedded in the skin. The paramedics who'd arrived had taken one look at her and bundled her into an ambulance, despite her protests that she wanted to stay and look for her daughter. The police had since told them that Jasmine had broken several ribs, her collarbone and her left arm, while the damage to her face would require plastic surgery. She was lucky to be alive, they'd said, but Alison couldn't help thinking that Jasmine might prefer to be dead than to face the ruin of her perfect face. At least Juniper would still have a mother, though, and that was worth something. *If* the kids were okay. Her gut clenched again.

Steph came into the area where they were waiting, and they all scrambled to their feet. Alison's heart beat fast, frantic prayers scrolling through her mind. Greg met her eyes from across the room, and she could see the tension in his body too.

'We found them.' Steph's face was wreathed with smiles. She looked happier than she had done since this whole thing had started, and it was that sight that made Alison finally believe that the kids really were safe. 'We found them, and they're all fine. Cold and wet, and very tired. But we've got them. They'd started trying to make their way out. Thankfully, they hadn't gone far from their original location. And Gabby...' she turned to Alison, 'Gabby is all right. We've given her an inhaler, and she won't need any more medical treatment. They just want to see you. They're on their way here.'

'Oh, thank God.' Alison slumped back into her chair, relief flooding through her.

'I'm afraid Tabitha isn't with them,' Steph said gently, and Fiona jerked towards her. 'The children said she managed to get away from Lou and went into the woods to try to find Gabby's inhaler. Lou went after her.'

Fiona sucked in air, and Alison reached out to her. What a brave girl, and all for Gabby. God, she hoped Tabitha would be okay. She thought of the shoe once more, and her gut twisted.

'But let's not jump to conclusions, all right?' Steph continued. 'She could be anywhere. We have police and search-and-rescue looking everywhere, as you know, and we'll distribute the child-rescue alert to the media. I'm sure we'll find her soon.'

Fiona nodded, her hands gripped together so tightly her knuckles were white.

'Officers on the scene said you all spoke with Lou before she entered the water,' Steph said quietly. 'Did she give you any indication as to why she was doing this?'

Alison met Fiona's eyes, and the two of them held each other's gaze for a moment. Then Fiona gave a small nod, as if she knew exactly what Alison was thinking: it was time. Time to tell the truth – not because they needed to save loved ones, but because they had to let the horror they'd submerged for so long reach the surface. Alison knew now that whatever else the waters might wash away, they couldn't take the love she had for her family.

That was what had given her strength, nothing else.

'We know why,' Alison said, glancing over at Nick and Greg now too. 'We know why, and we're ready to tell you.'

. . .

Only a few minutes later, there was nothing left to say. Steph had listened to her and Fiona as they told her what had happened, pausing only to jot down notes. Once they'd finished, she'd told them gently that she'd be referring the case on, and that for now, all they could do was wait. Alison had nodded, still uncertain what the future held. But even in the midst of everything, she felt lighter. Across the room, Fiona was holding onto her husband's hand, and it seemed she felt the same.

'They're pulling into the car park now,' Steph said, and Alison jumped to her feet, dragging Greg up with her. As she yanked on her coat, her eyes met Fiona's. They stared at each other for a minute in silence, as if they both knew there was nothing else to say, then she pushed out of the station and into the fresh air.

The clouds had cleared and the sky was blue, and she breathed in deeply. Her heart leapt as a police car came to a stop in front of her, the doors opened and Gabby tumbled out. Her daughter was pale, with dirt smeared across her cheek, but all Alison could take in was her face, glowing with love. She raced straight into Alison's arms, almost knocking her over with the force of her hug. Greg put his arms around both of them, and they stood that way for a long time, unable to let go of each other.

And despite the shock and trauma of the past twenty-four hours, Alison knew she was stronger now than she'd ever been.

THIRTY-SIX
JASMINE
4 P.M.

Jasmine lay in bed, floating on a cloud of painkillers. God, how she loved morphine. It was a blanket between her and the reality of what had happened. She lifted a bandaged hand to her face, wincing at the pain. The morphine might be strong, but it wasn't strong enough. Where the hell was that nurse when you needed her?

She closed her eyes, her mind skipping through all that had happened, as if she was watching a film play on her closed eyelids. Fiona telling her that she and Alison were going to the police. Her rush to get there to convince them to keep quiet, and then seeing the girl on the bike... and the crash. Crawling from the wreckage to spot Lou standing by the side of the river.

Except it hadn't been Lou. It had been *Mira*. It had been Mira, and she knew exactly what had happened that day. Jasmine shuddered now, trying to pull that blanket of morphine even closer around her as she pictured the look in Mira's eyes: loathing, hatred and disgust. And could she really blame her? Mira had reached out to her, after all, and Jasmine had pushed her back under. She might have tried to justify it all these years, but she knew the truth too: she was the one who had almost killed Mira. Not Fiona, and not Alison. She'd tried to make excuses for herself, tried to keep it all locked inside. But now the past had drowned her too, holding her under the surface until it bubbled out.

She blinked, an image of the little girl she'd been flashing into her head. Dirty blonde hair, ragged clothes... a bicycle she'd rescued from the tip the only way she could escape the estate. She jerked, then winced in pain. That bicycle. That girl. That was... She tried to get a grip on everything, but the thoughts kept sliding away. She chased them through the daze of morphine and whatever else they had given her, trying to hang on, wishing for once she was stone-cold sober. She needed to grasp this. She needed to understand. She took a deep breath and conjured the image once more.

Then she gasped.

That girl was her. The girl on the bicycle, the one she'd seen throughout the years, that hadn't been Lou's sister. It had been *her*.

She nodded slowly, piecing everything together as she held the image in her mind. She'd first seen the girl that awful day when she'd done such a terrible thing to Mira. The blurred face came into focus now: she'd been staring with wide blue eyes from the bank, greasy lank hair bunched messily in a ponytail, and so skinny that her knees and elbows looked huge. Jasmine cringed. She'd tried so hard to forget what she'd looked like; how poverty had twisted her features into something unrecognisable. She'd blocked out that girl who desperately wanted to do the right thing – to help her mother and be good – but was constantly beaten back, sneered at and looked down on by everyone. She'd tried so hard to forget that she hadn't even realised the girl on a bike watching that day was her.

Over the years, the girl had appeared in her nightmares – flashbacks to her terrible childhood, the days she'd come home from school and see her mother lying in her own urine on the sofa, so pale and still that Jasmine didn't even know she was alive. In the dreams, the girl would grab the bicycle and ride off, the very same way Jasmine had done. Sometimes, she'd even catch a glimpse of her when she drank, like she had today.

And today... today the girl had been the one to guide Jasmine to Lou – to Mira. Somewhere, buried underneath everything, she'd recognised that Jasmine hadn't wanted to kill Mira. She hadn't wanted to hold her down. She'd just been afraid: afraid that she'd never be able to be anything in this world. Afraid she'd never escape the poverty she'd grown up in; never be seen as anything but a poor kid from the worst estate in town. Jasmine had escaped, but...

She let out a breath. She hadn't really escaped, though, had she? Because her whole life had been driven by that fear – by the girl who lived on, despite being buried inside her. Everything she did had been about trying to cover her up, from her appearance to the house she lived in, her marriage and how she treated her daughter, her business and even her drinking... and what she had done to Mira.

She pictured Mira now walking so calmly into the rushing water and slipping under the surface, and she let out a cry. She *was* sorry for what had happened – for how it had ruined Mira's life. She'd meant it when she'd said it, and not only because she was scared of the consequences. And now... Mira had been right. It was too late. She was gone, and there was nothing she could do. That girl inside her would always be hurt, always stare at her accusingly, knowing she'd done the worst thing possible. That girl would never heal.

'Mum!'

Juniper's voice filled the room, and for a second, Jasmine thought she was still lost in her thoughts; in the cloud of morphine. Then she felt a hand on her arm, and she opened her eyes, drinking in her daughter's face. Juniper was tired and pale, with blood staining one side of her head and leaves caught in her hair, but Jasmine thought she'd never looked more beautiful. She blinked, hoping she wasn't hallucinating, reaching up to touch her daughter's cheek. Happiness flooded through her when her fingers met a solid object. She was real.

'They found you!' She tried to speak, but the words sounded garbled, and she saw Juniper shoot a fearful glance at Aidan, who was by her side. Jasmine swallowed, imagining how dreadful she looked right now. And not just right now. She would never look the same again. She wouldn't be that beautiful, successful woman Aidan had fallen in love with – if being with him was even a possibility once he found out what she'd done. She wouldn't be the gorgeous mum any daughter would be proud of.

'I'm here, Mum. I'm okay. I fell when I was running from the car.' Juniper touched her head and grimaced. 'But I'm safe now. I love you.' She squeezed Jasmine's hand, and love rushed through her. 'And I'm so glad you're okay too.'

Jasmine tried to nod, but even with the morphine, tears of pain pricked her eyes. *I'm so glad you're okay.* Juniper didn't care how she looked... whether she had scars; whether she'd ever be the same beauty again. All she cared about was having her mum here with her.

A tear splashed onto Jasmine's cheek, and she winced at the stinging sensation. She'd tried so hard to give her daughter everything – to be the perfect mum, so different from her own mother – that she'd missed what was really important: love. Juniper loved her, the same way Jasmine had loved her own mother. The old hurt speared her as she thought of how, for whatever reason, her mother had never been able to get past her demons to return that love. Jasmine had, though. She loved her daughter so much that she wanted to give her everything – so much that she'd almost ended up with nothing.

Would Juniper love her still when she told her what she'd done? Because she had to tell her now; tell Aidan. As much as her outside would never be perfect again, her inside never had been, and she couldn't keep covering it up any longer. It had been slowly killing her, whether she'd realised it or not.

She looked up at Aidan, her heart beating fast as she strained to reach her other hand towards him. Would he take it once he realised what she was; knew what she had done? Would he accept her with all her faults... with that vulnerable, fearful little girl still inside?

'I'm sorry,' she whispered, each movement of her lips like a thousand razors cutting them. She didn't know exactly what she was apologising for: for the million little things she'd done, or the big things that had let down both her and her family? For the mistakes in her present, or those in her past? Had Aidan heard about Mira? Did he know now why she'd taken their daughter?

Even if he had, she needed her family to hear it from her. She needed to say those words aloud.

'Lou... she's not Lou, but someone from the past. Someone...' she swallowed, trying to get the words out through the pain, 'someone I hurt. Because I was jealous of her. Because I was scared people would think I was worth less than she was.' She'd never admitted being jealous of anyone before. 'I thought she'd died, but she hadn't.' She let out her breath. 'I could have killed her. I almost did. That's why she took Juniper.' She swung her glance over to her daughter, who was watching with wide eyes. 'I'm sorry, Juni,' she whispered.

'It's okay, Mum,' Juniper said, squeezing her hand.

'I don't want to be scared any more,' Jasmine went on, desperate to speak through the haze closing in. 'I don't want to drink or try to be perfect all the time. I want... I want to be me. If I can figure out who that is.'

As if in slow motion, Aidan took her hand in his. 'That's what we want too,' he said, his eyes shining with tears. 'That's all we want.'

Jasmine blinked, another tear falling down her cheek. There was so much more to say, and so much more to explain. But finally, she knew that he had seen her. The people she loved most had seen what she really was, inside and out, in all her brokenness.

And they loved her still.

And that... that was enough to give her, and that girl inside, hope.

THIRTY-SEVEN

FIONA

5 P.M.

Fiona sat on the sofa next to Nick, every inch of her throbbing with fatigue. This was the longest day she'd ever experienced, but it wasn't over yet – not until they had Tabitha back, safe and sound. Tim was home, wrapped up in blankets beside them, huddling against her like he hadn't done since he was young. He hadn't left her side since they'd been reunited at the police station, where he'd clung to her in tears when they'd told him they hadn't yet found his sister. Without Tabitha next to him, his usual confidence seemed to have deserted him, as if he'd realised how much his sister buoyed him up.

He'd told them how Lou had chased after Tabitha in the woods, and how they'd waited for her to come back so Gabby could have her medicine. He and Juniper were really worried about how she was gasping for air. When neither Lou nor Tabitha returned, he'd decided he should try to find the motorway and flag down a car. But Juniper didn't want to be left alone with Gabby, and there was no way they could leave Gabby on her own. So even though Gabby was in a state, they decided to all three try to make it to the motorway.

The storm had stopped by then, he'd said, but it was slow

going having to climb over the broken branches and everything else. He'd had to help Gabby, and he wasn't sure they would make it by dark. He was starting to think they should turn back to the cabin when they heard people shouting their names. A policeman had an inhaler for Gabby, and after a few puffs and a bit of a rest, she was almost back to normal. Tabitha and Tim were heroes, and Fiona couldn't be prouder of both her children.

Both her children. Her stomach churned as she thought of Tabitha. Where was she? Was she all right? Social media was buzzing with appeals to find the missing girl, and the local TV and radio had broadcast her photo, but there was no news. Police were continuing to search the river and woods. So far, though, they hadn't found anything, not even Lou. No, *Mira.* God, it was still so hard to believe.

With her daughter missing, Fiona had barely been able to think about what might happen now that they'd told the truth. Pain shot through her as she thought of how what had happened that day had destroyed Mira's life. Maybe they hadn't killed her outright, but they had still ruined her. As she and Nick had left the police station with Tim, Steph had said that she would be passing the file on to another officer, and someone would be in touch soon. Whatever happened, though, Fiona just wanted her daughter back.

She glanced at Nick, wondering what he was thinking. How did he feel about her now, given what he'd learned? He'd listened as she'd explained to Steph exactly what had happened with Mira, and how she'd been responsible for not doing more. He'd reached out and taken her hand, the first time they'd touched since she'd told him about the work event. But did that mean he forgave her?

Did she forgive him?

'I'm so sorry,' she said, turning to face him now. 'I'm sorry for everything.'

He held her gaze, and panic flitted through her at his unreadable expression. 'I'm sorry too,' he said. 'I shouldn't have lied to you about where I was, and I definitely shouldn't have spent so much time over at Lou's... or whoever she is.' He dropped his head. 'What happened between me and her, well, maybe it didn't start all of this, but it never would have happened if I hadn't let her in like that.' His face twisted. 'I played a part in this too. It wasn't only you. It's me. It's *us*.'

Fiona felt tears come to her eyes. For the first time in ages, she felt the distance between them close.

Nick squeezed her hand. 'I want our family to be together again – really together.'

Pain twisted Fiona's gut as his words rang in her ears. Together again. Would they ever have that? Or would Tabitha... She stopped herself from going further.

'I want us both to fight,' Nick went on. 'We should be heroes for each other, like Tim and Tabitha were today.'

'I want that too,' Fiona said in a rush. She held his gaze, her heart thumping. Would he believe her? Would he see how much she meant it?

After what felt like for ever, he nodded. 'I know. I've seen it today – how you've stepped up to help get the kids back. It can't have been easy, facing what happened all those years ago, knowing it could have real consequences for you. But you did everything you could, and I hope...' he paused, 'I hope you will keep doing that for me too. I promise I'll be here, no matter what happens with all of this. I'll be here for you and the children, so much more than I have been. I want to have a life with you... a life that's full; a life that's whole. A life with my family.'

Fiona nodded, her eyes filling with tears as his words rang in her ears. *I want to have a life.* Mira would never have that, and Fiona would always live with guilt and regret. But while she would continue paying the price, she knew now that she didn't have to hide from what she'd done. There would be consequences, but hopefully she *could* have a life – a full one, like Nick had said. She could fight for what she believed in.

She owed that much to Mira. She owed it to her family.

And maybe... maybe she owed it to herself too.

'Come on,' she said, getting to her feet and pulling up Nick and Tim. They both looked at her in surprise. 'We're not going to sit here while Tabitha is still out there. We're going to find her.' She looked down at their linked hands. 'Together.'

THIRTY-EIGHT

TABITHA

I don't think I've ever been this tired, but I can't sleep. I'm tucked under my duvet after a lovely warm shower, the heat in my room cranked as high as it will go. Downstairs, I can hear the comforting rumble of Mum and Dad's voices, and on the floor across from my bed, the soft wheeze of Tim's breathing. We haven't slept in the same room for ages, but when he asked if he could bunk up beside me, I nodded. After all that's happened, I want to keep him close. And it feels so good that he came to my room – to me – for support, rather than me going to him like I used to. Somehow, it feels like what happened has made us equals. We're both able to lean on each other, and I love that.

I'll never forget how happy and relieved I was when I saw the torchlight coming towards me. The water had swept our car off the road and into a ditch that we couldn't drive out of. Even though we weren't injured, the woman who'd picked me up didn't think it was safe for us to get out – we'd tried to, but the ditch was full of water and debris, and the current was so swift it carried off my broken shoe. So we sat and waited, trying over and over to get through on 999 before her phone began to lose battery. It felt like for ever, and I couldn't help nodding off a few times.

When I saw the policeman's face appear at the car window, I wondered if I was dreaming. It took a while to get us out, but once I was free, Mum, Dad and Tim were waiting on the bank. They rushed towards me and hugged me so tightly that I could barely breathe, but I didn't want them to let go. Tim *didn't* let go, actually. He kept hold of my arm until we got back to our house, safe and sound. I didn't mind. I know now that I don't need him to protect me or lead me. I can think for myself.

But as happy as I am that I'm home, sadness sweeps through me when I think of Lou... and Mum. She didn't want to tell me and Tim today what happened between them. She said we should get a good night's sleep, and she'd tell us everything tomorrow. But I wanted to wake up with all of this behind me, and Tim said the same. So she sat us down once we were back home and wrapped up in blankets on the sofa, and she told us that Lou was dead. She told us why Lou took us... what Mum did when she was just a few years older than us, and why Lou wanted to punish her.

Tears started streaming down her face as she spoke, and I could see how sorry she felt. I've never seen her cry. If I think about it, I've never really seen her show any extreme emotion. She goes along with it all, calm and stable, taking whatever happens. But now... now I could see that maybe, underneath all of that, she does feel. She'd felt bad about this for ages, she said, and it was time now for it all to come out. Time for her to face whatever might happen. She didn't mean to be a part of it, but just standing by and doing nothing wasn't the answer; wasn't right. She wanted us to know that, but I think it's something I've already learned.

Dad reached out and touched her arm when she was saying all of this. It was nice to see him do that. I hope he understands that Mum didn't mean it. That she's not bad. And that she has learned now, like I have. I think the police will see that too.

I turn over in bed and draw the duvet even closer around my shoulders, one more thought coming into my mind. I hope that somehow, wherever she is, Lou knows my mum is sorry too.

THIRTY-NINE

FIONA

ONE YEAR LATER

Fiona parked the car and walked down to the river. It was exactly a year since Mira had died here – when everything had changed again. Unlike that day, when wind had whipped across the ruddy sky and rain had lashed down, this one was clear, with blue skies stretching as far as the eye could see. The river meandered through the grassy fields, calm and benevolent, instead of the rushing angry torrent it had been back then.

So much else had changed too. In the weeks and months that had followed that dreadful day, Fiona had spent a lot of time talking to investigators, explaining what had happened. Since Mira hadn't died years ago like they'd thought, and they'd all been so young at the time, the police had decided not to take the investigation any further. But with the police operation to find Lou's body stretching on into the days that had followed, the full story had got out to the media. Hell had been unleashed on them from all sides. Fiona had decided to stay in the town, but Jasmine had never returned to her home here – or her business. Fiona had heard she'd been having multiple surgeries to try to repair the extensive damage the windscreen had done to her face.

As for Alison, Fiona had seen a For Sale sign up on the house she and Greg had lived in. She wasn't surprised: after the revelation, how could Alison bear to stay in the place where Mira had grown up; a place that should have been hers if that day so long ago hadn't happened? Alison's business had closed down, too, and Fiona had heard through the grapevine that she, Greg and Gabby were planning a fresh start in southern Spain, where the weather would be better for Gabby's asthma and Alison could try to rebuild her gym.

She wrapped her arms around herself, thinking of her own life. She and Nick were slowly coming together, making an effort to be active participants in their marriage and their lives. It hadn't been easy, and there were times when they'd both fallen back into their old roles. But that day when the children had been taken was a constant reminder of how much they had to lose, and how they had to work to protect it. Eager to do something – anything – to help make amends for what she'd done, Fiona had started volunteering for an anti-bullying hotline at the weekends. It gave Nick a chance to have some one-on-one with the kids without her around, and although it would never make up for what had happened with Mira, it made her feel like she was helping someone. Hearing the stories from children who were being bullied made her only too aware how Mira must have felt.

She heard a noise behind her and turned, stifling a gasp when she saw Jasmine. She was wearing a pair of jeans and a T-shirt, and her face was criss-crossed with scars, but it was definitely her. Fiona nodded, unsure what to say, and they stood in silence, both staring at the river. Then a figure appeared on the far bank, and she looked up to see Alison. Their eyes met, then they both turned to gaze at the water below.

This wasn't about them, Fiona thought. They weren't here for each other. They were here for Mira – to remember. To remember what had happened, and the part they had played. The part they were finally able to own up to.

It was what Mira had wanted, but it hadn't been enough.

Fiona cast one last glance at the river, then walked back to the car. The past was the past, but it would never be buried. It *shouldn't* be buried. It would always be alive in her now, pushing her forward.

Towards her children. Towards her husband.

Towards life.

A LETTER FROM LEAH

Dear reader,

I want to say a huge thank you for choosing to read *The Mother Next Door*. If you enjoyed it, and you want to keep up to date with all my latest releases, just sign up at the following link. Your email address will never be shared and you can unsubscribe at any time.

www.bookouture.com/leah-mercer

I hope you loved *The Mother Next Door*. If you did, I would be very grateful if you could write a review. I'd love to hear what you think. It makes such a difference helping new readers to discover one of my books for the first time.

I really enjoy hearing from my readers – you can get in touch on my Facebook page, through Twitter, Goodreads or my website.

Thanks,

Leah

www.leahmercer.com

facebook.com/AuthorLeahMercer
twitter.com/leahmercerbooks

ACKNOWLEDGEMENTS

A huge thanks to Laura Deacon and the team at Bookouture for providing such solid support, both on this book and the ones before. Thank you to author and friend extraordinaire, Mel Sherratt, for continuing to be there for me on this publishing journey over the past decade and more! I also want to thank book reviewer Melissa Amster for her support for me and my writing, ever since the very early days. Thank you, too, to Hannah Todd for her enthusiasm and guidance. And finally, thank you to my son for being my invaluable technical and plot advisor, as always.

Made in the USA
Middletown, DE
08 March 2023

26411912R00149